Murder Boogies with Elvis

Murder Boogies with Elvis

A SOUTHERN SISTERS MYSTERY

Anne George

WM

William Morrow
75 YEARS OF PUBLISHING
An Imprint of HarperCollinsPublishers

This is a work of fiction. Names, characters, places, and incidents either are the product of the author's imagination or are used fictitiously. Any resemblance to actual events, locales, organizations, or persons, living or dead, is entirely coincidental and beyond the intent of either the author or the publisher.

Designed by Richard Oriolo

ISBN 0-06-019870-2

To Ruth Cohen, my agent, and Carrie Feron, my editor,
who have been with me, Patricia Anne,
and Mary Alice from the beginning.
My love and deepest appreciation. You're the best.

Murder Boogies with Elvis

Chapter One

I was lying on my stomach under the kitchen sink, eating a peanut butter and banana sandwich and listening to Vivaldi's "Spring" when icy cold hands grasped my ankles. I screamed, reared up, and banged my head on the drainpipe so hard that zigzag lights streaked across my vision. The next thing I was aware of was being dragged from under the sink and hearing a very familiar voice saying, "What on God's earth is wrong with you?"

My chin hit the kitchen floor with a clunk and the zigzag lights streaked again; pain from both blows met in the top of my head.

"Are you okay?"

Maybe, I thought, if I just lay there she would go away—"she" being my sister, the boss of the world. The pain would lessen, Vivaldi would move on to "Summer" and then to "Winter." Eventually I would get up, get some ice for the knot that was swelling like a balloon on the back of my head. If I were lucky, the brain damage would be minimal.

"You weren't trying to commit suicide, were you, like that poet woman? Tell me you weren't trying to commit suicide, Mouse. That would be a terrible thing to do to me."

"What?" I struggled to a sitting position and looked up at Mary Alice. Way up. She's six feet tall (she says five-twelve) and admits to two hundred fifty pounds.

"Well, I know I haven't been around as much lately since I've been seeing so much of Virgil, but I didn't think you were that depressed."

"What the hell are you talking about?" I touched the back of my head tentatively. "I may have a concussion, but I'm not suicidal."

"Well, what were you doing under the sink?"

"Putting down some of those tile squares. A couple of them weren't sticking good, so I was putting weight on them. Lying on them for a few minutes." I looked down and saw my peanut butter and banana sandwich squished on my T-shirt. "Actually I was eating my lunch. And the poet you're thinking of is Sylvia Plath. And it was a gas stove she stuck her head in, not a sink." I held up a hand. "Help me up."

Sister grabbed me with the cold hands that had started the trouble and pulled me up.

"How come your hands are so cold?" I asked, walking slowly to the kitchen table and easing into a chair. I quickly learned that if I didn't move my head suddenly, the pain was a simple throb. "You scared me half to death."

"I was getting ice for a Coke when I looked over and saw half of you sticking out from under the sink."

"Well, would you get me a couple of pieces now? Just wrap them in a paper towel."

She opened the refrigerator. "You want some Coke and some aspirin, too?"

I forgot and nodded my head. Pain rattled around in there.

"I may really be hurt," I said. I closed one eye and then the other. Was the left eye a little blurry?

"Of course you're not. It's just a bump."

Sister handed me the Coke, aspirin, and a paper towel with ice in it. I swallowed the aspirin and tried the eye test again. I looked through the bay window at Woofer's igloo doghouse. Right eye first. Okay. Left eye. A couple of floaters.

"I have floaters in my left eye," I said. "I think I've jarred my retina."

Sister sat down across from me. "Doesn't mean a thing. You're fine. I have floaters all the time. One looks like one of those little white mealy worms Grandpapa used to fish with. Caught all the crappie with. Comes and goes."

"You have a mealy worm floater?"

"Sometimes. Comes and goes."

I held the paper towel with the ice in it against the back of my head and looked at Mary Alice for the first time since she had come in. Really looked at her. The view from the floor didn't count.

"You look very spiffy today," I said. She did. She was wearing a pink pantsuit and her hair was a darker blond than usual. Her bangs were pulled to one side and her skin glowed.

"Thanks. I've been to Delta Hairlines, and there was a lady there giving free makeovers advertising some new cosmetics for seniors. I told her I was only sixty-four, but she gave me one anyway."

"Sixty-four, huh?"

Sister didn't answer that. The truth is that she's sixty-six, but on her last birthday she decided to start counting backward. I'm five years younger than she is, or at least I was. In a couple of years I'll be older than she is and soon she won't qualify for senior-citizen makeovers.

"I bought some of it and would have gotten you some but our skin tones are completely different."

She was telling the truth about this. Everything about us is different. She has olive skin and brown eyes, and I have fair skin and hazel eyes. I used to have strawberry-blond hair, and Sister was a brunette. Now I'm gray and she's usually strawberry-blond. Add to that the fact that I'm a size six petite—and Lord knows what Sister is—and is there any wonder that when we were children and she told me I was adopted, that I believed her? So did everybody else. I'm just grateful that we were born at home so there was no chance that we had been mixed up at the hospital.

I closed my right eye again. One of the floaters in the left did look a little like a mealworm. I looked from one side to the other.

"Are you doing that or are you having some kind of spell?" Mary Alice wanted to know.

"I'm doing it."

"Good, because I came by to tell you the news. Virgil and I have set the date."

"For what?"

"For our wedding, Patricia Anne. Don't be dense."

"Dense? I didn't even know you were engaged. What happened to Cedric?"

"Who?"

"The man you were engaged to last I heard."

"Oh, I think that's over with." She took a sip of Coke and looked thoughtful. "I mean, he's in England and all. I'll let him know, though."

"That would be thoughtful. You could invite him to the wedding."

"Well, our engagement never was very serious."

Sarcasm is totally lost on this woman.

"Anyway," she continued, "the wedding is going to be the fourteenth of May. Virgil's retiring the first of April, and we're going to buy an RV and go all over the West for our honeymoon. Doesn't that sound like fun?"

Virgil Stuckey, who might or might not soon be my brother-in-law, is the sheriff of St. Clair County. He is a very nice man, sixty-five years old, and larger than Mary Alice. The RV had better be a big one.

"It was Virgil's idea. Will Alec took me to New York for my first honeymoon and then Philip took me to Paris and Roger to St. Croix. Virgil said this would be something different."

"He's right." And a whole lot cheaper. Sister was breaking her pattern in marrying Virgil. The other three husbands had all been very rich and each had been twenty-eight years older than she was. But when you're sixty-four (-six), it's hard to keep that pattern going.

I wondered how closely Sister had looked at RVs. I shifted the wet paper towel on the back of my head and considered how my husband, Fred, and I would get along on a long trip in an RV. We've been married almost forty-one years and seldom have a cross word, but I had an idea that we would be at each other's throats by the time we reached the Mississippi River. The truth is that we don't travel well together.

"Do those things have bathrooms?" I asked, remembering a trip across South Carolina when Fred kept saying, "Next exit," and I thought I would pop.

"I'm sure they do." Sister frowned slightly. "Wouldn't you think?"

I shrugged. Pain shot up my head. Damn. "Find out."

"I will. Virgil doesn't need one often, though. He has a very good prostate. He says the doctor told him he has the prostate of a twenty-year-old."

"Good for Virgil."

"And for me." Sister grinned.

I ignored this and aimed Sister in another direction. "Have you made any plans for the wedding?"

It worked. She clasped her hands and leaned forward.

"It's going to be a small one, just family. And we want to have it at some little country church like John John Kennedy and Carolyn Bessette. Bless their hearts." She sighed and tapped a packet of Sweet'n Low against the table. "I was all set to vote for him someday."

I thought of the beauty and possibility that had been taken away so suddenly. Of the little boy saluting, the man kissing his bride's hand. Pain again slammed the top of my head.

"Anyway, that was such a nice wedding," Sister continued, "and I've had every other kind."

"True." I couldn't match the husbands and ceremonies, but there had been a big church wedding, a home wedding, and an elopement.

"I can see a cream silk dress for me—long, of course. And what about magenta for you? You're going to be the matron of honor. And I saw a wonderful color called sunflower for the girls. We'll look like a spring garden."

"The girls?"

"Debbie, Marilyn, and Haley. Virgil's daughter is going to be in it, too."

Magenta and sunflower? Dear Lord. I did a quick calculation. My daughter, Haley, would be more than five months pregnant on the fourteenth of May. I could imagine how excited she was going to be about wearing a sunflower-colored bridesmaid dress. About as excited as Sister's daughters, Marilyn and Debbie, would be.

"You haven't told them yet, have you?"

"I'm going to surprise them."

I put the wet paper towel on the table. "Mary Alice, I don't want to wear a magenta dress."

"Of course you do."

"I do not. I've never worn magenta in my life."

"Well, you should have. We'll put a rinse on your hair so you won't look so washed out. I swear, Patricia Anne, you need to take some iron or eat more. When I saw those skinny white pitiful legs sticking out from under the sink, it's no wonder I thought you were dead."

"Go home," I said.

"Okay." She stood up. "But I didn't tell you that Virgil, Jr., got Virgil and I tickets for the Vulcan benefit at the Alabama Theater tomorrow night."

"*Me*," I said. "He got Virgil and *me* tickets."

"You mean Fred and you? He sure did. Wasn't that nice? Four seats on the front row. We're all going out to dinner afterward. It'll give you a chance to meet him."

"Go home," I said.

Sister put on her jacket. "Virgil, Jr., is an Elvis impersonator. Supposed to be real good. Of course, the white jumpsuit and sideburns take some getting used to."

I threw the wet paper towel at her. She ducked.

"Your tiles are coming loose under the sink. I'll call you when you're not so cranky."

The only thing on the table to throw was the sugar bowl, and I didn't want to break it. She was going out the door anyway.

Magenta and sunflower. Yuck. I got up, careful not to move my head too quickly, and looked at the tile. Damn. A couple of them were coming unstuck. No way was I going to lie back down on them, though; I'd epoxy them later. I closed the cabinet door, scraped the peanut butter and banana off my chest with a kitchen knife, and pulled the T-shirt gently over the knot on my head. Then I threw the shirt in the washing machine and went to take a shower.

The hot water felt wonderful. By the time I got out and put on some clean corduroy pants and a turtleneck, I was almost cheerful. I went into the room that used to be our sons' room— and which has metamorphosed into a sewing, ironing, computer room—and checked my e-mail. No new messages. Haley had had her amnio test several days earlier, and I was hoping for news. But in a few weeks, this e-mail business would be over.

She and Philip were coming home. Home from Warsaw, Poland, where they had been since last August. Fred, Mary Alice, and I had gone to visit them for Christmas, and the e-mail lines had stayed busy, but it was going to be so good to have her home, to see her getting larger and larger with the baby she had wanted for so long. Haley's first husband, Tom Buchanan, had been killed by a drunk driver just as they were considering starting a family. It was a blow that she would never fully recover from, but she had met Dr. Philip Nachman at her cousin Debbie's wedding and had finally fallen in love again. Philip was almost twenty years older than Haley and had two grown children. He wasn't anxious to start another family, and their relationship was off and on for several months. Haley won. They're married, she's pregnant, and Philip is thrilled about it. He's an ear, nose, and throat specialist, and the day after their wedding they left for Warsaw, where he was teaching a seminar at the medical school.

I chewed on a fingernail. The amnio results should be in by now. And Haley had promised to let me know as soon as she heard something. Surely everything was all right. Surely. I took a deep breath, went into the kitchen, and fixed myself another peanut butter and banana sandwich.

April isn't the cruelest month in Alabama; March is. When Sister had come in, the sun had been shining. Now a bank of dark clouds had rolled in from the west, and it looked like it might rain soon. Woofer ambled from his house, shook himself comfortably, and went over to the elm tree and hiked his leg. The elm tree has a white stripe around it after years of this activity.

I opened the door and called him inside. He looked from me to his igloo, trying to make up his mind. That igloo is mighty comfortable on a windy March day.

"Treat," I promised. I grabbed the box of dog biscuits off the kitchen counter and shook them.

He sat down and yawned.

I shook the box again. "I won't let Muffin bother you."

He knew I was lying but he came in anyway. Muffin is Haley's cat, which I've been keeping for her. Muffin adores Woofer, purring and ducking her head against his. Woofer loves to lie down by the heating vent in the den, and Muffin curls up right by him. I've gotten several cute pictures of the two of them to send to Haley. In each, Muffin looks blissful and Woofer looks disgusted.

"See?" I said, giving him a couple of treats. "She's not even in here. She's in the middle of my bed, where she's not supposed to be."

Woofer ate one of the biscuits and took the other one into the den. I sat down at the table to eat my sandwich and make out a grocery list. I had planned on tomato soup and tuna sandwiches, but spring had turned into winter in the last couple of hours. Beef stew? Chicken potpie?

The phone rang and I jumped. The dull ache in my head pounded.

"Aunt Pat? Magenta and sunflower?"

"That's what she says."

"I can't believe Mama's really getting married."

"She's done it three times before."

"But Mary Alice Tate Sullivan Nachman Crane Stuckey?"

"Maybe this will be the last one. She's running out of room at Elmwood Cemetery."

Debbie, Sister's daughter, and I both giggled. Sister has all of her husbands buried together at Elmwood. They had each impregnated her once and died neat deaths—though Roger Crane's demise on a transatlantic flight had caused some problems. She's still complaining that on his death certificate the place of death is listed in terms of longitude and latitude. "And us so close to Atlanta. Now that would be a nice place to die. They could have put that."

"You haven't heard from Haley, have you?" I asked Debbie.

"Not yet. Everything's all right, though, Aunt Pat."

"I know." But I wanted reassurance. I wanted a copy of the amnio test in front of me saying the baby was fine, a healthy boy or girl. "I wish she would let them tell her the sex so we could plan things."

Debbie gave a snort. "Put Mama on the case. I didn't want to know about David Anthony, remember, and she went snooping in the files or bribed somebody or something and came in yelling, 'It's a boy! It's a boy!' "

"She gave a considerable donation to the neonatal care unit at University Hospital."

"Well, I guess I shouldn't complain."

"She means well."

Debbie and I giggled again.

"Have you heard about the honeymoon?" I asked.

"No. Tell me."

Which I did.

"Mama and Virgil in an RV? Oh, Lord, that's priceless. How far do you think they'll get?"

"Gardendale, maybe," I said, naming a suburb west of Birmingham and immediately feeling guilty. "I'm sorry, Debbie. I'm being mean. I think it's the knot on my head."

Which called for more explanations.

"Did you check your pupils? Are they dilated?"

I assured Debbie that I was all right.

"Well, you really might have a concussion if you were knocked out for a minute. Don't go to sleep for a while."

I promised that I wouldn't, Debbie said she would check with me later, and we hung up.

A light rain had begun to fall, more heavy mist than rain. The Piggly Wiggly could wait, I decided. I went into the den, lay down on the sofa, pulled up the afghan, and immediately fell asleep. So much for promises.

Chapter Two

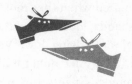

*L*ooks funny up on the mountain without Vulcan," Fred said, coming in and shaking out his jacket. "Dark." He came over where I was putting turkey bacon on the microwave grill, gave me a very nice kiss, patted me on the behind, and said, "Umm. I love breakfast for supper."

I leaned against him for a minute. Nice. "There's a benefit for the old boy at the Alabama Theater tomorrow night. Mary Alice got us some tickets. We've got to get him repaired and back up."

"What kind of benefit?" Fred went to the refrigerator and got a beer.

"It should be fun. Virgil's son's an Elvis impersonator, and he's on the program. He got us front-row tickets."

"Just so it's not a ballet," he called as he headed down the hall toward the bathroom. "You can see the men's hernias when they pick the girls up."

"Is that what they're called?"

I heard a laugh as the bathroom door closed.

Vulcan, the largest iron statue in the world, has stood on Red Mountain overlooking Birmingham for as long as any of us can remember. He's the god of the forge. Majestic from the front, an apron shielding vital parts from sparks, and bare-butted in the back, his tight rear end mooning the whole southern side of the city. We're used to the sun glinting off this huge behind, but visitors are frequently amazed when they look up at the statue.

"None of my husbands looked like that," Mary Alice remarked one day as we were driving down Valley Avenue and she glanced up at Vulcan. "Will Alec didn't have a butt, remember? He had trouble keeping his pants up. And Philip and Roger weren't much better. Men's hips are too low down on their bodies. Have you ever noticed that, Mouse?"

I've given up on the "Mouse" bit. It was my childhood nickname because I was so little and supposedly squeaked when I cried. I've tried to get Mary Alice to quit calling me that, but it's a lost cause.

"Fred's aren't," I said.

"Just looks that way because of the roll of fat."

I gritted my teeth. "Love handles."

"You wish."

Poor Vulcan and his magnificent behind have fallen on hard times recently. There was some worry years ago that he wasn't secure enough on his pedestal, that during a windstorm he might topple off, taking out visitors, the gift shop, the parking lot, and Twentieth Street—one of Birmingham's main arteries. The solution was to cut a hole in the top of his head and fill him halfway up with concrete. Smart. Rain came though the hole in his head. The concrete expanded and contracted in the heat and cold, and the iron didn't. So Vulcan began to crack up, bless his heart. He had to be taken down, piece by piece, and taken to iron statue intensive care where they promised to restore him to full health in a couple of years. In the meantime, the mountain is dark and we miss him. And the money has to be raised to bring him back.

"Heard from Haley?" Fred was back in the den.

"Not yet."

"Where's the TV thing?"

"The remote? Try the sofa."

I thought that in a moment I would hear Peter Jennings's voice. Instead, Fred surprised me by coming into the kitchen and sitting at the table.

"Maybe we ought to call her."

"It's two in the morning in Warsaw."

"They'd be sure to be at home."

I stuck the biscuits into the oven and looked at him. He seemed to be serious.

"Not a good idea, I said. "She'll let us know when she gets the test results."

I reached in the refrigerator. "Two eggs enough?"

"Sure."

"Mary Alice and Virgil are getting married in May." I took a bowl down and started breaking the eggs into it.

"I'll believe it when I see it."

"She just might do it this time. I'm to be the matron of honor and wear a magenta dress. The girls are wearing sunflower."

"Good Lord."

The rain had gotten harder. It was drumming lightly on the den skylight. The phone rang and Fred answered it.

I can always tell when he is talking to either Freddie or Alan, our two sons who live in Atlanta. He talks louder than normal, a Santa Claus voice. I can just imagine him calling them to tell them when I die. "Ho, ho, ho, Son. Your mother seems to have dropped dead on the kitchen floor. How's everything going with you?" Well, maybe I'm exaggerating with the "ho, ho, ho," but the tone is right. And Freddie and Alan are just as bad. They sound like sports announcers when they talk to each other.

Which brings me to the point that I knew he was talking to either Freddie or Alan.

"Haven't heard a word, but we're sure everything is fine. Absolutely. You want to speak to your mother?"

I wiped my hands on a paper towel to take the phone, but Fred said, "Okay, Son," and hung up.

"Alan on his car phone," he explained. "Just checking on Haley. Says he'll call you tomorrow."

"Okay. You ready to eat?"

"Let me go check the computer again. Sometimes there's a delay from overseas."

I was putting the food on our plates when he called, "Who's Joanna?"

"What?" I set the plates down and went into the den. Fred was standing in the bedroom doorway.

"Who's Joanna?"

"We got a message?"

"From Haley. It says, 'We're all fine and love you. Haley, Philip, and Joanna.' "

I rushed to the computer. There it was. Joanna.

"You dummy," I squealed. "It's a girl. Haley found out after all."

Fred and I looked at each other and then we were hugging and blubbering. Our daughter was having a daughter. Joanna.

It was a long time before we got around to eating supper. Long after we called Warsaw and did a lot of laughing and crying.

"She'll be Miss America for sure. Just think how beautiful she's going to be with Haley's strawberry-blond hair and Philip's eyes."

It was the next morning and my neighbor, Mitzi Phizer, and I were taking our morning walk. Mitzi and Arthur have lived next door to us for forty years, but it's only recently that Mitzi has been joining me every morning when I take Woofer for his stroll. I'm delighted. She's good company and swears she's lost eight pounds, though I can't believe it's the exercise. Woofer stops at every tree to mark his territory, so our hour walk may take us around three blocks.

"No. She's going to be President Joanna Nachman."

"She could be both. What's wrong with a beautiful president?"

"True."

It was a wonderful day. It smelled like early spring, that unmistakable combination of the first quince and forsythia and the sun drying last night's rain. I had called everyone in the family to tell them the news and had slept very little, but I could have run around the blocks instead of strolling. Fortunately Woofer and Mitzi weren't as hyper as I was. So we ambled and enjoyed the morning.

"Mary Alice says she's marrying Virgil Stuckey in May." I had just remembered the other big news.

"Do you think she means it? She's always getting engaged. Where does she find all these men?" Mitzi stepped over a small puddle on the sidewalk. "It was that Cedric fellow last I heard."

"She just might. She's made an awful lot of plans like what color dresses the girls and I are going to wear and where they're going on their honeymoon."

"Really?" Mitzi grinned. "What color?"

"Magenta and sunflower."

Mitzi pressed her lips together but gave up and burst out laughing.

"Are you the magenta?" she asked, reaching into the pocket of her jogging suit for a Kleenex and snuffling into it. Mitzi always cries when she laughs.

"I'm the magenta." I giggled. Mitzi's laugh was infectious. "We're going to put some stuff on my hair so I won't look so washed out."

"You're not." Mitzi reached for another Kleenex.

"And can't you just see pregnant Haley in sunflower? Sister says she'll look like she's in full bloom."

"Oh, Lord."

Woofer sat down and looked at us patiently. We had lost our minds, but that was okay.

"She won't really do it, get married," Mitzi said when we calmed down and started walking again. "This is just another one of her tangents, don't you think? Like buying the Skoot 'n' Boot because she liked to line dance."

"Maybe so." The country-western bar that she had bought was still a sore subject between Sister and me. "I'll have the lay of the land better tomorrow. We're going with Virgil and her to the Vulcan benefit tonight. It seems that Virgil, Jr., is an Elvis impersonator and is on the program."

The Kleenex came out again. Woofer gave up and sat down. We called this exercise?

"I saw them advertising that on TV," Mitzi said. "A whole line of Elvis impersonators doing that Rockettes kick."

"Well, Virgil, Jr., is one of them."

"Arthur and I ought to go. I wonder if it's sold out. We gave some money to the Vulcan restoration fund, but we haven't gotten in on any of the fun stuff."

"Call and find out. You can go with us."

We started walking again, two gray-headed ladies and a gray-headed dog. Which was fine.

"Did I ever tell you, Patricia Anne, that I dirty-boogied with Elvis once?"

"You what?"

"I dirty-boogied with Elvis. At least that's what my sorority sisters called it."

"You're kidding. You actually danced with Elvis? And, no, you've never told me."

"It was sort of embarrassing."

"We should all be so embarrassed."

Mitzi shrugged. "I guess so. Anyway, it was at a sorority party. You know I went to college in Memphis."

I nodded.

"And somehow Elvis got invited. And he came over and asked me to dance. He was absolutely the wildest dancer you ever saw. Actually, I think he was showing off some. Mostly I just stood there."

"With Elvis." I was astounded that Mitzi had never told me this before.

"There wasn't anything about him that wasn't going in different directions. I didn't have any idea what I was supposed to do."

"Just enjoy it."

"I would now."

"Well, have mercy, Mitzi. You dirty-boogied with the King and never said anything about it?"

"I guess so. He was just a kid, though. It's hard to realize he'd be in his sixties now, like we are."

"What was he like?"

"I don't know. We just went out on the floor and he danced like crazy and that was it. To tell you the truth, I thought something was wrong with him, the way his knees bent. But he seemed nice."

"Your fifteen minutes, Mitzi."

"More like four long ones."

"I'm jealous."

"I'm jealous of myself when I think about it. There I was, eighteen and dancing with Elvis Presley. I remember thinking Elvis was a strange name and wishing that he wouldn't wiggle quite so much."

"Amazing."

"Mary Alice is the one he should have gotten hold of."

I shook my head. "Boggles my mind to think of it. He probably wouldn't have gone on to be famous. She'd have worn the wiggle out."

"Possibly."

"So y'all come tonight. It'll refresh your memories."

"They're fresh."

We smiled at each other and walked along quietly for a while. Then Mitzi looked up at Red Mountain and said, "You know, Patricia Anne, on a sunny day like this, we'd be getting the full benefit of the moon. It seems so strange not to have Vulcan up there."

"We'll get that big bare butt back."

We turned the corner and headed toward home. Our neighborhood is the first of the "over the mountain" suburbs, built when the word "suburbs" probably hadn't been invented. With bedroom communities sprawling now into adjacent counties with hours of commuting time, we consider ourselves very lucky. Our houses have front porches, chain-link fences, sidewalks. And we're ten minutes from everything, even downtown. Okay, so we're not fancy, but we like it. And houses here seldom have "For sale" signs in the yards. Word of mouth sells them before realtors have a chance to list them. Mitzi and Arthur had recently come into a large amount of money and hadn't even considered moving. They had added on a sunroom.

"Come in for some coffee," I said.

"I can't. Bridgett is bringing the baby by for me to baby-sit."

"Tough job."

We grinned at each other.

"Why did they wait until we were in our sixties to have babies?"

"Well, Alan and Lisa had their boys early, but I was teaching and they were in Atlanta. Believe you me, Joanna Nachman is going to be one spoiled baby."

We had stopped in front of my driveway. Mitzi gave me a hug. "I'm so thrilled for all of you."

"Me, too. Let me know if you want to go with us tonight."

"If I can get Arthur up off of his behind." She gave a little wave and headed toward her house.

I took Woofer's leash off, gave him a couple of dog biscuits I had in my pocket, and went into the kitchen where Muffin was sitting on the table. I picked her up, hugged her, and told her she wasn't supposed to be on the kitchen table. She smelled like clean, healthy, sweet cat. How was I going to give her back to Haley? And how had I gotten so enamored of this cat anyway? I was a dog person. Mary Alice was the cat person. Her cat, Bubba, slept on a heating pad on her kitchen counter, which I had always thought was terrible. Granted, he was old. But on the kitchen counter? And he never moved. Several times I had been suspicious that he was dead and only the heat was keeping him flexible. Once I had even picked up his paw and let it drop, checking. Bubba had opened his eyes, yawned widely, and gone back to sleep. Now I hoped that Muffin didn't decide she wanted to sleep on the kitchen counter. I sat down in my recliner and held her, purring loudly, against me.

Sleep slammed against me. One moment I was sitting there holding Muffin and the next moment the phone was ringing, I was cold, and an hour had disappeared from the morning.

"Her name is Tammy Sue," Sister said when I answered the phone.

"Whose name?" I was still more than half asleep.

"Virgil's daughter. Are you all right? You sound loggy."

"I feel loggy. I was asleep. Wait a minute." I got a glass of water and came back to the phone. "Okay."

"Well, her name is Tammy Sue and she's thirty years old and her husband's an Elvis impersonator."

"I thought it was her brother who was an Elvis impersonator."

"He is. Apparently St. Clair County is just a nest of them."

I thought of rural St. Clair County: rolling hills, small towns, cattle farms. A nest of Elvis impersonators?

"How did that happen?"

"How did what happen?"

"How did St. Clair County get to be a nest of Elvis impersonators?"

"Well, my Lord, Mouse, how should I know? I'm not a historian or an anthropologist. Virgil just said there were a bunch of them up there. Maybe it's some kind of club or something."

"Like the Rotary."

"Could be."

Surely she didn't believe that.

"Anyway," she continued, "Tammy Sue is going to sit with us tonight because her husband's performing, too. And then we're all going out for dinner. Okay?"

"Fred can't eat dinner at ten o'clock because of his reflux. He'd be up all night hurting and making me think he was having a heart attack."

"Well, he can have a piece of pie or something."

"That wouldn't work, either. You've never seen him having one of his spells."

"And for that, I'm eternally grateful. But this is a big deal, meeting Tammy Fay and her husband. And we're telling them tonight that we're getting married. Y'all come with us, Mouse. Fred doesn't have to eat."

"I thought you said her name was Tammy Sue."

"It is."

"You just called her Tammy Fay."

"I'm sure she'll answer to either one."

"Well, look. When you tell her about the sunflower-colored bridesmaid dress, you'd better call her Tammy Sue. Okay?"

"Sure. Why?"

"Because it's her name."

"And you're being tacky. But we'll meet you in front of the Alabama at quarter to eight."

After I hung up, I remembered that I hadn't told her that Mitzi had dirty-boogied with Elvis. It was going to boggle her mind.

Chapter Three

The Alabama Theater is one of the great old movie palaces built in the 1920s. To enter it is to enter a Moorish castle, Alabama style. Every inch of the wall is decorated with plaster moldings of curlicues and flowers and gilded lattice grillwork entwined with lacy vines that look suspiciously like kudzu. Electric candles flicker in niches and when the lights dim, the gilded sky still glows with a pinkish light. Red carpeted stairs like those Rhett carried Scarlett O'Hara up soar from the Hall of Mirrors (the lobby included a concession stand with the best popcorn in the world). Rhett would surely have dropped her halfway up or had a heart attack, though. People huff and puff just getting themselves up those steps. But the principal attraction for Mary Alice and me, when we were children and Mama would take us to movies there, had been the lounge in the basement that had been decorated in someone's idea of a harem.

We spent more time in the lounge perched on the round, red velvet seats inhaling secondhand smoke than we did watching the movies. A lot of times the show was more interesting there. And the dialogue, too.

One thing we never missed, though, was the Mighty Wurlitzer. The lights would dim, a spotlight would come on, and the organ would rise like a red-and-gold calliope on great chords of music and applause. One o'clock in the afternoon, but Mr. Wurlitzer (we really thought that was his name) would have on a tux and would even invite us to sing along with the bouncing ball on the screen. Pure joy.

Like Vulcan, the Alabama fell on hard times. Fortunately it's in the process of being restored. It's not quite as bright as it once was, but the Mighty Wurlitzer once again rises in the spotlight and everyone's hearts beat a little faster.

Mary Alice and Virgil were waiting for us under an old movie poster advertising *Love Letters,* starring Jennifer Jones and Joseph Cotton. Beside them stood a buxom young blond woman wearing a green jacket and white flannel slacks.

"That's got to be Tammy Sue," I said to Fred.

"Tammy Sue looks corn-fed."

"She's pretty."

"I didn't say she wasn't. I said she looks corn-fed."

I gave him my schoolteacher look that, after forty years, bounces right off.

"What?" he asked. "What's wrong with being corn-fed?"

One more schoolteacher look and then we were smiling and shaking hands with Virgil, who looks like both General Norman Schwarzkopf and Willard Scott. A few tendrils of hair still cling to the top of his scalp; his face is etched with years of military service, including two wars and several awards that Mary Alice says he won't talk about, as well as almost twenty years as the sheriff of St. Clair County. Well over six feet tall, Virgil is a commanding presence with the sweetest smile I've ever seen.

Holding his firm grasp, I thought that Mary Alice had herself a prize.

Tammy Sue had her father's smile. She had a round face and pink cheeks that begged to be pinched. And she was probably a natural blonde with just a little drugstore help. The sunflower bridesmaid dress wouldn't do her in.

"Isn't this wonderful?" she said, gesturing at the crowd. "It's a sellout."

"I know," I said. "My next-door neighbor tried to get tickets this afternoon and couldn't."

"Larry, that's my husband, and Buddy, that's my brother, are going to be nervous wrecks."

"They'll be fine," Virgil said as we started into the theater.

"But there are two new guys who haven't practiced nearly enough. It has to be synchronized."

"Synchronized" came out as "thincronized." On her, it was cute.

"So Virgil, Jr., is 'Buddy'?" I asked as we worked our way through the crowd.

Tammy Sue nodded. "My mama always said he was her best buddy." She glanced at Mary Alice and Virgil, who were in front of us. It was a curious look, and I tried to remember how long Virgil had been widowed. Three years? It didn't matter. Tammy Sue would have mixed emotions.

She gave a slight shrug and turned to me with a smile. "You wouldn't believe the seats Larry and Buddy have gotten us. They're in the front row."

"That's wonderful. How did they manage that?"

"Larry's a theatrical agent. He booked half the people who are in the show tonight. Cock Fight is his biggest act." Tammy Sue beamed proudly.

Fred, who was holding my arm and listening, leaned around me and said he thought that was illegal.

Tammy Sue giggled. "It's a rock band, Mr. Hollowell. But

not far from being illegal. They get pretty outrageous sometimes."

"Sounds interesting." I turned and smiled at Fred. "And we're
in the front row."

He smiled back and mouthed, *You owe me.*

"I'll pay."

Mary Alice and Virgil were doing a great job of running inter-
ference through the crowd. Sister's good at this. Her formidable
size and elbows have opened a lot of paths for me. "Don't be so
damned polite," she'll say, snatching me along. "And why on
God's earth didn't you eat and grow?"

Sister is convinced that there are no small genes in our gene
pool. Therefore, I must be anorexic. Sometimes she'll poke me
in the ribs like the witch did Hansel and Gretel and say, "Pure
bone." Which can be scary and may, subconsciously, be the reason I haven't plumped up.

The Alabama has a large stage. When it was built, vaudeville
was still popular and no one had dreamed that the screen that
was rolled down for the movies would ever be the main attraction. Our seats were so close to the orchestra pit that we could
lean over and see the musicians who were tuning up and the
Mighty Wurlitzer with its red top and gold music rack. The man
we still called Mr. Wurlitzer, though surely there had been
dozens of them, had on a white tux and was reading a paperback
book while he waited to rise to the heavens.

"This is so exciting," Tammy Sue said as we settled down. She
was sitting in the middle, between Sister and me. With her lisp
it came out "ekthiting." She laughed and put a finger to her lips.
"Exciting." She leaned around Mary Alice. "Did you hear that,
Daddy?"

"I heard it, darling."

"Poor daddy spent a fortune on speech lessons for me, and I
still mess up when I get"—she paused—"excited."

I could learn to love Tammy Sue. As a teacher, I knew how much teasing she must have received. Virgil and his wife deserved a lot of credit for raising this happy, self-confident woman.

Sister was being unusually quiet. I was facing her as I talked to Tammy Sue and saw her glance around at us several times. But she didn't attempt to join in the conversation. Not like Sister at all. She was even wearing a black pantsuit and the rinse Delta Hairlines had put on her hair kept it from being quite as orange as usual. Hmm.

"No, Larry and I don't have any children yet," Tammy Sue was saying as the lights dimmed. I leaned over, saw Mr. Wurlitzer toss his paperback off of his platform and sit up straight. And then the magic words, "Ladies and gentlemen, the Alabama Theater proudly presents Henry Taylor at the Mighty Wurlitzer!"

I was a child again as he rose into the spotlighted air, feet pumping the pedals, fingers pressing the keys. The organ gleamed. Mr. Wurlitzer gleamed. Hot damn. Hello, my honey. Hello, my baby.

The audience was his and we sang along. He was the warm-up act, but if there had been nothing else, the audience would have been satisfied. He segued from "Take Me Out to the Ball Game" to "Stars Fell on Alabama," and we went right with him. He finished with "God Bless America" and half the audience, confusing it for a moment for the national anthem, stood.

"Irving Berlin and Kate Smith would be proud," I told Tammy Sue, who had jumped to her feet and sat back down slightly embarrassed.

"Who?" she asked.

"He wrote it. She sang it."

"Oh. Okay."

Mr. Wurlitzer began to sink into the orchestra pit as the audience belted out and held the last "home." I glanced over, saw him turn off the lights on his music stand, give a little wave to the orchestra leader, and hop off his bench even before it had totally reached the bottom. Then he grabbed his paperback and disappeared through a small door under the stage.

The applause died down when the gold curtain began to rise. We were greeted with a night scene. A full, bright moon shone against a backdrop of dark sky and against that moon a girl was silhouetted. Slowly she began to dance as a spotlight gradually lit a male figure on the stage watching her, reaching for her.

"Larry didn't book this act," Tammy Sue whispered into my right ear.

"Looks like ballet," Fred whispered into my left ear.

Whatever. It was lovely. And by the time the two were moving toward each other for an embrace, I was totally lost in the dance and unprepared for the whack against my head.

I jumped. Sister was reaching around Tammy Sue and hitting me with her program.

"What!" I was in no mood to be disturbed.

She said something I couldn't understand.

"What?" The couple met. He lifted her lightly.

Tammy Sue translated as the couple embraced.

"She says that's Dusk Armstrong."

"Really?" I looked at the beautiful spotlighted girl with interest. Mary Alice and I have an acquaintance, Bernice Armstrong, who has three daughters born ten years apart. Dawn was the first, then Day ten years later. That was fine. But Bernice obviously lost her mind when she had the last one or was sending not-so-subliminal messages to her husband, Jerry, when she named the baby Dusk. Dawn is a former Miss Alabama and a model; Day is an assistant manager of a Regent's Bank. Our prognosis for Dusk's occupation had never been optimistic. Fortunately we were wrong.

Great, I mouthed back at Sister.

"Here comes one of Larry's acts," Tammy Sue exclaimed.

The Briquettes danced onto the stage and did a reasonable imitation of The Supremes. I hoped Larry wasn't planning on making a living as their agent, but the audience gave them a good round of applause.

It was during this act that Fred dozed off. He missed the jugglers, the tap dancers, Miss Jefferson County, and Miss Point Mallard's duet. But there was no sleeping through Cock Fight.

All of the lights went out. Total darkness. Then one spotlight popped on to a single man center stage. He was dressed as an eighteenth-century dandy: tight white pants, knee-high stockings, waistcoat, and even a white wig. He stood still for a second, and then he did a slow bump and grind—ending with his pelvis stuck so far out it was unbelievable.

"Ready for loooove." He moaned.

The audience squealed its agreement. Then *pop, pop, pop.* Other spotlights on other guys about as ready for love as they could get.

"It's stuffing," Tammy Sue explained just before they blasted into an unrecognizable song with, for me, unrecognizable acoustical instruments. I slapped my hands over my ears and looked up nervously. That was old plaster up there on the ceiling. Vibrations like this could cause an avalanche.

Fred's eyes were open and he wasn't moving. I poked him with my elbow and motioned for him to put his hands over his ears.

He pulled my left hand down.

"Have I died and gone to hell?"

"Not yet."

He nodded and covered his ears.

Next to me, Tammy Sue was jumping up and down, squealing, and clapping. Beside her, Mary Alice and Virgil seemed as stunned as Fred and I were. We looked like four hear-no-evil monkeys connected by a jack-in-the-box. Then the spotlights changed colors and I closed my eyes. Thank God our cousin

Pukey Lukey wasn't with us. His motion sickness, which he has never outgrown completely, would never have survived this.

Fred pulled down my hand again.

"What?" I screamed.

"Are those men for real?"

"They're 'ready for loooove.' "

He looked so crestfallen, I took pity. "Tammy Sue says it's stuffing."

"Pass the word to Virgil."

But I clasped my hand back to my ear. Let Sister reassure Virgil about his masculinity.

The man, who I supposed was the lead singer since he seemed to be the one doing the most strutting, began to rip the brass buttons off of his waistcoat and throw them into the audience. He squatted and tossed one gently to Tammy Sue, who looked as if she might faint. Then he rose, straightened his stuffing, held out his arms, and sailed into the orchestra pit.

The audience gasped. All of us in the front row leaned forward or jumped up to see if he was all right. The orchestra pit was dark and empty. The other members of the rock band didn't seem perturbed, though, that one of their members had departed, quite possibly for good. They were making as much noise as ever.

"Reckon he's okay?" I screamed to Tammy Sue.

"Probably. That's Bobby Joe."

Bobby Joe, being a rock star, was immune to injuries?

As in answer, he strutted back onstage, a gold-tinsel halo bouncing above his head. The audience went wild.

"I thought for sure he'd broken his neck," Fred said. He sounded disappointed.

There were fifteen more long minutes. And then, thank God, it was time for intermission.

Tammy Sue's face was flushed. "Weren't they wonderful?

Can you believe that Larry's their agent?" She held up the brass button that Bobby Joe had thrown to her and looked at it as if she were a jeweler appraising a valuable stone.

"Must have been paying the preacher," Fred said.

I put my hand on Fred's cheek and turned his face toward me. "Enough."

He grinned and stood up. "I'm going to the bathroom."

"Take your time."

"He seems very nice," Tammy Sue said as he left.

"He usually is. Rock bands just aren't his type of music."

"What is?"

"You talking about Fred?" Mary Alice leaned over and joined in our conversation. Virgil, I noticed, had joined the crowd streaming up the aisle. "Last I heard he was into Tommy Dorsey."

"Oooh, I love Tommy Dorsey," Tammy Sue exclaimed. She turned to me. "Is Mr. Hollowell a good jitterbugger?"

"Absolutely," I said, smiling sweetly at Sister.

She smiled back just as sweetly. "You ever heard of the Hollowell Jive of Fifty-Five, Tammy Sue? Fred originated that. Of course, that was back when his joints worked."

Tammy Sue looked from one of us to the other. "Y'all are kidding me."

"Now, would I do that?" Sister asked.

"Yes."

"And you'd be right." Sister stood up. "Do either of you want to try for the bathroom?"

I shook my head. No way I was going to stand in the line to the ladies' room which I knew would be snaking up the steps.

"I don't want to miss the second half," Tammy Sue said.

The three of us nodded in agreement. Damn men architects.

"I wish I had a choice. Oh, well." Sister gave a little wave. "See you later."

"She seems very nice," Tammy Sue said. "I know Daddy's crazy about her."

I nodded. It was going to be interesting to see how Tammy Sue and Mary Alice worked out their relationship. I hoped Tammy Sue wouldn't be intimidated by her new stepmother.

"Do you think they're going to get married?"

I had forgotten that Mary Alice and Virgil hadn't told his children yet. That explained Sister's unusual quietness tonight. She was nervous about breaking the news. A new role for Sister.

"Maybe," I said.

"Well, maybe it'll work out. Daddy's been needing someone. And Mary Alice seems so easy to get along with. I really like her."

Easy to get along with? Lord have mercy.

"I just hope, if they do, that it's a little wedding, and that she's not planning on me wearing a bridesmaid dress. I'm done with that. Last time I was in a wedding I had to wear the most god-awful yellow dress you ever saw, and I said to myself, 'No more, Tammy Sue.'"

Oh, joy. Welcome to the family, Tammy Sue.

We had a wonderful fifteen minutes of conversation. I told Tammy Sue about Haley and the baby. She told me about her job as a realtor, that she and Larry had been married for five years, that her brother, Buddy, was still drifting, she thought. An Elvis impersonator? Get real. It was fun for Larry, but sometimes she thought Buddy really believed he was Elvis. He needed to settle down, get a good job, and find a nice girl to marry.

Members of the orchestra began to wander back into the orchestra pit. Fred and Virgil came down the aisle.

"Did you see Mary Alice?" I asked.

Virgil nodded. "In the line outside the ladies' room. You ought to see that line."

"We see them every day," Tammy Sue said.

Neither man looked concerned. Hah. Nicholas and Alexandra hadn't been concerned, either. Soon the great bladder revolution, boys.

The lights dimmed and the Mighty Wurlitzer rose from the floor again to begin the second half of the show. The organ was so well lighted that the women trying to get back to their seats weren't having too much trouble. By the time we sang "Cuddle Up a Little Closer," "Alexander's Ragtime Band," and Mr. Wurlitzer had segued into what he announced was the *hymn du jour*, "How Great Thou Art," the audience was settling down—even Mary Alice, who was breathing heavily and fussing, "Who the hell's idea was it to put the bathrooms in the basement?" as she stumbled over Virgil's feet.

Fortunately the audience was belting out the last line of "How Great Thou Art."

Tammy Sue patted her on the arm sympathetically.

We sat back to enjoy the rest of the show. There were the usual jugglers, comedy routines, one spectacular group of contortionists that Fred said it hurt him to watch and which Tammy Sue said was one of her husband Larry's acts. And then, according to the program, it was time for the dancing Elvises.

The music was "Jailhouse Rock," and fifteen Elvises came from each side of the stage, thirty Elvises in all. They were short, tall, skinny, paunchy, but still eerily alike with their black hair, sideburns, and white jumpsuits. They danced onto the stage with a sort of sidestep, then joined arms, bowed to the audience's applause, and then broke apart. We soon caught on that there were four stars who got to come to the front of the stage and do their version of Elvis dances. One turned cartwheels and did splits, which I had never seen Elvis do, but he was good at it and got a round of applause. One was wonderful, dirty-boogying and sweating.

"That's Larry." Tammy Sue squealed. "Hey, Larry!"

Larry's hips moved even faster.

I poked Tammy Sue. "Where's Virgil, Jr.?"

"That's him coming up now."

He wasn't dancing like Larry had done. His movements were

slower, more sinuous. He was Elvis, the slight sneer on his face, the lock of hair across his forehead. The audience went crazy.

And then the line was back together again. The music changed to "Love Me Tender," and the Elvises began the chorus-line kick. Since they weren't all the same size, it was ragged but effective nonetheless. Thirty Elvises advanced toward us. Twenty-nine stopped at the edge of the stage, held up their arms, and then bowed. But one kept coming, staggering sideways for a moment, then advancing. For a second he looked straight at me, his face contorted. Then he reeled and fell backward into the deep orchestra pit.

There was the screech of musical instruments in the pit, silence from the audience, and then an uneasy stirring. This was just another stunt like the Cock Fight guy had pulled. Right? Then twenty-nine Elvises rushed over and looked into the pit, some of them in eminent danger of following their cohort as they jockeyed positions to see what had happened.

"Larry, don't you fall off that stage," Tammy Sue screamed. "Get your ass back." She jumped up and looked down into the pit. "My God. He's hurt bad."

Virgil, too, was leaning over and looking.

"Daddy!"

Virgil looked up. Virgil, Jr., who was okay, was yelling at him. Virgil closed his eyes and sat back down.

The audience had caught on. Several people rushed down the aisle toward the stage. Doctors, I hoped.

"Don't look," Fred told me.

"Are you crazy? No way."

Tammy Sue was keeping us apprised of what was happening anyway.

"His head's in the bass fiddle. He's not moving. I'll bet those strings cut the hell out of him. Looks like he bounced off the organ, though. The corner's smushed."

"Let's go. I hate this." Fred said, standing and taking my hand.

"We're going," I said to Mary Alice, who had her hands over her face. She nodded.

"Looks like there's blood everywhere," Tammy Sue announced. "I'll bet it was one of those new guys who didn't know what he was doing. Probably dead."

"Sit down, Tammy Sue," Virgil ordered. He had an arm around Sister's shoulder.

Tammy Sue looked startled, but she sat.

Fred and I got the hell out. Most of the people in the audience were still seated, waiting to find out about the Elvis, to see what was going to happen next, hoping against hope that he would prance back onstage with a tinsel halo. So the aisles were still fairly clear. We got out of the parking lot easily and were almost home before either of us spoke. Then Fred said, "Stuff like that gets to me. Did you see the expression on that poor man's face? I never saw anything like it. Weird."

"I think he was dying before he fell."

Which was true. The story made the eleven o'clock news. Not only was the Elvis dead of an apparent heart attack, but 911 had received a record number of calls. The name of the man was being withheld until relatives could be notified.

I fixed us some hot chocolate with a lot of tiny marshmallows, and we sat by the fire talking about Haley and the baby, trying to dim the too vivid picture of the man with the contorted face staggering toward us.

It was midnight before we went to bed. It had been an unnerving evening, but the last thing I thought about before I went to sleep was Tammy Sue, and I had to smile. Mary Alice just might have met her match.

Chapter Four

E-mail from: Haley
To: Mama and Papa
Subject: Homecoming

Oh, happy day! We've made our plane reservations. The three of us will be on a Delta flight that gets into Birmingham at 4:15 on April 1. I didn't know how homesick I was until I realized that this time next month we'll be settled in our own house in Alabama. I can't wait to see all of you. I know the twins have grown so much, and we haven't even set eyes on David Anthony. Debbie's been sending us pictures, but I can't wait to hug him. To hug all of you.

Mama, I've got a favor to ask. Could you go over to Philip's house (I haven't started thinking of it as our house yet. Guess I will soon.) one day soon and open it up? Don't do any cleaning, just air it out. We'll get a maid service when we get home to clean it up. We've got to straighten everything out first. We got married and left in such a hurry that I just sort of threw my stuff in.

I'm feeling fine. I can't wait!

Hugs and kisses to both of you and to Woofer and Muffin, too.

Love,

Haley

E-mail to: Haley
From: Mama
Subject: Can't wait to see you

Honey, I can't wait until the first of April. I'll be happy to go over and open up the house. All sorts of things are happening here. Your aunt Sister has set the date for her wedding, but I'm sure that she or Debbie has e-mailed or called you. It's May 14. We are all to be bridesmaids. More details on this later. You're really going to like Virgil. We met his daughter last night. His son is an Elvis impersonator. Not bad, either. We went to see him perform last night at the Alabama, a fund-raiser for Vulcan.

Take care, honey. Love to you, Joanna, and Philip

There was no reason to tell her all of the evening's details. I hit the send button and delivered her hugs and kisses to Muffin, who was lying in the bay window in the kitchen watching the birds at the feeder.

"I'm keeping you, though," I said. It was the first time I had voiced this, but I knew it was true. There was no way that Haley was going to get Muffin back. Muffin's tail slashed back and forth as my elbow accidentally hit the window and the birds flew away.

She gazed up at me with a look-what-you've-done-now look.

"I'm sorry," I apologized.

She might or might not forgive me.

"I'm keeping you anyway," I said.

It was almost 8:30. I had slept the night before but not a deep, restful sleep. Fred hadn't slept well, either, and at some time during the night he had gotten up. The afghan crumpled on the den sofa told me that was where he had finished the night. I hadn't heard him leave. I'd check with him in a little while. He'd want to hear Haley's news, too.

Fred had brought the morning paper in and left it on the table. The Metro Section had been pulled out and I saw what he had probably been looking for. The headline announced: ACCI-DENT AT ALABAMA KILLS PERFORMER.

Accident? No way. Heart attack, maybe.

I poured myself a glass of orange juice and a cup of coffee and sat down to read the story. There was nothing new. An Elvis impersonator had fallen into the orchestra pit of the Alabama Theater during a performance the previous evening. He was pronounced dead at University Hospital. The name was being withheld pending notification of next of kin.

Suddenly the man's face, contorted as it had been the night before, was superimposed on the story. Damn. I pushed the paper aside, reached over, and turned on the TV on the kitchen counter.

"An accident at the Alabama Theater last night claimed the life of an unidentified man."

I switched off the TV and made myself think about Haley coming home. Her refrigerator would need to be stocked, and she wouldn't feel like going to the grocery. It had taken me a week to get over jet lag when we got back from Warsaw, and I wasn't pregnant. Some flowers would be nice, too.

I got a pencil and a piece of paper from the junk drawer. In a few minutes, I was lost in list making.

A spatter of rain against the window startled me. I glanced out at the thermometer on the deck and saw that it was forty-two degrees. A raw day. March. I got my raincoat from the hall closet, slipped my feet into my sneakers, and went to check on Woofer. He was snuggled up warm and cozy in his igloo. I handed him a couple of treats, promised a walk if the weather improved, and invited him into the house.

He declined the invitation. I gave him the hug and kiss that Haley had sent and scurried back into the house, where the phone was ringing.

"You okay?" Fred asked.

"I'm fine. You okay?"

"Fine. Didn't get much sleep last night."

"Me neither."

"Have you heard anything more about that man at the Alabama?"

"They're saying it was an accident, and they haven't given his name yet."

"That was no accident."

"I know."

"Let me know if you hear anything."

"I will. And, honey? We got an e-mail from Haley. They're getting in on April the first. She wants us to open up the house for them."

"How about that."

"I know."

I could imagine how Fred's face had brightened at the news. Her absence these last few months had left a giant hole in our lives.

The phone rang again just as I hung up.

"Egg McMuffin or sausage biscuit?" Sister asked.

"Egg McMuffin."

I put on a pot of fresh coffee.

She must have been calling from the drive-in window, since she was at my kitchen door before the coffee had finished perking.

"Damn," she said, holding out a McDonald's sack for me to

take while she closed her umbrella. "So much for the sunny South." She stepped inside and pulled off her raincoat.

"What on God's earth have you got on?" I asked. "You look like Yul Brynner."

She swirled so I could get the benefit of the outfit from all directions. Yards of white material, tied at the waist with a yellow scarf, ballooned out as she turned. I was wrong. She looked more like the Pillsbury Doughboy than she did Yul Brynner. She hung the raincoat on the back of the pantry door.

"I'm taking a class in the martial arts. It's a mixture of karate, tae kwon do, and some other stuff. It's Virgil's idea. He says every woman should be able to protect herself."

"You've been doing a pretty good job." I got plates down, put them on the table, and started unwrapping Egg McMuffins.

"I think he's right, though. You ought to go with me. Little as you are, you're a sitting duck."

"But I have you to protect me."

Sister pulled a chair out and sat down. "True. Actually, Virgil wanted me to get a gun, too, but I told him I didn't like them. He said he didn't like them, either, but being a sheriff it was pretty important to have one."

"But you're not, are you? Getting one?" I poured the coffee.

"Of course not. I'm just going to learn how to break necks. Incidentally, you need a new bathrobe. That thing is pitiful. I didn't even know they still made chenille."

"Penney's found some somewhere." I took a big bite of my Egg McMuffin. Delicious.

Sister pointed to the newspaper I had placed on the counter. "Did you see the article about the man who fell in the orchestra pit last night?"

"Don't want to talk about it while we're eating. That was pretty gruesome."

"I was just going to tell you who he was. His name was Griffin Mooncloth."

"Mooncloth? What kind of name is that?"

"Just a name. Pretty, isn't it?"

"How did you find out? They're still not releasing it on the news."

"Virgil called me this morning. He stayed last night to help the Birmingham police out. Tammy Sue took me home."

What I was supposed to do then, what Sister was waiting for me to do, was to ask her to tell me more, but I didn't. Death and Egg McMuffins don't mix. A man with a name is too real. I concentrated on my food and told her that Haley was coming in on the first.

"Good," she said, wiping her hands on a paper napkin. "We'll give them a party."

I had taken exactly two bites of my Egg McMuffin. Sister had polished hers off.

"Can I tell you some more stuff that's not too bad?" she asked.

I nodded. Might as well.

"Nobody knew who he was."

"He just boogied out onstage with the other Elvises and none of them knew him?"

"Apparently. He was in Bud McCracken's place in the line, and nobody noticed that it wasn't Bud because he's new anyway."

I finished chewing my Egg McMuffin, swallowed, and crumpled up my paper napkin.

"What happened to Bud?"

"He's disappeared." Sister tapped her fingers on the table. "Can I tell you now what happened to Griffin Mooncloth?"

"Don't be too graphic."

"Would 'somebody slit his gizzard out' be too graphic?"

The Egg McMuffin stuck about halfway down my esophagus. I reached for my coffee. "You're lying."

Mary Alice shook her head. "That's what Virgil said. He said,

'Mary Alice, honey, somebody just slit the gizzard right out of that poor boy.' "

I glared at Sister. "That can't be right. Virgil's putting you on. That man was dancing right toward us in a white satin suit and there wasn't a drop of blood on it."

Sister reached down and picked up Muffin, who was rubbing against her leg. "You going to let Haley have this cat back?"

"No. I've got squatter's rights."

Muffin settled down in Sister's lap. Sister scratched her under the chin and said she reckoned that Griffin Mooncloth had had his gizzard cut out from the back.

"Oh, for heaven's sake." I pushed my chair back so quickly that Sister and Muffin both looked up in surprise. "People don't have gizzards." I snatched my plate and Sister's and put them in the dishwasher. "Gizzards are what come in the plastic bags they stick up frozen chickens' rear ends."

"Well, my goodness. Don't get testy. Maybe Virgil was speaking metaphorically."

Metaphorically? If I hadn't been so upset, I'd have been impressed. Instead I asked, "What in hell would a gizzard be a metaphor for?"

"Some important organ that he couldn't get along without. Why is it making you mad, anyway?"

"Because." I reached for the coffeepot. "Because last night we were sitting in the Alabama Theater, having a nice time and watching a bunch of Elvises dance, and one of them named Griffin Mooncloth, and I don't believe that name for a minute, whom nobody knew, got killed right in front of us, and Virgil treats it lightly by saying he got his gizzard cut out." I pointed to Sister's cup. "You want some more?"

She nodded. "You take your estrogen today?"

I ignored that and poured the coffee. "I didn't get much sleep last night."

"You must not have."

I sat back down. Muffin deserted Sister and got in my lap. That made me feel better. I rubbed her head with one hand and reached for the sugar with the other.

"I don't know. It's just that I saw his face and kept seeing it all night." I stirred my coffee. "How did they find out his name if nobody knew him? There sure wasn't room for a wallet in that jumpsuit."

"Dusk Armstrong knew him. Turned out he was one of her old boyfriends. Virgil said they asked everyone in the show to stay to see if anyone could identify him. She was the only one who knew him. She's been studying dancing in New York and says he was in her class."

"He was from New York?"

Sister nodded.

I thought of Dusk outlined against the moon the night before, how beautiful she had been. Lord, I hoped this wasn't something she was involved with.

There was a tap on the backdoor and Mitzi Phizer stuck her raincoat-covered head in. "Hey," she said. "I saw your car, Mary Alice, and thought I'd find out what happened at the Alabama last night. I heard on TV that one of the performers died onstage."

"Fell into the orchestra pit," Sister said.

"Oh, my Lord!" Mitzi shook raindrops from her gray curls.

"But he was already dead." Sister looked at me. "Someone had removed one of his vital organs."

"What?"

I got up, took Mitzi's raincoat, and hung it on the door by Sister's. It was raining so hard now that water dripped on the floor from the coat. I had a sudden memory of the old cloakrooms at Lakeview School, could even smell the damp of the coats and galoshes, the bologna sandwiches in tin Mickey Mouse lunch boxes. Damn. I shook my head, which I realized was throbbing dully. I felt the knot from the day before yesterday when I had slammed into the drainpipe. It was slightly sore. Did concussions take forty-eight hours to show up?

"We had seats in the front row, and he fell right in front of us," Mary Alice said. "He was one of the Elvis impersonators."

Mitzi sat down at the table. "And someone killed him?"

"Dead as a doornail."

I picked up the coffeepot. Mitzi motioned that she didn't want any.

"Who was he?" she asked.

Sister was happy to relate the story again. I leaned against the kitchen counter and listened. The rain hitting the skylight sounded loud. I felt cold.

"Well, my goodness," Mitzi said. "Dusk Armstrong? Bernice's baby?"

I nodded. "Dawn, Day, and Dusk. Bless her heart."

"Bernice should have had better sense," Mary Alice said. She pushed her chair back. "I've got to go to class. Martial arts," she explained to Mitzi.

"I figured. Or trying out for *The King and I*. You look like Yul Brynner."

"The better to kick ass. *Yaaa!*" Sister jumped and gave a karate chop. Muffin skittered into the den and down the hall.

"What did you think of Tammy Sue?" she asked me, putting her coat back on and ignoring the fact that Mitzi had jumped halfway out of her chair.

"Very nice."

Sister nodded. "We're going to get along fine."

"You haven't told her about the wedding yet, have you?"

"We're going to tonight."

"Be sure to tell her she's going to be a bridesmaid."

"I will. Bye, Mitzi." A wave and she was gone.

"She's wonderful," Mitzi said admiringly as the door closed behind the karate kid. "I wish I had half of her energy."

"She may have met her match with Tammy Sue, Virgil's

daughter. The sunflower bridesmaid dresses may be on their way out." I shivered. "Why don't we go in the den? I'll light a fire."

"Are you feeling all right?"

"Just no sleep, I think. But will you check this knot on my head? Can concussions take a couple of days to show up?"

Mitzi ran her hand carefully over the bump and then looked at the pupils of my eyes.

"Are they supposed to be dilated or undilated?"

"Dilated, I think."

"Well, these aren't my reading glasses, but they look okay. Why don't you put on your reading glasses. That ought to magnify them."

Which I did and was pronounced normal.

"Why don't you go curl up on the sofa with a book," Mitzi suggested. "I'm going to the store. Do you need anything?"

I needed sleep. I shut off the ringer on the phone and sacked out. One of the great pleasures of being retired. I miss my students, I'll admit, but tutoring math a couple of mornings a week at the local middle school helps. I wish someone had clued me in to math thirty years earlier, though. One answer. One. I was grading research papers. Footnotes. Bibliographies. English grammar. And the math teachers were checking one answer. Of course I had become very good friends with *Beowulf* and Walt Whitman. No small perk.

When I woke up, I felt loggy but better. The rain was still pelting the skylight, so taking Woofer for a walk was out. I checked the phone. No calls. I was convinced that Mary Alice would have had a dozen. I swear she belongs to every club in Birmingham and is on the board of the museum, the botanical gardens, and the Humane Society. You name it. I belong to an investment club that meets once a month, and she belongs to it, too.

I fixed a peanut butter and banana sandwich and sat down to watch *The Price Is Right,* but I couldn't concentrate on it. I gave up and turned it off when a woman overbid on a pickup truck by ten thousand dollars. My Lord. What did she think it was made of? Gold? I went to the desk and fished out the list of things to do for Haley. I should buy something special for the baby. But what? Something they would see when they walked into the house that would let them know how thrilled we were about our granddaughter.

A rocking chair? I'd look while I was at their house and see if there was a rocking chair just the right size for holding a baby to nurse her and, later on, to read to her and rock her to sleep. I was daydreaming so hard that the phone's ring startled me.

"Hey, Aunt Pat," Debbie said. "You okay? You sound out of breath."

"I'm fine, honey. Just thinking about buying Haley a rocking chair to rock the baby in. Maybe have it there in the house when they come in."

"That's a great idea. I'm wearing mine out."

"Is Brother okay?"

"He'd be better off if the twins would leave him alone. They think he ought to play with them."

The twins, Fay and May, are almost three. Two-month-old Brother would have to grow up quickly to protect himself.

"Each of them had him by a leg last night pulling him across the floor."

"My Lord!"

"He seemed to be enjoying it. Henry sat them down and explained that Brother is not a doll, though, and that they could hurt him."

"I hope they listened."

"I'm sure they did. The novelty of having a baby around just hasn't worn off."

Novelty?

"Where are they now?" I asked. I'm sure I sounded fearful.

Debbie giggled. "Asleep. All of them. Listen, Aunt Pat, I

called for a couple of reasons. One is that y'all were at the Alabama Theater last night, weren't you? Mama told me she had tickets."

"In the front row. You've heard about the man getting killed? He fell in the orchestra pit right in front of us. It was horrible, Debbie."

"Well, that's what I wanted to know. On the news this morning they said he died of a heart attack. Then on the noon news, they said it was a murder."

"Your mother was by here earlier and informed me the man's gizzard was cut out. I think that classifies as murder. Why? Why do you need to know?"

"Well, they said his name was Griffin Mooncloth. That's not your usual everyday name. And I talked to him yesterday. He had an appointment with me this afternoon at three."

"Really? What was it about?"

"I don't know, Aunt Pat. He called and left a message and when I called back he just said he needed some legal questions answered and made the appointment." She paused. "He said it wouldn't take long, so I figured it couldn't be too complicated."

"I hope he wasn't planning on changing his will."

"I hope not, too. Tell me what happened."

The story got shorter each time I told it. It reminded me of teaching. For first period classes you had more than you could cover. By last period, with the same material, you had time left over. In my version to Debbie of Griffin Mooncloth's death he was stabbed and fell into the orchestra pit. Period.

"Then we left," I ended.

"Hmm."

I could hear a tapping noise. "Are you hitting your teeth with a pencil?" I asked.

"Guilty."

"Well, quit it. Your mother's got a fortune invested in your teeth."

"True." The noise stopped. "What did he look like, Aunt Pat?"

"I wasn't paying much attention to him until he left the Elvis chorus line and fell forward. That's what they were doing, that chorus-line kick all together and he kept coming. He didn't look too good then."

"Young?" Middle-aged?"

"I'd guess thirtyish. Why?"

"I don't know. It's just that he sounded so nice on the phone."

"You remember Dusk Armstrong? She identified him. Said he was in a dance class with her in New York. She can probably tell you about him."

"She's here in Birmingham?"

"She was in the show last night. Beautiful."

"Always has been."

There was a moment of silent agreement.

"Aunt Pat? The other reason I called was because I got a strange message from Marilyn. Some of it was garbled, probably talking on her car phone. All I could make out was 'Debbie, don't tell Mama.' Have you heard from her?"

Marilyn is Mary Alice's oldest child. Her father was Will Alec Sullivan, the chinless husband. Fortunately Marilyn has a beautiful chin. In fact, she is a beautiful woman, tall like her mother, but thin, elegant. She lives in Pensacola, where she has worked most recently as a financial planner. She has had some fairly long-lasting relationships with men but says she's not interested in marriage. Ever. Somehow I believe her.

"I haven't heard a word from her, honey. Let me know what she's up to."

"I will. Love you, Aunt Pat."

"Love you, too, darling."

Just as I hung up the phone, the doorbell rang. Most unusual. Nobody comes in our front door.

I looked through the peephole and saw a man drenched by the rain. He was running his hands through wet, dark, curly

hair, scattering raindrops. I left the chain on the door and
opened it.

"Yes?"

"Mrs. Hollowell?"

"Yes."

"I'm Charles Boudreau, Mrs. Hollowell. I'm here to impregnate your niece."

"You're what?" Surely I hadn't heard right.

"Oh, God," he said, a look of pain on his face. "I'm too late,
aren't I?"

Chapter Five

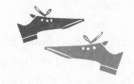

The man looked to be in his late thirties. He was well dressed, and while I stood there with my mouth open, he pulled a bright white handkerchief from his pocket and wiped the rain from his face. Or maybe it was tears.

Surely he hadn't said he wanted to impregnate my niece. Maybe the music from the Cock Fight group the night before had damaged my ears. I tapped them and said, "What?" again.

"I'm Charles Boudreau, Mrs. Hollowell. Marilyn's beau."

Not boyfriend. Beau. Men hadn't been beaux in my lifetime. Was he putting me on?

"Has she mentioned me?" He had the most beautiful eyes I had ever seen, a dark, soulful brown with lashes that any woman would kill for.

"Not that I remember."

"Is she here? In Birmingham?"

"Not that I know of."

He reached in his pocket and handed me a damp business card across the chain on the door.

"Well, if she shows up, will you please tell her that I'm at the Tutwiler Hotel and that if it's not too late, I'm ready and willing. Not just willing but thrilled. Anxious. Ecstatic."

I glanced at the card. Charles Stewart Boudreau, Attorney, Boudreau and Associates, Lafayette, Louisiana.

"I'll tell her, Mr. Boudreau."

"I thank you mightily, ma'am."

I swear he gave a slight bow before he turned and headed back toward the red Nissan parked at the curb, walking slowly as if the sky weren't pouring buckets of rain on his head. He looked so bedraggled that, for a moment, I considered calling him back and fixing him some hot chocolate.

Never let a stranger in the house, my common sense said.

But he looks so pitiful. I waffled.

The man is nuts. What kind of a person comes to the door announcing that he's there to impregnate your niece?

A nutty one, I agreed. *Best not invite him in.*

I went into the den and dialed Debbie's number.

"Have you ever heard Marilyn mention a Charles Boudreau from Lafayette, Louisiana?" I asked when she answered.

"Seems like the name's familiar. Why?"

"He's here to impregnate her."

"At your house?"

"I'm not sure where the event is supposed to take place. But he's staying at the Tutwiler. We're to tell her that he's ready, willing, thrilled, anxious, and ecstatic."

"What?"

I repeated the adjectives, adding that he was also afraid that it was too late.

"What does he mean by 'too late'?"

"Trust me. I have no idea."

"Maybe she's already pregnant, and this is what I'm not sup-posed to tell Mama."

"Could be."

"But Marilyn is the sensible one, Aunt Pat. She wouldn't do anything like just up and get pregnant like I did."

"You thought it out, honey. You wanted children and the UAB sperm bank was a good solution. You had no idea that Henry would show up in a couple of years."

"True. And if I hadn't done it I wouldn't have my precious girls."

"Let's not even think about that. But listen, if you hear from Marilyn, let me know. In the meantime, I'm not going to men-tion this to your mother."

"I won't, either. She'd be down at the Tutwiler grilling Charles Boudreau." Debbie paused. "He sounds Cajun, doesn't he?"

"He may be. He has gorgeous, dark eyes."

"Marilyn has always found great-looking men."

"You haven't done so bad yourself."

"True. Well, let the good times roll, Aunt Pat."

We both hung up laughing.

I brushed my teeth, combed my hair, and slapped on some lipstick, the minimum I figured I could get away with if I were hit by a truck on the way to Philip's house. Every woman in the world knows you have to wear clean underwear in case you are hit by a truck, but the lipstick may be a Southern thing. You want to look pretty when the firemen unhinge your door with the jaws of life, and the paramedics rush you to the waiting hel-icopter for the trip to Carraway or University Hospital. The con-dition of your underwear might be questionable by that time but, by damn, your lips would be Shimmering Coral, and there's something to be said for that.

The rain hadn't slacked at all. At this rate, Village Creek would be over its banks in time for the TV weather people to announce it on the five o'clock news. One of them would be standing under a huge umbrella with rain popping against it. "Looka there," they would exclaim excitedly, pointing to the debris toward the rushing creek. Years ago the city bought the houses that were threatened by the flooding, but it's still a favorite TV shot. I've seen a reporter standing there pointing at a floating foam cooler while lightning zapped around him. "Looka there."

I got my old yellow vinyl poncho with the hood from the hall closet and ran to my car. The poncho is not the outfit I would want to be wearing if I were pulled from my car after the proverbial collision with the proverbial truck In fact, I think it makes me look like a commercial for frozen fish sticks. But this was a poncho day.

Philip's house (it was going to take me a long time to think of it as Haley's, too) is not far from Mary Alice's in a part of town called Redmont. It's a beautiful old section of Birmingham atop Red Mountain, overlooking the whole city. The steel barons built their homes up there. From their windows they could see their mill furnaces lighting up the valley at night. Philip's grandfather, who had built his house, had not been one of the industrial barons but had founded one of Birmingham's first banks and had handled the steel accounts very well. His father and his uncle Philip (Mary Alice's second husband) had carried on in their father's footsteps in the bank. But the younger generation had sold it. Sister and Debbie had gotten a pretty penny from the sale. Debbie had been a child and has never been the type to be impressed with wealth, but Fred laughed until he cried when Sister burst into our kitchen fluttering a check and declaring that, as God was her witness, she would never go hungry again.

"You've never missed a meal in your life," he snorted.

"And now I never will, thanks to my darling Philip."

At the time she was married to her darling Roger, who was richer than Philip.

I pulled into the circular driveway and looked at the house.

Dark brick, it was a generic large house, fitting no specific type of architecture. On a rainy day like this, it seemed downright gloomy, and I thought of the contrast between this and the house Haley and Tom had owned. It had been all white with splashes of bright colors, orange kitchen chairs, abstract paintings. She sold it a month after Tom had been killed and had moved into an apartment. Now I studied this house, trying to figure out some way to make it more inviting and homey. I smiled. A swing set in the front yard would do wonders.

As I was getting out of the car, a new Mercedes pulled up behind me and Yul Brynner got out. We both dashed for the porch.

"I saw your car," Sister said, as I unlocked the door. "I was on my way home."

I looked back at the Mercedes. "How's your new car doing?"

"I miss my Jag. I may have to swap this one in—I don't care if it does help the state's economy."

Sister had hit a mailbox with her beloved Jaguar a couple of months earlier (she swears it was all my fault), and Virgil had talked her into buying the Mercedes because it was made in Alabama. Him being able to talk her into something was the first clue I had that she was really serious about him.

"Did you have a good workout?"

We stepped into the dark hall. I pulled my yellow vinyl poncho over my head, trying not to scatter too much moisture.

"Let's just say that if a big man came up behind and grabbed me, I could pick him up and throw him into tomorrow."

"That sounds good." I looked around for a place to put the poncho, finally laying it on a throw rug just inside the door.

Mary Alice nodded and glanced around. "I don't remember this place being so gloomy. I swear I've been to parties here and it looked good and smelled good."

"Well, Philip's been living here by himself for years since Lorraine died, and it's been closed up for seven months."

"Even so." She sniffed. "Haley's going to have her work cut out for her. It smells terrible."

"Just musty. Let's turn the heat up." I went down the hall to turn up the thermostat, and Sister followed me, pausing to look into the powder room.

"Yuck. Black. And come look at these deer on the wallpaper, Mouse. Aren't they dead?"

There was a reassuring click as the furnace came on. Good. I joined Sister in the powder room and looked at the wallpaper, tan and white deer lying in a dark green woods.

"They're just resting," I said. "They've had a hard day gamboling through the forest."

"Gamboling, hell. They're dead as Bambi's mother."

"No they're not. Besides, there's no blood."

"It's on the side we can't see, like that Moonflower guy last night."

"Mooncloth." I shivered. "Come on, let's get some tea."

Sister followed me into a very nice kitchen. Windows on two sides allowed a wonderful view of the valley and, when Vulcan was back on his pedestal, Haley would be able to see him, too, the majestic side view.

"Have you talked to Virgil any more about what happened?" I searched in vain for a tea kettle and finally filled two cups with water and stuck them in the microwave.

"He said they don't know anything else." She held up the two boxes of tea bags she had located and looked at me questioningly.

I pointed to her right hand. "Lemon Zest."

"Probably old as the hills."

"It'll be warm, though." I had worn a heavy blue sweater over a T-shirt, but I was still cold.

"What are they doing?" I asked. "Talking to all the Elvises?"

The microwave dinged and we took our tea to the kitchen

table. Below us, Jones Valley and the city of Birmingham were shrouded in rain and fog.

"And Dusk Armstrong. Apparently she hadn't known he was here in Birmingham, though. She said she hardly knew him, anyway."

"Well, somebody knew him and didn't like him." I sipped the Lemon Zest carefully. It was delicious.

Sister stirred her tea with her finger. "And they had to stick the knife in him just as they started the chorus-line kick toward the front of the stage because he lined up with the others and seemed okay."

"Which narrows it down to the Elvises on either side of him, wouldn't you think?"

"That's what I told Virgil and he said no, that when they were lining up, anyone could have sneaked up behind him. The one on his left was Larry Ludmiller, remember. Tammy Fay's husband."

"Tammy Sue."

Mary Alice shrugged.

"Who was on his right?" I asked.

"Virgil didn't say. I don't think whoever it was knew him, though. The Mooncloth guy, I mean."

"Well, Larry didn't, either, did he?"

"Says he never saw him before in his life. Wondered who the hell he was when he danced out onstage."

"Strange." I sipped the hot tea carefully.

"I told Virgil. I said, 'Virgil, maybe it was someone with a bad case of Elvis envy.' "

"Elvis envy?" I nearly spit the tea out.

Sister frowned at my reaction.

"Elvis envy?" I repeated when I had swallowed safely. "Is this some kind of psychological problem that leads to violent behavior?"

"How should I know?"

I rubbed my forehead. I felt a headache beginning.

We both jumped when the doorbell rang. Mary Alice spilled tea on her Yul Brynner outfit and muttered, "Shit."

"Who could that be?" I wondered.

"Probably a Girl Scout selling cookies. Isn't this the time of the year?"

"In the pouring down rain during school hours? You're nuts."

"Well, go see,"

For a moment I thought it might be Charles Boudreau, that he had followed me looking for Marilyn.

The bell rang again. For the second time that day I looked through a front door peephole. This time I was delighted at what I saw. I opened the door to Officer Bo Mitchell of the Birmingham Police Department.

"Bo! Come in." I started to hug her, but she held up her hand.

"I'm wet as a duck's butt." She stepped into the foyer. "You know, something just told me it was you when the call came in."

"What call?"

"Breaking and entering. Burglary. Various and sundry. I told myself, I said, 'Bo, if it's various and sundry it's going to be Patricia Anne and Mary Alice. You can bet on it.' "

"What are you talking about?"

"The burglar alarm, Patricia Anne. The one you have thirty seconds to enter the code before we start calling, which we did and you didn't answer."

"Oh, shit." I rushed back to the kitchen, opened the pantry door and punched 5-7-7-2.

"What's the matter? Who is it?" Sister was standing at the sink rubbing her martial arts top with a wet paper towel.

Bo grinned at Sister's outfit. "Shall we dance, dum dum dum?"

Sister twirled around. "Hey, Bo. I'm taking a martial arts class."

"Good, you're going to need it in prison because you're under arrest for breaking and entering."

"Damn. The burglar alarm? Why didn't you call us?"

"We did. The phone's disconnected."

"That's one more thing I need to do." I reached in my purse, got out my little notebook, and wrote, *Call phone company.* "They're coming home the first of April, Bo. And Haley's pregnant."

"Well, I declare." She pulled out a chair and sat down at the table. "Boy or girl? Or does she know?"

"A girl." I got another cup from the cabinet, filled it with water, and put it in the microwave. "Her name is Joanna because she was blessed by the pope."

"Joanna Paula?"

"Hmm. I hadn't thought about that." I got a tea bag from the box. "Lemon Zest?"

She nodded and shrugged out of her raincoat.

"What have you been doing, Bo?" Sister asked, sitting down beside her.

"This afternoon? Fishing a dog out of Village Creek. Either of you want a dog? Woofer could use the company, Patricia Anne."

"He's too old to learn to share, Bo." I handed her the cup of hot water and the tea bag.

"I think Joanie's going to take him, anyway, if nobody claims him. He kissed her when she wrapped him up in a towel."

"She's not out in the car, is she?" Joanie Salk is Bo's partner. Joanie is tall, thin, and white; Bo is short, plump, and black, though not as plump as she had been when we first met her. She has decided that she is going to be the first woman chief of police in Birmingham and has started working toward that goal. I think she'll succeed.

"No. She's taking a course at UAB. I dropped her off. She said to tell y'all hey."

"You really knew it was us?" Sister asked.

Bo grinned and sipped her tea. "I guess y'all were at the Alabama Theater last night when that Elvis guy was killed, too, weren't you?"

"In the front row," I admitted. "How did you know?"

"Stands to reason the way you find bodies. You know folks are going to quit inviting you to their parties, don't you?"

Sister gave me a dirty look. "It's Patricia Anne's fault. I never saw a body in my life until she retired."

I swatted at Yul Brynner with a paper napkin.

Bo burst out laughing.

"What?" we both asked.

"I saw Sheriff Stuckey down at the station, y'all. He was telling me about last night. He's a nice man, Mary Alice."

"So nice I'm marrying him in May."

"Well, I do declare." Bo swirled her tea bag gently in her cup. "Congratulations."

"Thanks. You'll be getting an invitation."

"She's planning on the attendants wearing magenta and sunflower," I grumbled.

"Have mercy. I wouldn't miss that for the world." Bo put her tea bag on the saucer and smiled at me. "I'll bet you're the magenta, Patricia Anne."

"She's acting a fool about it, too." Sister said. "You know what a beige person she is."

"I'm not a beige person." I pointed to my blue sweater.

"Nothing wrong with beige." Bo took a sip of her tea. "Umm, that's good."

"Have the police found out anything about the man who was killed last night?" I asked. "Like what he was doing here? We heard that none of the other Elvises even knew him."

"Y'all know more than I do. Y'all saw it happen. All I've been doing is fishing dogs out of Village Creek."

"All we saw was him falling in the orchestra pit," Sister said. "That was enough to give me nightmares all night."

"Me, too. We thought he was having a heart attack. We didn't know about him being stabbed."

Bo nodded. "Probably a switchblade the way it went in and then up. You can get such a good grip on a switchblade, you can do a lot of damage in a second."

Sister and I both put our tea down.

"They haven't found it?" I asked.

"Not that I know of. I'm just guessing about the switchblade anyway. We haven't gotten the report back."

"But someone would have had blood all over them wouldn't they? I mean your hands would be right up against the body if you were gripping a switchblade, wouldn't they? And all the Elvises had on white suits. Looks like that would be easy to check out."

"Might not have been much blood at all," Bo said. "A punch, a little push up and across, and then out. Real quick, and you've got the aorta that's bleeding inside, not out."

"My Lord," Sister said. She had turned a greenish color. "Y'all change the subject. This is gruesome."

"God's truth," Bo agreed. "Tell me about the wedding."

Which Sister did, in detail. A lot of details that I hadn't heard. I swear I think she was making it up as she went along. No sane person would plan a wedding reception in a pasture. There's bucolic and there's idiotic. Sister was opting for the latter as far as I was concerned.

Bo finished her tea and said she had to get back to work, that probably folks were sitting on top of their cars under the Fifth Avenue viaduct waiting to be rescued. Lord only knew why, but it seemed like they aimed for that spot every time it rained hard. She put on her coat and told us to behave ourselves. We promised that we would. It wasn't until she had driven off that I remembered that I hadn't told her about Griffin Mooncloth's appointment with Debbie. I was sure Debbie had already called and reported it, though.

"I'm going to go upstairs and see if there's a rocking chair," I said. "I wonder which room they'll use for the baby."

"That little room next to the master bedroom. The one Philip uses for his office. The one with all his computer stuff in it."

"Of course." We grinned at each other. Dr. Philip Nachman's life was in for some big changes.

"A switchblade," Mary Alice said as we went up the steps. "Sounds like *West Side Story*, doesn't it? With those rumbles. Sort of old-fashioned."

"Old-fashioned, my foot. The kids at school call them flicks. And they're easier to hide than guns."

"You're just full of information, aren't you?"

"You're full of it, too." I expected her to swat me on the behind, but she had apparently missed the barb. I had just relaxed when she yelled, *"Yaa!"*

I leaped over two steps to avoid whatever my sister, who had suddenly turned into Chuck Norris, was about to do to me.

"It works, doesn't it?" she said, smiling.

Chapter Six

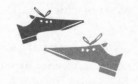

"Impregnate Marilyn?"

Fred and I were sitting at the kitchen table eating the barbecued chicken, baked beans, and potato salad without mustard (we hate potato salad with mustard in it) that I had picked up at the Piggly Wiggly on my way home. Rain was still hitting the windows and Woofer was lying under the table. I had pulled off my shoes and was rubbing him with my sock feet.

"I swear that's what he said. He even repeated it."

Fred frowned. "Sounds like a crazy man. I'm glad you didn't let him in. What did Mary Alice say when you told her?"

"I didn't tell her. I talked to Debbie, and she'd had a message from Marilyn saying not to tell her mother."

"That some man was showing up to impregnate her?"

I helped myself to more potato salad. "Debbie's not sure. Marilyn must have been calling from her car phone and the message was garbled. But that might have been what she was talking about." Under the table, Woofer rolled over and gave a little sigh of pleasure as my feet massaged him. In the den, Muffin was stretched out on the sofa asleep, her head resting on a pillow.

"I'm not giving that precious cat back," I said, pointing toward her.

"I know." Fred wiped his hands on a paper napkin before he reached for another piece of chicken. "Did Debbie know this man?"

"No. She doesn't have any idea what's going on."

The sound of the rain was steady, hypnotic. I was suddenly grateful for my warm, dry house, for the furry body beneath my feet, for the lovely man scarfing down barbecue chicken across from me. It was one of those moments that you want to save, when you realize how lucky you are.

"Well, Marilyn's always had good sense. She can take care of herself. You don't think this man is dangerous, do you?" Fred asked.

"He just seemed upset."

"Well, we'll find out what it's all about eventually." He took a bite of chicken and said, "Umm, that's good. You need to get the Piggly Wiggly's recipe, honey."

There went the moment. I hesitated and decided not to take offense. I've learned in forty-one years of marriage that half the time I get mad at Fred, he has no idea what he's said or done that could possibly have upset me. Besides, it's hard to get mad at a man with barbecue sauce on his nose.

"Wipe your nose," I said.

The evening continued peacefully.

We took our coffee into the den and turned on the news. We had had three inches of rain. Village Creek was flooded. Tonight's designated challenge-the-elements reporter pointed toward the rushing water, rain pop-popping on her umbrella. "A train of rain choo-chooing from the Gulf is causing this," the windblown reporter—obviously the mother of small children—explained.

Then back to the studio and the story of the murder at the Alabama Theater. Griffin Mooncloth, Elvis impersonator, killed at a benefit for the restoration of the statue of Vulcan.

A tape: Mr. Wurlitzer pointing toward the floor of the orchestra pit. "Right here. Missed smushing the organ by inches." A look of sadness. "That would have been a great loss."

"Lord," Fred grumbled, clicking over to *Wheel of Fortune*.

"We forgot to turn off the burglar alarm today at Haley's," I said while Vanna was turning over three S's. "Bo Mitchell came to investigate and told us that the Mooncloth guy was probably stabbed with a switchblade knife."

Fred was interested enough to turn down the volume. "From the back? What did it do? Hit a kidney?"

"Bo said he wouldn't have died as quickly as he did if it hadn't hit something like his aorta."

"From the back? What about ribs? Wouldn't the blade have been deflected?"

I clasped an imaginary switchblade and held my hand slightly sideways. "Put the side of your hand beside the spine, turn it, click the knife, in, up, and jiggle a little sideways. If the blade is long enough you get the aorta."

"And there's blood everywhere. We didn't see any blood."

"He's bleeding inside. The knife makes a small entrance slit."

"Did the police find the knife?"

"No. Whoever did it probably snatched it out, closed it, and put it in his pocket."

Fred tapped his chin thoughtfully with here's-the-church hands. "There still had to be blood on the knife, maybe not much, but some, and that lets all of those Elvises in the white suits out."

"Probably," I agreed.

Fred nodded and turned the volume back up on *Wheel of Fortune*. Then he turned it down again. "What's Tammy Sue's husband's name?"

"Larry Ludmiller. Why?"

"I'll bet he had some blood on his arm, and I'll bet the fellow on the other side did, too. You know how they had their arms around each other in that line."

"Probably. But you know, they didn't form that line until the end. They were doing those individual dances and then they all came together in the line facing the audience. That had to be when it happened. The Mooncloth guy wouldn't have been dancing around with a stuck aorta."

Fred looked over at me. "Don't you get involved in this, Patricia Anne."

"What?" I was startled. "Why should I get involved?"

"I don't know. I just have a feeling."

"Well, you can forget it. There's no reason for me to get involved."

Vanna turned over an *N*.

"You got any idea what that is?" Fred asked, pointing toward the TV.

"The Princess of Wales." I really do need to get on that show. Not only can I solve all the puzzles, I'm so short I would make Pat Sajak look tall.

The pleasant evening continued. Fred dozed in his chair. Woofer got up and went to the back door, wanting out.

When I opened it, I realized the choo-chooing of rain had slowed down some. Woofer ambled over to his favorite tree, marked it, and headed for his igloo.

"Night, night," I called. He wagged his tail and disappeared into his warm igloo, one of the best buys I ever made.

I covered Fred with an afghan and curled up on the sofa with Muffin to watch *Who Wants to Be a Millionaire*, another show that I needed to get on with my trivia-clogged brain. A man was stuck on the $125,000 question and I was telling him to quit, fool, take your $64,000 and run, when I heard a knock on the back door.

"Fred," I said, "someone's at the back door."

He pulled the afghan higher around his shoulders and gave a little sigh.

The next knock was more insistent. Probably Mary Alice, I thought. She was like the post office. Neither rain, sleet, nor snow could keep her from her appointed rounds—and, God knows, I was one of her appointed rounds.

I got up just as the man on TV came to his senses and took his money. Good. I went into the kitchen and turned on the back light. A tall, black-hooded figure stood at the door, hand raised to knock again. My heart skipped a couple of beats.

"Aunt Pat, it's me!"

I opened the door. "My Lord, Marilyn, all you needed was a scythe in your hand."

"What?"

"Never mind, darling. I just didn't know who you were for a minute. Come in. You're soaking."

There was an awkward moment of trying to hug each other and keep the wet raincoat out of the way. We ended up laughing, with Marilyn leaning down to kiss me on the head. Like her mother, she is a foot taller than I am. Unlike her mother, she is thin. She is also beautiful with naturally curly dark brown hair, olive skin, and big brown eyes. She is the exotic-looking one in our pale family; and she has always had the sense to emphasize this by wearing bright colors and long, flowing skirts.

"She looks like a gypsy," I've heard her mother complain. "And why won't she cut her hair? It sticks out like a long black Brillo pad." I've also heard Haley and Debbie wishing that they looked just like Marilyn.

But this night she looked nothing like a gypsy. When the black raincoat came off, I saw that her hair was pulled back and caught at her neck with a barrette. She was wearing jeans, a red sweater, and running shoes, and her eyes were puffy as if she had been crying.

"Did I scare you? I'm sorry."

"Just for a second." I hung her coat on the pantry door. "Have you had any supper?"

"I had a cheeseburger in Montgomery. Where's Uncle Fred?"

"Asleep in the den. Montgomery was a long time ago. Why don't you go dry off, and I'll fix you something to eat. We've got potato salad and baked beans left over. And I can grill you a cheese sandwich."

"That sounds wonderful."

Just then the phone rang.

"If that's Mama, you haven't seen me. Please, Aunt Pat."

"Okay, honey." But it wasn't Mary Alice, it was the Hannah Home. Their truck would be in our neighborhood on Wednesday. I was relieved. Whatever was going on, Mary Alice was Marilyn's mother. I didn't want to have to keep anything from her.

"Hey, Uncle Fred," I heard Marilyn say. The phone must have awakened Fred.

"Hey, sweetheart. What are you doing here?"

"Long story. I'm going to go get dried off. I'll tell y'all then."

I plugged in the grill and got the cheese, butter, and dill pickles from the refrigerator. If the coffee wasn't still hot, I could stick a cup in the microwave. Unless Fred wanted some more, in which case I would have to make another pot. I looked in the den and saw he was already asleep again. The theme song for *Millionaire* was playing.

Was Marilyn running away from Charles Boudreau? Or running to him? That was certainly a strange message I was given to pass along to her. And why didn't she want her mother to know she was here? Why was she here?

"It was terrible driving tonight," she said, coming back into the kitchen. "Solid rain after I left Montgomery." She reached over the counter and took a bite of the potato salad I had already put on her plate. "Umm. That's good."

"It wasn't raining in Pensacola? The weather lady said it was choo-chooing up from the Gulf."

"Not when I left."

"Sit down, honey. Everything's ready." I lifted the sandwich from the grill with a spatula. Melted cheese oozed from the side. It looked so good, I decided to fix one for myself. But first I handed Marilyn her plate and took her coffee from the microwave.

"This looks great, Aunt Pat. Thanks."

"You're welcome." I sliced the cheese for my sandwich while Marilyn started eating. Questions could wait for a few minutes.

Muffin strolled in and went over to her water bowl.

"That's Haley's cat, isn't it?" Marilyn asked.

"Not anymore. Seven months gives me squatter's rights."

Marilyn smiled. "I'm thrilled about Haley's baby. Debbie told me."

I put my sandwich on a plate and joined her at the kitchen table. "Joanna. That's a nice name, isn't it?" I said it again, savoring the sound, "Joanna."

"It's a beautiful name."

I took a bite of my sandwich, which I needed like I needed a hole in my head, but which was delicious, chewed, swallowed, and said, "Marilyn, a man named Charles Boudreau came by here today. He said he was here to impregnate you, that he would be willing, happy, ecstatic, and that he hoped it wasn't too late."

Marilyn put her fork down carefully and looked at me. "Charlie was here?"

I nodded. "There were some other adjectives, but I can't remember them all. They all had to do with his willingness to participate in conception, though."

Marilyn nodded but didn't say anything.

Finally I asked her if she would clue me in on what was going on. "The poor man was crying at one point."

She looked startled. "Charlie was?"

"Into a very nice, white handkerchief."

"Well, I'll be damned." Marilyn picked up her fork and began to eat again as if we had been discussing the weather.

"He said to tell you that he's at the Tutwiler."

"Tough." Marilyn shoveled a forkful of potato salad into her mouth and chewed slowly.

"Who is he?"

Marilyn held up her hand signaling that she was chewing and unable to answer. Finally she took a sip of coffee, pushed her plate back, and patted her lips with her napkin.

"It's a long story, Aunt Pat."

"I've got time."

"You're sure he was crying?"

The scowl on my face told her that she had better get on with her story.

"You remember about fifteen years ago when I first moved to Pensacola that I took some courses at West Florida?"

I nodded that I remembered; I didn't.

"Well, one was a speech course, and Charlie was in it. One night he asked me if I would go to dinner with him that Saturday, that it was his birthday. I told him it was my birthday, too, and we found out that we were exactly the same age to the day." Marilyn hesitated, examining a red fingernail so perfect that it had to be acrylic. I wondered if she had had any fungus problems. I had let Sister talk me into getting fake nails several years earlier and had ended up going to the doctor.

"Anyway," Marilyn continued. I pulled myself away from the thought of greenish-black nails and listened. "We had a wonderful time, and we ended up with a relationship that lasted for a couple of years. Then Charlie went back to Lafayette because of his mother's and father's health. He asked me to marry him and go with him, but I think he would have been surprised if I had said yes. What we did do, though, was promise to see each other every year on our birthday. We made a pact that if we weren't married and didn't have children by the time we were forty, that we would get together."

"Sounds like Julia Roberts in *My Best Friend's Wedding*." I could have bitten my tongue when I said it. But Marilyn didn't take offense.

"It does, doesn't it? Their deadline was thirty, though. We weren't in any hurry." Marilyn poked at the fingernail, which popped off and landed on the remains of her potato salad. "Damn," she said, picking it up and wiping it on her paper napkin. The real nail, I noticed, looked pink and normal. "That thing's been feeling funny all day," she said. "I'll have to get it glued back on before I go to the hospital."

"You're going to the hospital? What's wrong?"

"Nothing. I'm going to the fertility clinic, Aunt Pat. I'm going to be artificially inseminated like Debbie was."

"Tomorrow?" I gave up on the cheese sandwich, which I hadn't needed anyway.

"For tests. They have to make sure I'm ovulating okay and that everything's all right. Then they'll set the date."

"But honey—" I actually felt a little dizzy.

"Ma'am?"

"What about Charles?"

"I called him last weekend and said, 'Charlie, we're going to be forty next month, and I don't want to get married, but I do want to have a baby, and you promised.'"

"And?"

"He said he thought our pact had always been a joke. So I told him that was fine, that my sister had gotten her twins at UAB and, by damn, so could I. And that *you* would understand."

"Apparently he's regretted his decision."

"I don't care." Tears filled Marilyn's eyes. She reached for her paper napkin, placing the fingernail on the table.

A hard shower of rain hit the bay window. Muffin came and jumped in my lap.

"Maybe you should give him a call anyway," I said. "He certainly seemed upset."

"I don't think so. And, Aunt Pat, please don't tell Mama I'm here."

"But why not? She would understand."

"Like hell she would. I mentioned the possibility of going to the clinic once, and she said she couldn't understand why her daughters couldn't get pregnant out of the usual conduits."

"Conduits?" I grinned. "I don't think I've ever heard them called that before."

Marilyn snorted into the napkin, a half-laugh, half-sob. "Damn."

"I won't tell her, but I wish you would."

Marilyn shook her head no.

"Does Debbie know?"

"Not yet, but I'll tell her." She got up, splashed water from the sink faucet onto her face, and dried it with a paper towel. "She knows about the conduits. She thought it was funny."

I forced back a giggle, which resulted in a hiccup.

Marilyn sat back down. "Okay, enough about this. Tell me what's been going on, Aunt Pat."

"You're going to see your mother while you're here, aren't you?"

"Oh, sure. I'll see her after I go to the clinic. I'll just tell her I'm here on business. Which is the truth."

"Then she can update you on the wedding plans."

"They're so bad you can't tell me?"

"How do magenta and sunflower strike you?"

"Oh, Lord. Are you the magenta?"

I nodded. "She'll tell you all about it."

"You like Virgil, don't you?"

I nodded. "Very much. Fred and I saw his children last night. They seem nice, too. His son's an Elvis impersonator."

"Really?"

I told Marilyn about our evening at the Alabama Theater, about Griffin Mooncloth, the switchblade, the fall into the orchestra pit.

"Dusk Armstrong knew who he was," I added.

"Dawn's little sister? I was in school with Dawn. I think Debbie was in school with Day." Marilyn shook her head. "I can't believe she named the last one Dusk."

"Well, she was Bernice's last gasp before menopause."

Tears welled again in Marilyn's eyes. "Oh, Aunt Pat. I hope I haven't waited too long."

"You haven't, honey. Everything will be fine."

Another burst of rain.

"You're staying here tonight, aren't you?"

"If it's okay."

"It's more than okay."

"Then I'll go get my overnight bag."

Marilyn got her raincoat from the pantry door and darted to her car. I woke Fred up and he headed down the hall to bed.

"Marilyn spending the night?" he asked.

I said that she was.

It was a couple of hours before I joined him. Marilyn and I had a lot of catching up to do. Finally though, I slid into bed beside Fred and was about to drift off to sleep when he snuggled up against me.

"Honey?" he whispered.

"What?"

"Let's talk about conduits."

"You jackass," I laughed. "You were eavesdropping the whole time."

"Just part of it."

"Well, tell your conduit to behave himself."

"I think he needs a schoolteacher to tell him."

So a schoolteacher did.

Chapter Seven

The sound of Fred taking a shower woke me up the next morning. I reached for the remote, clicked on *Good Morning America,* and promptly went back to sleep. By the time I woke up, Fred was gone, and the program was almost over. Oh, the joys of retirement.

I opened the blinds and saw that the rain had stopped, but the sky was still sitting on us, dark with layered clouds. It was possible that more rain was in the offing. The outside thermometer with the huge numbers read forty-eight degrees. I had found it at Home Depot and bought it immediately. It's wired to our fence, and Sister frequently remarks about how tacky it is. But hey, we can see it.

The door to the guest room was closed, so I assumed Marilyn was still asleep. I was wrong. She was sitting at the kitchen table

drinking coffee and reading the paper. She had on flannel pajamas that had seals balancing balls on their noses all over them.

"I want a pair of those pajamas for Christmas," I said, head-
ing for the coffee.

"Morning, Aunt Pat. I'll put it down on my list."

"You want some more coffee?"

"Not yet." She folded the paper and put it on the table. "I was
just reading about that Mooncloth guy, the one who got killed.
There's a long article about him in the paper. Did you know he
was a Russian dancer? A real prominent ballet star."

I reached for the sugar. "A Russian named Mooncloth?"

"According to the paper, it's a translation of his name that he
used on the stage."

"A Russian ballet star dressed as Elvis dancing onstage at the
Alabama? What in the world?"

Marilyn pushed the paper toward me. I didn't recognize the
picture of the handsome young man on the first page. But the
only time I had seen him his face had been contorted. RUSSIAN
BALLET STAR SLAIN AT ALABAMA THEATER, the headline pro-
claimed, the lead story of the day. I sipped my coffee and read
the article that stated Mr. Mooncloth, one of Russia's premier
dancers, was in the United States on a cultural exchange. He
was currently appearing with the New York City Ballet, where
he had received rave reviews for his performances in *Prism* and
Symphony in C. Mr. Mooncloth, the article continued, had
been finishing his second and final year as an exchange artist
when he was killed.

"Oh, Lord," I said. "Birmingham's going to make all the head-
lines again. Probably an international incident. Why couldn't
whoever stabbed him have done it in New York? What was he
doing here anyway, jumping around on the stage at the Alabama
with Larry and Buddy and those other Elvis impersonators?"

"If we knew that, we'd probably know why he was murdered."
Marilyn pushed her chair back. "You want a bagel, Aunt Pat?"

"Sure." I read while Marilyn put the bagels in the toaster and got out the cream cheese.

"They don't even know where he was staying or how he got here." I said in disgust. "And he had to get that Elvis costume somewhere. Seems like the police would be looking into that."

"None of it makes sense," Marilyn agreed. "You want some more coffee?"

I held out my cup. "No wonder Dusk Armstrong knew who he was. I thought she said he was in one of her classes. She must have meant that he was teaching it."

Marilyn poured the coffee and took the bagels from the toaster. "You know what I remember, Aunt Pat? I remember you keeping candy sticks on the counter to stir coffee with. It would give it the best flavor."

"Look on the second shelf of the pantry. They're in a red tin can."

Marilyn put the bagels and cream cheese on the table and went to the pantry. She came back smiling, holding a peppermint stick and looking about twelve years old in her flannel pajamas.

"Honey," I said, watching her stir her coffee. "What are your plans for the day?"

"My appointment at UAB is at two o'clock. Is it okay if I spend another night with you? It might be late when I get through."

"Of course it is. It's our pleasure. You know that."

I spread cream cheese on my bagel and took a bite. "Have you thought any more about Charles Boudreau? I'm sure he's still at the Tutwiler."

The peppermint stick clinked against the side of the cup. "I've thought about him."

"And?"

"I told you what he said when I asked him if he would father my child, Aunt Pat. He stuttered like crazy, said he thought the pact was just a joke."

"But he's changed his mind."

"Probably because he thinks I'll marry him if I get pregnant." I'm sure I looked puzzled.

"It's a long story, Aunt Pat. Suffice it to say there's no way on God's earth that I could live with Charlie Boudreau." Marilyn took a bite of bagel and chewed viciously.

So much for Charles Boudreau's chances.

"You want me to go with you this afternoon?" I asked after we finished eating.

"No, but thanks. I'll be fine." She got up and put her plate and coffee cup in the dishwasher. "Right now you know what I'm going to do for you?"

"Vacuum the house?" I asked hopefully.

"Take Woofer for his walk. The weather's too raw for you to be out this morning."

I suddenly felt a hundred years old and fragile as glass. "I'm sure I'll be all right with my walker. And I'll bundle up."

Marilyn laughed. "Oh, Aunt Pat. That's not what I meant at all."

But, of course, it was.

I took the paper and settled on the sofa in the den while Marilyn was dressing. I wished that she would call her mother. I knew that the back door was going to fly open at any minute, and Mary Alice would come in and discover Marilyn was there and would get her feelings hurt as well as become mad. I'm used to her getting mad, but Sister's feelings aren't easily hurt, and in this case they would be. I was sure.

"Marilyn," I said as she came back through the den, "your mother is going to call or show up here any minute. I wish you'd call her."

Marilyn shook her head. At that moment, the phone rang, and she disappeared like a shot out the back door.

"Have you read the paper?" Sister didn't wait for me to answer. "Can you believe a Russian spy getting killed right in front of us? And what the hell would he be spying on in Birmingham? All of our nuclear warheads in the caves under Vulcan?"

Marilyn reopened the door, snatched Woofer's leash from where it hung at the end of the counter, and took off again. Coward.

"The paper said he was a ballet dancer. It didn't say he was a spy."

"But you know he was. What would a Russian ballet dancer be doing in Birmingham?"

"Doing Elvis impersonations?" I sighed. She was going to be furious with me when she found out Marilyn was here and I hadn't told her.

"Don't be silly, Mouse. He could do that in Russia. But, listen, the reason I called is that Virgil is going to cook steaks here tonight. Debbie and Henry, and Tammy Sue and her husband, and Virgil, Jr., are coming." She paused. "And you and Fred, of course. A nice family evening. I'd thought we'd wait until Haley and Philip got home and maybe Marilyn could come up, but the weather's so god-awful and after what happened at the Alabama we all need something to cheer us up. We can do it again later on."

Guilt. Guilt.

"What time?" I asked.

After I hung up, I got out the vacuum and threw myself into housework with a vengeance. There's something about cleaning a house that soothes the conscience.

I was cleaning the toilet when Marilyn came down the hall and leaned against the door watching me.

"Let's go to the Hunan Hut for lunch, Aunt Pat," she suggested.

"Nope, your mother will be there."

"What about the Anchorage then? Get some veggies."

I flushed the toilet and straightened up. "She'll be there, too."

"And get mad at both of us?"

"I'm not worried about the mad. I just don't want to hurt her feelings."

"Well, I don't, either, Aunt Pat." Marilyn followed me down the hall to the other bathroom. "I think I'll call Debbie."

"Good idea." Spread the guilt around. I sprayed cleaner into the sink and sneezed. "Did you and Woofer have a good walk?"

"He marked every tree we passed."

"Good boy."

"And he didn't want to come in. He went in his igloo."

"I'll take him some treats in a few minutes."

Marilyn stood in the doorway looking as if she wanted to say something but was hesitant.

"What?" I asked.

"Has it ever occurred to you that Mama is a force of nature?"

I burst out laughing. "Frequently. Now go call your sister." I was getting a load of washing from the hamper when she came in to tell me that she was going over to Debbie's.

"Everything okay?" I asked.

Tears welled in her eyes. "I'm just confused."

I dropped the clothes and hugged her. Hell, I'd be confused, too, if I were about to go to a fertility clinic to be impregnated with a baby that I would have to raise by myself. A baby whose father I knew nothing about. I'd opt for Charles Boudreau in a second, whether I could live with him or not. Maybe that was what Debbie would tell her. On the other hand, Debbie had gotten the most precious twins in the world at UAB.

"Well, you don't have to commit to anything today."

"True." She was still sniffling when she left, though.

I put the washing on and went out to give Woofer his treat. The sky was getting lighter. By afternoon the sun would probably be out. Hopefully it wouldn't be so cold tonight that the peaches would freeze. We have to worry about that every year. Most people think of Georgia as the peach state, but Alabama's peach crop is one of our leading farm products. A late March freeze and it's wiped out.

"Patricia Anne?" Mitzi called over the fence. "You want to go out for lunch?"

"The Club?"

"See you in an hour."

The Club sits atop Red Mountain with the best view in the state. From the dining room you can see Jones Valley and Birmingham on one side, and on the other, you look across toward Shades and Double Oak Mountains. This was where Debbie and Henry had had their wedding reception and a helicopter had landed on the terrace to whisk them off to their honeymoon. It was also where my Haley had met Philip. As Mitzi and I sat down at our table, I remembered I hadn't checked my e-mail this morning.

"Only a couple of more weeks, and Haley will be home," I said. "A couple of weeks."

"I wonder if she's looking pregnant yet."

"Probably a little paunch."

The waiter set our food in front of us. You know you're in the South when the nicest restaurant in town has collard greens on its menu. Mitzi and I had both ordered them.

"I saw Marilyn walking Woofer this morning," Mitzi said, her fork poised above the collards. "Is she here for a meeting or something?"

"A meeting." Well, it wasn't exactly a lie.

"She's such a beautiful woman."

I agreed that she was, and then changed the subject by asking her if she had read the morning newspaper.

She had. "Can you believe that Mooncloth guy was Russian?"

"Mary Alice says he had to be a spy, that there wouldn't be any reason for a Russian ballet dancer to be in Birmingham."

Mitzi looked puzzled. "Why would a Russian spy be here?"

"God knows. Just one of Sister's flights of fancy."

"Is she still writing fiction?"

"She had a story accepted. I thought I told you."

"No. That's wonderful."

Lunch was good; the company was good. I was relaxed and enjoying myself when I heard, "Hey, y'all," and looked up to see Bernice Armstrong standing by our table.

"Hey, Bernice," Mitzi and I said together.

"I thought it was you over here," Bernice said. "Day and I were having lunch. She had to leave to go back to work, and I told her I was going to stop and speak to you."

"Have a seat," Mitzi invited.

"Just for a minute." Bernice pulled a chair out and sat down. When she was young, Bernice had been the most beautiful girl in Birmingham. Tall and elegant, she is still beautiful in her mid-sixties. Her hair is now white instead of blond but styled so it cups her ears. She was wearing a simple blue suit and her makeup was perfect. I remembered how Mary Alice had hated her when they were in school together. Looking at that perfect skin (the woman didn't even have any spots on her hands, for heaven's sake), I could understand why. Even her scarf was tied artfully, something that deserved hatred. Tying a scarf so it looks right is, as far as I am concerned, impossible.

"How are y'all doing?" she asked.

"Just fine," we chorused.

"Is Dusk still here?" I asked. "We saw her dance at the Alabama the other night. She's very good, Bernice."

"You were there? Wasn't what happened awful?"

We nodded.

"Dusk couldn't believe it. She's been in bed ever since it happened, bless her heart. I tried to talk her into coming to lunch with Day and me, but she said she didn't feel like it. She's supposed to go back to New York day after tomorrow. I hope she'll be up to it."

"He was taking a class with Dusk?"

"Not really. I think he was dating one of the girls in her class and would come down and dance with them some."

"The paper said he was quite an outstanding dancer," Mitzi said.

"Apparently." Bernice wiggled her fingers at a waiter who was pasing by. "Could I have some coffee, please?" She turned back. "Day has seen him dance when she's been in New York. She said he's the best."A slight hesitation. "Was the best."

"And they have no idea why he was in Birmingham dressed like Elvis?" I asked.

"Lord, no." Bernice's coffee arrived, and she reached for the cream. "They think it's the craziest thing they've ever heard of. He was Russian, you know."

"Well, he was here for something other than doing an Elvis impersonation," I volunteered. "He had an appointment the next day with Debbie for some business he wanted her to help him with. An appointment he didn't keep, obviously."

Bernice frowned. "Mary Alice's daughter Debbie? The lawyer?"

I nodded. "She didn't have any idea what it was about."

"Well, I guess it doesn't matter much now." Bernice gave a small shrug. "How are both of your husbands?"

"Just fine."

"I heard Arthur got shot, Mitzi, but that he's all right."

"Couldn't sit down for a few weeks."

"Mama?" Day Armstrong approached the table. She resembled her mother, tall, willowy, blond. I remembered Marilyn saying that Debbie had been in school with Day, which would make her in her mid-thirties. She looked ten years younger.

Bernice glanced up in alarm. "Something wrong?"

"Dusk called me on my cell phone just as I got in my car. She says she's feeling terrible."

"Oh, my. I was scared I shouldn't have left her. She was too quiet. Did she give any specifics?"

"Just that she's sick." Day turned to us. "Hi, ladies."

We nodded. Bernice got her purse that was hanging on the side of her chair and stood up. "Why didn't she call me?"

"She said she tried to."

"I'll bet I don't have the damn thing turned on. Well, you go on back to work, honey. I'll go see about her and let you know. Bye, y'all."

"Let us know, too, Bernice," Mitzi said.

She nodded. "Bye, y'all." She and Day hurried out.

"It doesn't matter how old your children are, does it?" Mitzi said.

"No. Thirty years from now, Haley will still panic if anything is wrong with Joanna."

We smiled at each other.

"Want another orange roll?" Mitzi asked.

"I'll half one with you."

> **E-mail from: Haley**
> **To: Mama and Papa**
> **Subject: Happy. Happy.**
> Just think. This is one of my last e-mails from Warsaw, y'all. We're flying KLM to Atlanta and then Delta to Birmingham. The flight gets there just in time for supper, and I want fried chicken and biscuits and milk gravy. I know that's terrible, but I can just taste it. Morning sickness isn't getting me down at all, Mama. Obviously. In fact, I've already gained four pounds.
>
> We've still got a lot of packing to do and friends to say good-bye to. There's so much about this place that I love and will miss. But I'll be HOME!
>
> I e-mailed Freddie and Alan about the baby, and they

both e-mailed back that you had called them and how happy
they are for us. Maybe this will give Freddie some ideas.

Got to go. Just think, y'all. April.

I love you,

Haley

There was one more e-mail. Martha Stewart and I have
become good friends since I signed on to her website. I get nice
chatty notes from her about big cookie cutters and nesting rab-
bit dishes. When I retired from teaching, Sister gave me a sub-
scription to *Martha Stewart Living,* saying it would perk up my
appetite and maybe I would gain some weight.

Well, to give Martha credit, the pictures do perk up my
appetite, but Fred drew the line when I served him lettuce and
herb soup declaring that men didn't eat boiled lettuce. Actually,
I thought it was right tasty.

Today Martha was telling me what fun the children would
have drawing on the windows with her crayons, easily removed
with window cleaner. Ha!

While I had the computer open, I looked to see if there was a
website for Griffin Mooncloth. There wasn't. I clicked on to the
New York City Ballet. He was listed, but not as one of their
principal dancers. Hmm.

I glanced at the clock. It was two-thirty. Marilyn would be at
UAB. I wondered what they would tell her, what she would
decide. I wondered if Dusk Armstrong was all right and who had
killed Griffin Mooncloth and why. I wondered if it would freeze
tonight and ruin the peach crop.

The only thing to do was to take a nap, which I did, with Muffin curled beside me on the sofa and the afternoon sun dimming
through the kitchen window.

Chapter Eight

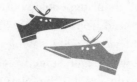

While I was out walking Woofer, Marilyn called and left a message that everything was okay and that she would fill me in on the details later. She was eating supper out so I shouldn't worry. She knew where the key was.

It was freezing outside and the clouds had lowered again. If it weren't March, I could have sworn that it was going to snow. I brought Woofer inside, and he immediately lay down on the heat vent. Muffin, as always, was delighted to have him in the house. She rubbed against him adoringly; he sighed and put up with her attentions.

I turned on the early news to hear the weather report. Thirty-four degrees tonight with wraparound clouds from the cold front that had come through. No precipitation. All of those extensive green blobs on the radar were virga, the weatherman explained, precipitation evaporating before reaching the ground.

I was considering a hot bubble bath when the phone rang.

"Bring garlic bread," Sister said and hung up.

Fred came in the back door, kissed me on the neck, and got a beer out of the refrigerator.

"It's not supposed to snow, is it?" he asked.

"Not according to the weatherman. Did you have a good day?"

"Fine. Has Marilyn gone?"

"She's having supper out. And we're having steaks at Sister's. Don't forget that Sister doesn't know Marilyn's here."

"I know nothing. Is Henry bringing the hors d'oeuvres?"

"Probably."

Henry Lamont, Debbie's husband, is a chef at one of Birmingham's finest country clubs. Fred loves Henry's cooking so much that I think if he hadn't asked Debbie to marry him, Fred would have gotten his shotgun out.

"Good." He took a swig of his beer. "Hear any more from Haley?"

"We got an e-mail. I printed it and put it with the rest of the mail on the desk."

"Good girl." He slapped me on the behind.

I slapped him back on his and went to look in the freezer to see if we had a loaf of garlic bread.

Three cars were already parked in Mary Alice's circular driveway, and lights glowed from all of the downstairs windows.

"Looks like a sure enough party," Fred said. "I thought it was going to be a little family cookout."

"Virgil's kids and Debbie and Henry. We're getting to be a pretty big family." I stepped from the car and admired the house, which I think is one of the most beautiful in Birmingham. Sister has always wanted a house like Tara with columns and a veranda. This house fit its setting, though. Elegant and sturdy.

Something damp hit my face. I held out my hand and looked toward the porch light. "Fred, I think it's snowing."

"Couldn't be snow. It's way above freezing."

I wasn't so sure.

Sister opened the door before we knocked. She was dressed in a purple velour pantsuit, and the porch light made her hair look more golden than usual. Or maybe she had made a trip to Delta Hairlines today. She thrust out her hand. "You got the garlic bread?"

"And a good evening to you, too, dear sister-in-law. What a pleasure it is to see you this evening and don't you look lovely." Fred handed her the sack. "We stopped by the Piggly Wiggly and got two loaves."

"Fool." She took the sack and hurried down the hall. "Y'all come in," she called over her shoulder.

"Southern hospitality," Fred said. "May I take your coat, dear?"

"Yes, you may, dear, and then I'll take yours." We grinned at each other. I hung the coats in the hall closet, and we went back to the den.

Five people were gathered in front of the fire. Debbie, Tammy Sue, and a girl we hadn't met were seated on the sofa. Larry Ludmiller and Buddy Stuckey were standing with their backs to the fire. Larry had on a plaid shirt and khaki pants and his black hair was combed back, lessening the Elvis look. Buddy, however, had on a black turtleneck and black jeans. His hair was combed Elvis style and his full lips curled on one side when he greeted us. Elvis himself couldn't have done it any better.

Debbie stood up, hugged us, and made the introductions. The girl was Olivia Ludmiller, Larry's sister. Olivia was thin, pale, and didn't seem to care whether she met us or not. She said, "Hello," and went back to studying her fingernails.

"Where's Henry?" Fred asked. God forbid that Henry and his food not be present.

"He's running a little late. I brought the hors d'oeuvres,

though, Uncle Fred." Debbie pointed toward a game table in the corner of the room. "I was helping Mama and forgot to put them over here."

"I'll get them," Fred offered. I hoped the plates were full.

"Maybe I'd better go in the kitchen and see what I can do to help," I said.

"The person who needs help is Daddy." Tammy Sue pointed to the patio where a bundled figure huddled over a grill.

"I offered," Buddy said.

Fred put a plate of what he calls "pinwheel patties" on the coffee table, helped himself to two of the patties, and walked to the French doors. "That's Virgil out there?"

"Mr. Macho himself." There was a slightly unpleasant tone in Buddy's voice. Tammy Sue gave him a hard look.

"Well, hell, it's snowing." Fred put both of the patties in his mouth, opened the door, and went out to join Virgil. Just then, Tiffany, the Magic Maid, came in from the kitchen. Tiffany is supposed to work for a maid service, but she spends more and more of her time at Mary Alice's. Tonight she had on red capri pants and a tight red-and-white striped sweater. Her blond hair was French-braided. Tiffany is twenty-three. Need I say more?

"I'm taking drink orders," she announced as both Larry and Buddy snapped to attention. "Hey, Mrs. Hollowell. I know you want Coke, and you do, too, Debbie, since you're breast-feeding. Brother. But what about the rest of you?"

"You got any vodka?" Buddy asked.

Tiffany gave him an are-you-kidding look. "We got everything, Bud."

"Buddy," he corrected her.

"He wants it with orange juice," Olivia said, marking her territory.

"And so does Larry," Tammy Sue said. "I'll have white wine."

Tiffany smiled. "We got plenty of beer. Sure you hadn't rather have that? Light, of course."

Debbie and I glanced at each other. This was going to be a long evening.

"Mary Alice and Daddy have been telling us about the wedding," Tammy Sue said after Olivia had also opted for white wine. "It's really quick, isn't it? They only met a couple of months ago."

So that was why Mary Alice was hiding in the kitchen and Virgil was freezing on the patio. Tammy Sue had been expecting the news, but when it came, the news hadn't gone over well.

Tammy Sue turned to Debbie. "What do you think about it?"

"I think it's fine. There's plenty of room at Elmwood for three more husbands."

"No, there's not," I said. "Fred and I have been offered two of the plots and we've accepted."

"What?" Tammy Sue looked from Debbie to me to see if we were serious.

"All of Mama's husbands are buried at Elmwood together," Debbie explained sweetly. "My daddy was the second one."

"All?" Tammy Sue chewed on a cuticle.

"Just three."

Tammy Sue looked so alarmed that I took pity on her. "They were all a lot older than Sister," I explained.

Tiffany came in with the drinks and then passed the hors d'oeuvres around. "Mrs. Crane said to tell you that we'll eat when Henry gets here. He just called and said it would be about a half hour."

"We don't have to wait on Henry," Debbie said. "The steaks will be cold." She pointed toward Fred and Virgil on the patio.

Tiffany offered me a pinwheel patty. "The steaks aren't on yet. Sheriff Stuckey's just warming up the grill."

Oh, for heaven's sake. Well, Virgil could get pneumonia if he wanted to, but Fred wasn't going to. I put my Coke on the coffee table and went out to the patio to tell Fred to come in right this minute. The two of them were huddled over the open grill.

"Larry said he couldn't tell if it was a man or a woman," Virgil was saying.

Fred looked up and saw me. "Hey, honey. Virgil was just telling me that Larry caught a glimpse of the person who stabbed the Russian guy. The only problem is Larry's about blind without his glasses."

"Hey, Patricia Anne." The hood of Virgil's jacket was tied under his chin, making his face look as round as a baby's.

"Y'all come in. It's freezing out here. You could cook these steaks in the kitchen, you know."

Virgil closed the grill. "I guess we'd better. What's Mary Alice doing?"

"I don't know. She hasn't come out of the kitchen."

Virgil sighed. "I'd better go see about her."

"Did y'all have a fight?" my tactful Fred asked.

"I'm not sure. We told my kids to come a little early, so we could tell them we were getting married and what the plans were, and they said they didn't think it was a good idea, and Mary Alice said, 'Tough titty,' or something like that, and Buddy said they'd better leave, and I said, 'Hell, no, you're not leaving. I spent sixty dollars on these steaks. You're going to eat them if it kills the king.' And Mary Alice went in the kitchen and said I didn't take up for her."

"Well, they sound like great steaks," Fred said. I gave him *the* look.

"They are," Virgil agreed.

"I'll go see about Mary Alice," I said. "Y'all come on in by the fire. What do you want to drink, Virgil? I know Fred wants beer."

"Anything." Virgil looked grateful. "Find out how mad she is and what I did wrong, will you, Patricia Anne?"

"That'll be the day," Fred said, pushing his luck.

Mary Alice was standing at the kitchen island crumbling bacon bits over a huge bowl of spinach salad when I came in.

"Don't you say a word," she said. "I'm sick and tired of being nice and sweet."

"God forbid." I stopped at the counter and petted Bubba Cat who was asleep on his heating pad. I picked up one of his legs slightly and let it fall. He opened one eye and glared at me. Good, he was still alive. One of these days that cat is going to pass on to his heavenly feline reward, and no one is going to know for days.

Tiffany came in, glanced at us, and disappeared back into the dining room.

"I kowtowed to three husbands." Sister went to the sink and turned on the water. "Well, no more. I don't have to kowtow to anybody, certainly not to somebody who won't take up for me."

The idea of Mary Alice kowtowing to any of her husbands was laughable. If she lifted her finger, each of the three had jumped to do her bidding. Now didn't seem to be the time to argue with her though.

She soaped her hands viciously. "Who wants to be Elvis's stepmother anyway? Now that's just tacky."

She had a point there.

"And them acting like their father had lost his mind because he wants to marry me."

"Well, it was a shock to them. Tammy Sue seemed real nice the other night at the Alabama. How did you break the news to them anyway?"

Sister ripped a paper towel from the holder to dry her hands. "They came in and Virgil said something like 'Kids, the good Lord has seen fit to bring Mary Alice and I together, and we think the best thing we can do is make it legal.' "

"Mary Alice and me," I corrected.

Sister scowled at me. "Don't hand me any of that English teacher shit, Mouse."

"Well, he ought to know better than to say 'bring I.' "

"He could have said the whole thing better, if you ask me.

And every one of them looked at me like I was a big bug or something, and the Elvis guy even said, 'You're kidding. I don't think this is a good idea, Daddy.' " She wrung the paper towel as if it were a chicken's neck. "The pissant."

"What did Virgil say then?"

"He said 'Y'all come on in. We'll talk about it.' He didn't say kiss my foot about how it was our business, not theirs." She slammed her hand down on the counter so hard that Bubba actually moved. "Lord, I wish Mama hadn't taught us to be polite. You know what else I wish?"

I shook my head.

"You're not going to believe this, but sometimes I wish we were Yankees, Mouse. A Yankee would have just booted them out of her house with a clear conscience, and more power to her."

"Did Virgil talk to them anymore? Tell them he loved you, not just that God wanted you to make it legal stuff?"

"I don't know what he said. I came in the kitchen." She propped against the counter. "And that Olivia Ludmiller wearing patent-leather shoes—and it was way after five o'clock. Did you notice that, Mouse?"

I had.

"Virgil came pussyfooting in and said he was going to light the grill to warm it up, and I said fine and handed him some matches. I wasn't about to tell him there's a perfectly good grill in here. Let him freeze." There was a hint of a smile on Sister's face. "What's going on in the den?"

"Debbie and Tiffany are holding their own. And I hate to tell you, but I told Fred and Virgil to come in. I think there are a few flakes of snow falling."

"That's okay." Sister squared her shoulders. "I'm going to go in there and be the proper hostess. You remember Glenn Close in *Sarah, Plain and Tall*? She was from New England wasn't she?"

"I think so. Why?"

"That's the kind of Yankee I'm talking about. She didn't take any foolishness." Sister looked thoughtful. "She really should have done something with her hair, though. She looked good in *Fatal Attraction* when it was curly."

Mine hostess swept out of the room.

The dinner party turned out better than I had hoped for, given the circumstances. We ate at the dining-room table, but Mary Alice had kept it informal. She had used peach-colored place mats and her everyday pottery dishes.

"I did the centerpiece," Tiffany whispered, putting a foil-wrapped potato on my plate.

"It's lovely," I said. And it was. She had taken a basket and filled it with bedding plants, begonias, and impatiens, which were available at all of the grocery stores and being bought by optimists who thought winter was over.

"I'll plant them in a couple of weeks." She moved on to Fred.

"Sit anywhere," Sister had said, and we had arranged ourselves like opposing teams. Larry, Tammy Sue, Buddy, and Olivia were on one side, Henry, Debbie, Fred, and I on the other. Mary Alice sat at the head, and Virgil at the end. Henry, who had just come in, was the only one who was unaware of the tension.

I had taught Henry in high school in Advanced Placement English and, to tell you the truth, he was this teacher's pet. Smart, a gifted writer, a wonderful chef, his entry into my family had been a joy.

"I hear Haley and Philip are coming in a couple of weeks," he said, handing me the butter. "Debbie says we're all going to the airport to meet them."

"I hope she doesn't get as big as I did with Brother," Debbie said. "And the twins. Oh, my Lord."

Across the table, sour cream and butter were being passed down the line. Larry and Buddy piled both on their potatoes. Tammy Sue opted for sour cream, and Olivia turned up her nose at both. None of them had said anything since we sat down.

"Buddy is an Elvis impersonator, Henry," Mary Alice said.

Henry chuckled. "You know, I thought you looked familiar."

Buddy curled his lip

"Hey, that's good." Henry took a piece of garlic bread and passed the basket. "Were you at the Alabama the other night when the Russian guy was killed?"

"Right next to him." Buddy pointed toward Larry. "He was on the other side."

"We couldn't figure out what was wrong with him," Larry added. "He just kept getting heavier and heavier."

"I'll bet he did." Henry turned to Debbie. "Eat your salad, honey. You need it."

I glanced over at Tammy Sue. She had on a pink outfit tonight, pink flannel pants and a matching pink sweater. She looked very pretty, but the spark that had been there the first night I met her was gone. She looked sad, diminished. And yet at the theater she had said that her father needed someone. Why was she taking it so hard? Mary Alice was a damned good catch. He could have gone for someone Tiffany's age.

Which Fred would probably do. I turned and looked at him. He was shoveling a piece of steak into his mouth. I kicked him on the ankle, and his eyes widened.

"What?" he asked, his mouth full.

"Just behave yourself."

He nodded.

"Where do you suppose he got the Elvis outfit?" Henry asked.

"That's about the only thing I can answer," Larry said. "We all get our suits cleaned at the same place on Southside. The lady gives us a discount so she can hang them in the window. She says it gets a lot of attention. Anyway, when Bud McCracken called and said he wasn't feeling good, I said I'd pick his up and he could come straight to the Alabama. It was Bud's."

"Ruined," Olivia said, startling us with the first word she had uttered since we had come into the dining room. "Absolutely ruined." She gave a thin smile and sipped her wine. I looked from her to Buddy Stuckey. Okay, he was strange with his Elvis look and his curling lip, but I got the impression that he was having fun with it. Olivia was unpleasantly strange. Were they really a couple?

"Let's change the subject," Virgil said. "Let Mary Alice tell you what she and I are going to do for our honeymoon."

"We're going to rent an RV and travel through the West," Mary Alice said.

The news was met with silence. Virgil looked at his kids anxiously. Finally Tammy Sue asked, "Are you going through Biloxi? I have a friend who won $1,300 there at the casino the other night."

"On what?" Mary Alice wanted to know.

"A slot. She said bells didn't go off, but it lit up."

A line had been crossed. We relaxed and began to enjoy our food. Buddy surprised those of us who didn't know him well by telling some funny stories about things that had happened to him while he was impersonating Elvis. The strangest, he said, was that he had been asked to conduct a funeral service for an avid Elvis fan.

"He didn't do it," Tammy Sue giggled. "He told them it wasn't legal."

We all laughed with the exception of Olivia, who gave a vague smile.

The phone rang, and Tiffany answered in the kitchen.

"It's for you, Sheriff," she said, sticking her head in the doorway.

"Damn." Virgil got up, but was back in a minute. "I've got to go. We've got a hostage situation in Springville. Some guy with his ex-wife and her new boyfriend." He came around the table and kissed Mary Alice on the cheek. "Sorry, sweetie, but I'm still the sheriff."

"I know. You be careful."

"Be careful, Daddy," Tammy Sue echoed.

He kissed her, too. "Behave yourself."

"I will."

Mary Alice pushed her chair back. "I'll walk to the door with you."

The room was quiet when they left. Then Henry, bless his heart, said, "We've got two desserts, chocolate pie and raspberry tarts. Who wants what?"

"I want one of each." Good old Fred.

Chapter Nine

Marilyn was asleep when we got home, or at least I assumed she was. Her door was closed and no light shone under it. Fred put on his pajamas, went looking for the Tums, chewed a couple, and was in bed asleep before I had cleaned my face, brushed my teeth, and settled down to read. I envy him his ability to sleep anywhere and anytime. If we are out at night, it takes me ages to calm down enough to doze off. Tonight, especially, my mind refused to shut off. Though the evening had ended pleasantly with Tammy Sue and Debbie insisting on clearing the table (Tiffany had left for a date), there was still a feeling of tension. The rest of us sat in front of the fire making small talk. Think it will freeze tonight? Remember the blizzard of '93? Eighteen inches on our porch. Stuck for days.

From the kitchen we heard the sounds of the disposal and of

the dishwasher being loaded. We could hear Debbie and Tammy Sue talking. At one point we heard laughter. Good, I thought. If these two could hit it off, half the battle would be won.

Mary Alice turned toward Olivia who was snuggled so close to Buddy on the sofa that she was almost invisible.

"What do you do, Olivia?" she asked.

Olivia looked up from nuzzling Buddy's arm. "Do?"

"Do you have a job? Are you in school?"

"Between jobs." She looked at Mary Alice as if she had insulted her in some way. Which, of course, didn't faze Sister.

"Between what kind of jobs?"

"Singing."

Larry laughed. "She sings 'Happy Birthday' while she's bringing in the cake. The last place was at Ruby Tuesday."

"There's nothing wrong with that," Henry said. "A good waitress is a prize. Believe me, I know."

"I'm a singer," Olivia said, glaring at her brother and at Henry. She returned to her nuzzling. Buddy seemed uncomfortable.

"Any of y'all fish?" Fred asked after too long a silence. "Know any good places up there in St. Clair County?"

The ice was broken. Thirty bream and ten largemouth bass later, Sister and I moved over to the game table.

"I saw Bernice Armstrong at the Club today," I said. "She and Day were having lunch. She says Dusk has been sick ever since the Russian guy was killed. In fact, she had to leave because Dusk called her."

"It made me sick, too, and I didn't even know him." Sister nodded toward Buddy and Olivia and said in a low voice, "Tell me she's not going to be part of my family. She reminds me of a lemon."

"She'll get squeezed out," I said. I thought it was pretty clever and laughed. Sister frowned at me.

"I don't think so. I think she's a leecher."

"A leecher?"

"Like a tick. You know. The type who has to be pulled off with tweezers."

"You're getting your metaphors mixed up."

"I swear he was *this* long." Buddy threw his arms apart, dislodging Olivia. "Must have weighed twenty pounds."

"Good God almighty," Fred said in awe.

"I think you're going to be all right," I told Sister.

So here I was, three hours later, wide awake reading a Peter Robinson book, which was a mistake. Chief Inspector Banks's exploits are not conducive to sleep. But it's hard to put him down. I finally took the book into the den, got a glass of milk, and curled up on the sofa under the afghan where I was joined by Muffin.

"Good book?" Marilyn asked, coming in barefooted and rubbing her eyes.

"Great." I held it up for her to see. "You okay? I didn't wake you up, did I?"

"No. I'm having trouble sleeping. I think I'll get some milk, too." She was back in a minute and sat in the recliner.

"Did everything go okay today at the clinic?" I asked.

"I'm fine. They're not even going to have to give me fertility drugs."

"Good."

She nodded. "I'll probably be back next week to get it done. I have to keep up with my temperature, make sure I'm ovulating."

It sounded so cold. I thought of my own children who had been conceived in passion and love. In fun. I thought of Charles Boudreau and wondered if he were still at the Tutwiler Hotel, ready, willing, able. Hadn't he used the word ecstatic? I took a chance. "Charles Boudreau is definitely out of the picture?"

"Definitely." Marilyn drank some of her milk. "How did the evening go?"

I told her that Virgil's children had been none too pleased to hear about the wedding, but that by the end of the evening, things had seemed to be more pleasant.

Marilyn nodded. "You know what I've been lying in there thinking, Aunt Pat? I've been thinking that in the morning before I leave, I'm going to go and have a talk with Mama. Tell her what I'm doing. I mean, hell, Aunt Pat, I'll be forty years old on my next birthday. I shouldn't still be intimidated by my mother. It's not like she's an ogre."

"You're going to tell her that you've been staying here?"

"I'm going to tell her everything."

"Oh, shit." I groaned.

I finally went back to bed and to sleep. When I awoke, both Fred and Marilyn were gone. It was after nine when I pulled on some sweats and went out to get Woofer. If Marilyn had left at eight then I could expect a visit or at least a phone call from Sister by eleven. But, like Marilyn, I would not be intimidated by her. I was sixty-one years old and a strong woman. Sister would not make me feel bad about not telling her that Marilyn had been at my house. She would not call me Mouse anymore or claim that I had lost her Shirley Temple doll fifty-five years ago.

The weather had done its usual March change. A brilliant sun shone in a cloudless sky; the temperature was around sixty degrees. Just right for a brisk walk, which was what Woofer and I had. I'd go shopping for Haley's rocker as soon as I got home, I decided. Go to the library. Maybe even take in a movie. Stay away from home.

But as we turned the corner toward our house, I saw that Sister's car was already in our driveway.

"It's okay, Woofer," I said. "I'm a strong woman."

Sister was sitting at the kitchen table eating a sweet roll. "Get dressed, Mouse," she said calmly. "We're going to an Angel-sighting Society meeting."

So I did.

I think it should be clear by now that my sister is a joiner. The Angel-sighting Society is new on her agenda, though. In fact, it may be new to Birmingham. Mary Alice has been trying to get me to go with her for a couple of months in spite of the fact that I've never seen an angel. She hasn't, either, she says. All you have to do is believe in them and clap when people tell of their sightings. Shades of Tinkerbell. So far I've managed to stay clear, but Sister knows when I'm vulnerable. She assured my cooperation by mentioning on the way over that she and Marilyn had had a nice conversation and that she understood why I hadn't told her that Marilyn was in Birmingham.

So there I was, sitting in a meeting room at the Vestavia Library, listening to a woman read a poem about sighting an angel. Before she read, she had handed out photocopies of it, so we wouldn't miss a word.

Oh, angel, flying above the earth
You bring such joy, laughter, and mirth.
Landing on the foot of my bed
To bring us all our daily bread.

There were many verses of it, and I clapped with everyone else when it was over. But the night's lack of sleep was catching up with me. A couple of times during the reading, Sister had to poke me with her elbow.

"You're drooling," she muttered.

I wiped my chin and tried to perk up. One of the sightings caught my attention. A nicely dressed lady told of picking up a young woman standing by the entrance to the Red Mountain Expressway with a sign that read: WILL WORK FOR FOOD.

"My grandson was in the front with me," the lady explained, "so the girl got in the back. I told her I had some windows that needed washing and that I would pay her, and she said, 'God bless you' and disappeared." The woman paused. "I turned my head and she was gone." A longer pause and a look toward the heavens. "An angel thanking me for my kindness."

Everyone clapped.

"Did you ever get your windows washed?"

Mary Alice and I smiled at each other at hearing the familiar voice right behind us.

"No, Miss Bessie,"

"Then I got a number for you to call."

The angel-sighter held out her hands, palms up. "You see, ladies? That's how it works."

More clapping.

As Mary Alice and I turned to speak to Bessie McCoy, she leaned over and whispered, "It's going to cost her a fortune."

"What are you doing here, Bessie?" Sister asked our favorite member of the investment club.

"The Lord's work. Hey, Patricia Anne."

"Hey, Bessie. I like your hat."

"My new spring model."

Actually every one of Miss Bessie's hats is exactly alike, crocheted with little brims. She wears them all the time. Rumor is that she was scalped when she was a child, a rumor that has gained her a lot of respect, though no one has ever come up with a believable version of the scalping. Today's hat was crocheted with multicolored acrylic yarn. Fortunately, being crocheted, there were a lot of holes to scratch through, which Miss Bessie proceeded to do.

"Have lunch with us," Sister said.

Miss Bessie nodded.

I was immediately more cheerful. With Miss Bessie along, Sister wouldn't harp on the fact that I had harbored her daughter without her knowledge for two days.

"Let's go to the Hunan Hut," I said. "Lunch is on me."

"Then let's get Bonnie Blue, too, since the Hunan Hut is right down the street from the Big, Bold, and Beautiful Shoppe."

I smiled at Sister. "Great."

"The ebony and ivory twins," Miss Bessie murmured to me as we followed Bonnie Blue Butler and Sister down the street to the Hunan Hut.

It's true. The two of them are the same size, have the same walk, the same mannerisms. The big difference is that Bonnie Blue's skin is a lovely dark chocolate color and that she is younger than Sister. She used to work at the Skoot 'n' Boot, the country-western bar that Sister had lost her mind and bought for no other reason except that she loved to line dance. After the Skoot's unfortunate end, Bonnie Blue had gone to work at the Big, Bold, and Beautiful Shoppe and had quickly become the manager. No surprise. Bonnie Blue's customers adore her because she's honest with them. If Bonnie Blue tells them an outfit looks good on them, they know that it does.

The Hunan Hut, which used to be a Pizza Hut, has a wonderful lunch buffet. One doesn't come in here for the ambience, which is Chinese-Italian, but to eat. And to talk. The first thing that Bonnie Blue wanted to know after we had heaped our plates and sat down was about Sister's wedding plan.

"You and Virgil really going to do it?" was the question.

"Absolutely. And it's going to be different this time. Will Alec and I got married at Trinity Methodist Church, Roger and I got married at City Hall, and a rabbi married Philip and I at Temple Beth-el."

"A rabbi married me," I said.

Mary Alice put down a forkful of fried rice. "He did not. You and Fred got married at home by that Baptist preacher with the real red face. I thought he was going to have a stroke at any minute. And we didn't even have nine-one-one at the time. All I could think of was how on God's earth are we going to get this huge man to the hospital if he collapses on us."

"You said a rabbi married Philip and I. It's Philip and me. Objective case, for heaven's sake. And while I was getting married, all you were thinking about was how red the preacher's face was?"

"Rabbi Newman married Philip and I. I, I, I. Screw the objective case."

Miss Bessie laughed. "You two sound like me and my sister."

"They do it all the time." Bonnie Blue took a bite of egg roll. "Eat your lunch, girls."

"I can't remember my wedding," Miss Bessie said, "I hardly remember my husband, but I sure as hell remember my mother-in-law."

Sister buttered a Parker house roll. The Hunan Hut's cuisine is somewhat eclectic. "That's one thing I never had to worry about, a mother-in-law."

"Your husbands were all too old," I said.

"But virile. I didn't get those three children out of the air."

"Parting shots."

Bonnie Blue frowned at me. "Tell us about the wedding, Mary Alice."

"We're thinking about having it at the little church at Tannehill Park. You know that old church they moved there from somewhere out in the woods? And I want you to find me a dress like the one Carolyn Bessette wore because I want a picture on the steps of Virgil kissing my hand and I want the dress swirling around."

Bonnie Blue rubbed her forehead as if she were getting a headache. "She was pretty skinny, Mary Alice."

"Well, it doesn't have to be exactly like hers." Mary Alice shoveled the forkful of fried rice into her mouth and chewed thoughtfully. "But what I can't decide," she said, after she had swallowed and taken a sip of tea, is whether to have it at eleven o'clock and have lunch afterward, or at four o'clock and have a cocktail reception."

"I vote for the cocktail reception," Miss Bessie said.

"But there's a problem with that, Bessie. The church is in a state park, so we can't serve alcohol. I was thinking about talking to the folks who live across the road from the park and seeing if we could set up a tent over there by that little lake."

I thought about the land across the road from Tannehill State Park. "That's a cow pasture, Sister, and a pond."

"No. Farther down where the sign says FISHING, TWO DOLLARS A DAY. That little gravel road."

"Still a cow pasture."

Bonnie Blue frowned in concentration. "Have the reception at your house, Mary Alice. You can set up a large tent in the front yard, and everybody wouldn't have to be watching where they stepped. Somebody would probably show up dead in the pond, anyway, the way you two have been finding bodies."

Mary Alice pointed a fork at me. "It's her bad karma. The only dead people I ever saw were laid out until Patricia Anne retired. Except for my husbands, that is."

"Didn't one of them die on an airplane?" Miss Bessie asked.

"Roger. He didn't even tell me he couldn't breathe until we were halfway across the Atlantic. And by that time I could hardly make out what he was saying."

By this time I had eaten my egg roll. Damned if my karma was going to take the blame for the bodies. I pointed my fork back at Sister. "It was your son who married Sunshine Dabbs, Miss Smarty. And I've got a permanent knot on my head from falling over that turkey she left on your stoop." I leaned over to Miss Bessie. "See my knot?"

"Hmm," she said.

Bonnie Blue frowned in concentration. "Can we back up here a minute? The problem is the time and place to have the reception. Right?"

"Just don't serve potato salad," Miss Bessie said. "That stuff is dangerous in the summertime, especially when you make a big batch. Folks would be falling out with food poisoning right and left. I was at a family reunion one time where that happened. Lord. Worst thing I ever saw."

"That's true," I agreed. "I wonder if corn salad would be as bad."

Miss Bessie nodded. "It's the mayonnaise."

"Would you two just hush?" Mary Alice said. "I'm sure the caterers will make sure that everything's fine."

We concentrated on our food for a few minutes. Then Bonnie Blue said, "Well, if they do have potato salad, I hope they don't put mustard in it. I hate mustard in potato salad. My auntie always puts mustard in her potato salad and wonders why nobody eats it. She sure knows how to make chicken pie, though. The best crust. Everybody fights over it."

Another few minutes of eating. The waitress came over and freshened our tea.

"Actually, there's another slight problem," Mary Alice said. "Virgil, Jr., is an Elvis impersonator, and he's going to be the best man."

Bonnie Blue looked up from her almost-empty plate. "He'll be wearing a tux, won't he?"

Mary Alice shook her head. "Virgil says Virgil, Jr., always wears the white jumpsuit on dress occasions. He says nobody will notice it. Now can you believe that for a minute? We're standing up there, the wedding party at the front of the church all dressed up, with Elvis in the middle, and nobody noticing?"

"Some things you just have to accept," Miss Bessie said

philosophically. "I wish I could remember my wedding. I wonder if there was an Elvis in it."

"Y'all ever seen a black Elvis impersonator?" Bonnie Blue asked. "Used to be one around Birmingham. Had that white suit and big belt. And sweat! That man squished in his shoes. Looked like a fool marching down Fourth Avenue."

"Well, hopefully Virgil, Jr., won't sweat like that." But Mary Alice looked worried.

"Too bad about what happened to that Elvis at the Alabama the other night," Bonnie Blue said.

Sister and I looked at each other, but neither of us said anything. We didn't have to. Bonnie Blue had caught our glances.

"Y'all were there? Should have known."

"Let's not talk about it," I said. "Anybody want some more sweet-and-sour shrimp?"

Sister said, "Get me some."

As I left the table, I heard her saying, "In the front row. He fell, *splat*, right into the orchestra pit."

I was in no hurry to get back to the table and hear the saga of Griffin Mooncloth again. I went to the restroom and washed my hands, came back to the buffet, and loitered while the three women at my table still had their heads close together, engrossed, I was sure, in the Russian spy story. Finally Sister looked up as if wondering where I was. I got her some more sweet-and-sour shrimp and headed back to the table.

"I don't want to hear any more about it," I said, shoving the plate in front of her.

"Can't say that I blame you," Miss Bessie said. "You sure something isn't wrong with your karma?"

"My karma's fine."

And I really believed that until later at the Big, Bold, and Beautiful Shoppe.

I keep my credit cards in a little leather card case that Haley had given me one Christmas. It gets lost sometimes in the bottom of my purse, which means I have to dig around for it. That is what I was doing when the back of my hand brushed against something metallic. I paid the lunch bill, and we walked back to the Big, Bold, and Beautiful Shoppe, where Mary Alice wanted to look at some pictures of wedding dresses. Miss Bessie and I sat down to wait and I casually looked in my purse to see what it was that my hand had touched when I was rummaging for my credit cards.

"I've got to quit dumping change in my purse," I told Miss Bessie. "I need a smaller purse, too. This one is heavy as lead." That was next to the last sensible thing I said. The last sensible thing I said was, "Call Bo Mitchell."

And then, for the first time in my life, I fainted.

Chapter Ten

ortunately I was sitting in one of the wicker chairs that Bonnie Blue has arranged in the corner of the showroom for people who are waiting for customers. So I just slid to the floor, the room reeling around me. I'm not even sure I totally lost consciousness because I heard Miss Bessie saying, "Patricia Anne?" and then yelling, "Mary Alice!" I remember Bonnie Blue propping my feet up in the wicker chair Miss Bessie had been sitting in and Sister wiping my face with a cold wash-cloth.

"I'll call nine-one-one," I heard Bonnie Blue say.

That revived me. "No," I said, struggling to sit up but fighting nausea. "I'm all right."

"What happened?" Sister asked.

Miss Bessie answered. "She just looked funny, said to call Bo Mitchell, and fell out of the chair."

"Bo Mitchell? She's a policewoman." Bonnie Blue rubbed my legs as if I had frostbite.

"Confused," Sister said. "We'd better get the paramedics over here. It may be a reaction to the Chinese food." She put the washcloth against my throat. The coldness felt good. "Can you breathe, Mouse? You're not having a heart attack, are you? Chest pains?"

"Sister," I said. "I need Bo."

"Don't you dare try and sit up," Bonnie Blue said, holding my feet in the wicker chair.

"But y'all, there's a switchblade in my purse."

Bonnie Blue held me even tighter. "And there's a pistol in mine, but I'm still not gonna let you sit up."

"You packing, Bonnie Blue?" Miss Bessie looked pleased. "I used to. Damn it was fun."

Fun? Miss Bessie and a gun wouldn't do to think about.

Sister leaned over me. "What do you mean there's a switchblade in your purse?"

"There is."

She picked up my purse and turned it upside down. Lipsticks, combs, wallet, receipts scattered. And *thunk,* a switchblade knife hit the floor. Six inches long with a brown bone handle with a swirled design, the knife's switch was a small gold crown. Sister picked it up, mashed the crown, and the blade erupted almost cutting my arm.

"Damn!" I jumped back, dislodging my feet from the wicker chair and Bonnie Blue's hold, and jarring my whole body as they hit the floor. "Be careful with that thing."

"Lord have mercy," Sister said, looking at the knife with awe. Bonnie Blue, Miss Bessie, and I also looked. "It's rusty," Sister said.

Bonnie Blue held out her hand. "Let me see that," Sister handed it to her carefully, and she held it to the window and examined it. "That's blood, sure as anything. Not rust."

I had known when I saw the knife where that blood had come from, what the knife had been used for. But how the hell had it gotten in my purse? The room reeled again, but I closed my eyes and willed myself to be steady.

"We'd better call Bo," Sister said.

Einstein was right about time being relative. I'll vouch for the old fellow. The twenty minutes that we waited for Bo lasted for hours. Vicki Parker, Bonnie Blue's assistant, had left for lunch as soon as we had walked in from the Hunan Hut, so Bonnie Blue had to help the customer who came in looking for an outfit to wear to the Museum Ball. Sister, Miss Bessie, and I sat huddled in the reception area, Sister and Miss Bessie in the wicker chairs, and me semistretched out on the love seat. I felt better, not as if I would faint again or throw up, but every now and then I had a cold chill. The knife was back in my purse, which was lying on the end of the love seat. I was very aware that it was there.

"No, honey, that beige won't get it," Bonnie Blue said to her customer. "Everybody there's going to have on beige or black. Let me show you this emerald green we've got back here. Cut down to your belly button, but you've got the figure for it."

"I think I had an emerald green dress once cut down to my belly button," Miss Bessie said, scratching her head through the holes in her hat with a crochet needle she had pulled from her purse. I wished that was all that was in my purse.

Sister got up and walked to the plate-glass window that overlooked Twentieth Street. "I wish Bo would hurry up," Then to me, "You know we're jumping to conclusions here."

"What conclusions are we jumping to?" Miss Bessie wanted to know.

"That this is the knife that killed that Russian spy at the

Alabama Theater the other night." She turned back to the window.

"I haven't jumped to that conclusion," Miss Bessie said. "There must be hundreds of thousands of switchblade knives in Birmingham. Any one of them could have ended up in Patricia Anne's purse."

Hundreds of thousands? Lord. I closed my eyes and tried to concentrate. The first thing that Bo was going to ask me was where my purse had been for someone to drop a knife into it. The Hunan Hut? It had been hanging on my chair there. But one of us had been at the table the whole time. The Angel-sighting Society? The purse had been on the floor by my feet and Sister had been sitting on one side of me and a woman who had introduced herself as a Unitarian minister on the other side. Not likely. Last night at Sister's? In a chair at the game table where the snacks were. Totally unwatched. I had just picked it up when I left and hadn't opened it until I got ready to pay the bill at the Hunan Hut.

I shivered again. Surely not. Maybe, just maybe, like Sister said, I was jumping to conclusions.

"Here they come," Sister announced.

The bell over the door jingled merrily as Bo and Joanie Salk came in. Joanie has been Bo's partner for only a few months and the two couldn't be less alike. Joanie is tall, blond, and hangs loose while Bo is short, black, and tends to be a perfectionist. Bo's ambition is to be chief of police someday, and the odds are that she will be.

They spotted us and came over. Joanie had a lollipop in her mouth that she pulled out, wrapped in its original wrapper, and stuck in her pocket.

"Thinks she's Kojak," Bo said.

Joanie smiled. "I'm hooked on Dum Dum root beer suckers."

Miss Bessie shook her head. "Just don't chew them. All of my children used to chew Dum Dums. Stayed at the dentist. Drove me crazy."

"No, ma'am. I won't."

"Ice, too. They chewed ice."

"You rang?" Bo asked, sitting on the love seat beside me. "What's up?"

I reached in my purse, pulled out the switchblade knife, and mashed the crown. The blade swooshed out.

Bo jumped back, startled.

"Uh, that's ugly," Joanie said. "Where did you get that, Mrs. Hollowell?"

"Found it in my purse. I was looking for my credit card at the Hunan Hut and felt something. When we got here I checked, and there it was."

"She fainted dead away," Sister added, leaning forward to see around Joanie, who had knelt in front of me to examine the knife. "Probably not taking her iron."

Bonnie Blue said good-bye to her customer, who left carrying a garment bag. The woman looked over at us curiously as she went out of the door. Then Bonnie Blue joined us. "It's got blood on it."

"They think it belongs to a Russian spy," Miss Bessie said.

Bo and Joanie looked at each other, puzzled.

"The Russian spy who was killed at the Alabama the other night," Sister explained. "We were in the front row. I guess when he fell, the knife could have landed in Mouse's purse."

I tried to imagine that scenario: the man falling into the orchestra pit with a knife in his back, which somehow became dislodged and flew through the air to land in my purse, which had been closed and on the floor under my seat.

"The Mooncloth guy?" Bo asked. "He was a Russian spy?"

"That's what I heard," Sister said.

Bo took the knife from me carefully and closed the blade. "I suppose all of you have been looking at this, passing it around."

We nodded that we had.

Bo handed it to Joanie. "Bag it anyway."

Joanie reached into the large black leather case that was hanging from her shoulder, took out a plastic bag, and dropped the knife into it.

"And it just showed up in your purse, Patricia Anne?" Bo stood up.

I nodded. "I felt it in the Hunan Hut and didn't know what it was."

"Well, we'll see what we find out. You go on home and get some rest now."

"And take your iron, Mrs. Hollowell." Joanie reached in her pocket for her sucker.

The bell jingled their departure.

"Well, that sure didn't take long," Bonnie Blue said.

"I guess that's the end of that," Miss Bessie added.

Of course we all knew better.

On the way home, Sister asked me if I wanted to stop by the doctor. "You're still looking peaked," she said.

I said I didn't, that I just had a headache. Which was true. Plus the sore throat I'd been battling for a couple of days.

We rode in silence for a few minutes down the tree-lined streets. The green of new leaves contrasted with the darker magnolias and pines. Several people were working in their yards; one man was giving his grass the first cutting of the year. And last night a few snowflakes had fallen. Spring.

"I'm sorry about Marilyn," I said.

"It's okay. She told me she asked you not to tell me she was here."

I glanced around at Sister. She was being very understanding. I must look like death warmed over.

"Did she tell you about Charles Boudreau?"

I nodded that she had. "She said there was no way that she could live with him."

"I don't think living with him was what he had in mind." Sister dodged a pothole and nearly hit a pickup. "Get out of the way, fool," she yelled at the hapless man driving the pickup. "Did you see that? He almost hit us."

I closed my eyes and tried to remember my mantra.

"He comes from an impeccable gene pool. His grandfather or great-grandfather, I don't remember which one, was governor of Louisiana."

"Hmm."

"Not the one who wrote 'You Are My Sunshine' or the one who took all his friends to Europe." She turned onto my street. "Another one. You know, Mouse, sometimes I think Louisiana's governors are more interesting than ours. Some of ours are just downright dull."

I tried to remember a downright dull Alabama governor but couldn't.

"But Marilyn may really be making a mistake. She's got a bird in the hand here."

"As compared to two in the bush at UAB?" My heart was slowing down. I could see my house.

"You know what I mean. Now don't worry about supper tonight," she continued. "I'll bring something over around six-thirty. That's when *Wheel of Fortune* comes on, isn't it?"

I pulled the visor down, looked in the mirror, and pinched my cheeks. No candidate for Miss America, but I didn't look like I was about to step through the pearly gates.

Sister turned into my driveway and stopped. "I know you're upset about the murder weapon being found in your purse, Mouse, but we'll get you the best lawyers in Birmingham. Debbie will know who they are."

"What?"

"Not a thing to worry about. Now, how about some nice

salmon croquettes for supper? You want dill sauce?" She clicked
a button to unlock the door.

"What?" I asked again stupidly. How had we segued from
Charles Boudreau's gene pool to my imminent arrest for murder?

"Dill it is, then. Hop out, so I can go make some calls."

The murder weapon? The best lawyers in town? What happened to jumping to conclusions?

I didn't hop out of the car, more like a stumble. Mitzi was
waving to me from her yard, and I headed toward her as if she
were a beacon of sanity.

"Dumbest thing I ever heard of," Mitzi said. "To start with
nobody knows if that was the knife that killed the Mooncloth
guy. And even if it is, you were sitting in the front row of the
theater with a hundred people around you who can swear that
you were there. Mary Alice shouldn't scare you like that."

I was sitting on the sofa with the thermometer in my mouth.
"Unf?" I asked.

Mitzi glanced at her watch. "Okay."

I took the thermometer out. Almost 101. Damn. I was really
sick, and I'd been blaming my symptoms on being upset about
Marilyn and on Griffin Mooncloth's murder. Even on the excite-
ment of Haley's homecoming. The fainting today I had blamed
on the switchblade.

Mitzi took the thermometer and looked at it. "Yep. We're calling the doctor, girl. I knew when I felt your arm that you had a
fever."

"I'll just take some aspirin. I'll feel better."

Mitzi shook her head. "You told me the day before yesterday
that you weren't feeling good. You had me look at your eyes."

I rubbed the knot on my head, which had almost disappeared.

"That's not what's wrong," Mitzi said, noticing my gesture.

"And you'd better go see about it. You don't want to expose anybody."

As if I hadn't exposed a hundred or so people. I reached for the phone to call the doctor.

"I'll drive you," Mitzi volunteered.

"I've just got the sinus," I said.

Which, of course, was true. Given the high pollen count, plus the humidity and the change in temperatures, half the population of Birmingham snuffles through the spring. And to us, it's not sinusitis. It's the sinus. Haley's husband, Philip, is an ear, nose, and throat doctor, one reason that Fred happily blessed the marriage. Free treatment for the sinus. Imagine.

But free treatment was a few weeks away, so it was our GP who, after a quick strep test, which was negative, informed me that I had the sinus.

"I won't be contagious long, will I?"

"You're probably not contagious now." She handed me some sample packets of medicine and a prescription. "This will take care of it."

"Now all I have to worry about is being accused of murder," I told Mitzi on the way home.

"Tell me the whole story again," Mitzi said.

Which I did, starting with Dusk Armstrong and ending with the dinner party the night before with Virgil's family.

"One of them had to put the knife in your purse, didn't they?"

"It stands to reason. It was sitting there on the game table." I thought for a minute. "My guess is Larry Ludmiller. He was the one standing next to the Mooncloth guy in the line."

Mitzi stopped at a light. "But what would his motive have been?"

I shrugged. "I guess it's up to the police to find out."

"But it's interesting, isn't it, that the Russian guy had an appointment with Debbie. Out of all the lawyers in Birmingham, why Debbie?"

"He got her name out of the phone book?"

"What are the odds against that, Patricia Anne?"

"Pretty far-fetched."

"So let's say somebody recommended her. Who would it have been?"

"All of Virgil's family would be familiar with her name and the fact that she's a lawyer." I thought for a moment. "With the exception of Larry's sister. She probably wouldn't know." I sighed. "I hate to think of someone in Virgil's family being mixed up in this."

"I'm sure Mary Alice does, too."

I agreed. "Virgil seems like the nicest man in the world, but she's only known him a couple of months. I'm sure she's beginning to realize that there's a lot about him that she doesn't know."

"And vice versa."

We looked at each other and grinned. I wondered how many of the wedding plans Sister had told Virgil.

Mitzi turned into her driveway. "Why don't you go get on your nightgown and crawl in bed? I'll walk Woofer for you."

It was an offer I couldn't refuse. I took two of the doctor's pills as instructed, fixed myself a cup of hot tea, and put on my nightgown and robe. I had just settled on the sofa when the phone rang.

"Aunt Pat?" It was Marilyn's voice. "Is everything all right?"

"I have the sinus. I've just gotten back from the doctor."

"Oh, I'm sorry."

"But if you mean is your mother speaking to me, yes."

"Good. When are Haley and Philip getting home?"

"The first of April."

"I'm going to come back to meet them."

"They'll be jet-lagged."

"I just want to see them."

"Okay, honey, I think it's a great idea."

"Get to feeling better, Aunt Pat, and thanks for putting up with me."

"I will, honey. And you're welcome anytime. You know that."

"I know. Bye, Aunt Pat."

I hung up the phone thinking about my three children and Sister's three, all of whom were in their mid to late thirties. With the exception of my Alan, they had all put off marriage and having children until recently. When I was Marilyn's age, I had had a son in college and two teenagers right behind him.

I pulled the afghan over me and rubbed Muffin between the ears, remembering how old I had felt. On my fortieth birthday I had known there would be no more children. And here were my nieces and daughter just starting their families. Which way was better?

"I'm keeping you," I whispered to Muffin.

And then I slept.

Chapter Eleven

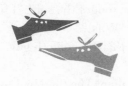

$\mathcal{F}$red woke me up when he came in around five-thirty. I told him I had the sinus, and he felt my head to see if I had any fever. I told him that Mary Alice was bringing supper. I didn't tell him that someone had dumped a switchblade in my purse. There was no use worrying him and, besides, for some strange reason I felt guilty about it. How many wives greet their husbands when they get home from work with, "Guess what, honey? A bloody switchblade knife showed up in my purse today."

Muffin deserted me, following Fred down the hall. I turned over on my side and drifted, neither awake nor asleep, but caught in that in-between state where dreams seem real and reality seems like a dream.

I heard Mary Alice come in the back door and I smelled salmon croquettes, but I was at her house. I was sitting on her sunporch and Charles Boudreau sat across from me telling me that he had impeccable genes.

"Don't tell me, tell Marilyn," I said.

"Tell Marilyn what?" Sister asked.

I opened my eyes, and she was standing over me.

"I was talking to Charles Boudreau," I said.

"You're sick, aren't you?"

"I have the sinus. Mitzi took me to the doctor."

She sat down at the foot of the sofa. "I found out something."

I was still drifting. "What?"

"Something about that Mooncloth guy."

"What about him?"

"He was an illegal alien. The time had run out on his cultural-exchange visa, and he hadn't left."

I turned over, opened both eyes, and looked at Sister. "How'd you find this out?"

"Virgil. He said the Birmingham police called the New York City Ballet to see if they could get in touch with his family, and the folks up there said the immigration people had been there looking for him."

"Well, couldn't he just have gone to the state department and told them he wanted to defect?"

Sister looked at me as if I had lost my senses. "Not if he was a spy."

"Who said he was a spy?"

"Didn't you?"

"Of course not."

"Well, somebody must have."

I rubbed my forehead. Sister asked if I wanted some more aspirin. I nodded that I did.

She was back in a minute with two aspirins and a glass of water. I propped up against the pillows and took them from her.

"You know what this means, don't you?" she asked.

I had no idea. I swallowed the aspirin and shook my head. Sister sat on the end of the sofa, folded her hands, and said, "It means that a Russian killed him. They knew he was going to defect and spill all of their secrets, and they couldn't have that happen."

Sister had a faraway look in her eyes.

I said, "You're writing a new story, aren't you?"

"I'm getting an idea for one."

"Well, in your story, was it a Russian agent who stashed the switchblade in my purse?"

"Could have been."

"Was this Russian agent's name Larry, Buddy, or Tammy Sue? They were the only ones who had access to my purse, Sister."

"I think her name was Olivia." Sister looked at me and grinned.

"What did Virgil say about the knife?"

The grin disappeared. "He said he didn't like it."

I hadn't liked it much myself.

"You told Fred?" Sister asked.

I shook my head. "I haven't had a chance yet." Which was a lie.

"Told me what?" Fred was standing in the doorway.

Sister didn't miss a beat. "That a Russian agent dropped the switchblade that he used to kill that Mooncloth guy into Mouse's purse."

Fred looked puzzled. Then his face brightened. "Are you working on one of your stories?"

Sister nodded.

"Sounds like a good one. Is that salmon croquettes I smell?"

Sister nodded again. "With dill sauce."

He couldn't say later that he hadn't been told. And the evening was peaceful. Fred and Sister ate the croquettes and I ate yogurt. The guy on *Who Wants to Be a Millionaire* won $500,000 and could pay off his student loans, and Griffin

Mooncloth's name wasn't mentioned again. All in all, a nice evening, even with the sinus.

Of course, the next morning all hell broke loose.

I was sitting at the kitchen table drinking orange juice and looking at the newspaper when the doorbell rang. I glanced at the clock. Nine-thirty. I had been up only a few minutes, had on my old pink chenille robe, and still felt miserable. Probably that Charles Boudreau again or a UPS package. I put Muffin down from my lap and went to the door.

When I looked through the peephole I saw two well-dressed, middle-aged men. Mormon missionaries? Jehovah's Witnesses? I opened the door, leaving the chain on.

"Yes?"

"Mrs. Hollowell?" The older of the two men said. He looked to be in his early forties, but he had a lot of white hair. The other man reminded me of Ron Howard, still little Opie to me, with a bald head and a fringe of red hair.

"Yes?"

White Hair held out a wallet with a badge in it. "Mrs. Hollowell, I'm Detective Hawkins, and this is Detective Blankenship. Would you open the door, please?"

"I'm not feeling well this morning. How can I help you?"

"Oh, hell, Mrs. Hollowell," White Hair said. "Excuse the language, Mrs. Hollowell, but I was scared it was you. I told Jasper here, I said, 'Jasper, I'll bet you anything it's my favorite English teacher from Robert Anderson High.' It's me, Tim Hawkins, Mrs. Hollowell. Second row on the left. Long black hair. Wrote my research paper on Matthew Arnold. 'Dover Beach.' Ah, love, let us be true to one another."

Jasper Blankenship snickered. Tim Hawkins gave him the look that probably turned Lot's wife into stone.

The pieces began to fall into place. The white hair had

thrown me. "Timmy? My goodness." I took the chain off the door. "Of course you can come in. Just don't look at me or the house. I've got the sinus."

The two men stepped into the living room.

"Y'all want some coffee?" I asked.

Timmy ducked his head. "No, ma'am. Mrs. Hollowell, I hate like hell to tell you this, excuse the language, but we've come to arrest you."

Detective Blankenship pulled some handcuffs from his pocket. "You have the right to remain silent. You have the right to an attorney—"

"Oh, shut up, Jasper. She doesn't need that crap." Timmy turned to me. "Mrs. Hollowell, we've got to take you in."

"For what, Timmy? Are you serious?"

"Suspicion of murder, Mrs. Hollowell. Seems they found a murder weapon in your handbag."

"I found it myself. It just showed up there."

"I know. It's just something we've got to do. They want to ask you some questions."

I looked down at my pink chenille robe. "Do I have time to get dressed?" I was feeling remarkably calm.

"Of course you do." Tim Hawkins gave his partner a look that dared him to stop me.

"And may I call my niece? She's my lawyer."

"Yes, ma'am."

"Well, y'all have a seat. There's coffee in the kitchen. Make yourselves at home."

The machine picked up at both Debbie's office and at her home. I left messages at both places that I was being arrested. I took a quick shower and put on my navy blue suit and heels. I might be under arrest, I might feel like hell, but I was going to be a neat criminal. I started to put on eyeliner but realized that my hands were shaking so much that I might blind myself. I guess I wasn't as calm as I thought.

Timmy and Detective Blankenship were sitting in the kitchen drinking coffee.

"I like your bay windows," Timmy said.

I looked out and saw Woofer marking his tree. "I need to call my neighbor," I said. "She'll be worried about me."

Mitzi's machine answered. I left word that I had gone to the police station. I didn't add that I was under arrest. I considered calling Fred, but surely I would be home in a little while.

"You ready?" Jasper Blankenship stood up. There was a tinge of sarcasm in his voice.

Timmy pointed to the table. "Rinse out your cup and saucer."

We went out and Timmy held open the front door of a Buick LeSabre for me. There was nothing to identify it as a police car, unlike Bo Mitchell's car that has "City of Birmingham" on the side. Jasper got in the back, and while Timmy was walking around the car, he reminded me that he had read me my rights.

I agreed that he had.

"Just wanted it clear."

"Exactly why am I under arrest, Timmy?" I asked when he got in the car. "And why couldn't you question me at home?"

"You were at the scene of the crime, Mrs. Hollowell, and the murder weapon was in your purse. So you're considered a murder suspect. Procedure says we have to hold you. And what they'll do at the station is give you a voice-stress analyzer test."

"A polygraph?"

"Not exactly." Timmy waited until a pickup had passed and then pulled out into the street. "Works sort of the same way, though. When they ask you a question that shakes you up, it'll show up on the machine."

"Timmy," I said. "I didn't know this Mooncloth man from Adam's house cat. We were sitting in the front row at the Alabama, and he fell over into the orchestra pit."

"I believe you, Mrs. Hollowell. What we're most interested in is the switchblade and how it ended up in your purse."

I considered this. "Have they had time to do a DNA test? Are they sure it's the murder weapon?"

Timmy shook his head. "The DNA won't be back for a few days, but the guy had B negative blood, which is fairly rare, and that's what's on the knife. And it fit the entry wound. Perfectly. It's the weapon, all right."

I was just grasping at straws. I had known it was the murder weapon when I pulled it from my purse and fainted.

"How long does it take? This voice-stress analyzer test." I asked. "And will the two of you be asking the questions?"

Timmy ran his hand through his white hair. Imagine. One of my students with white hair. "Depends. And no ma'am. There's a technician who does it. We'll talk to you afterward, though."

"Well, if it depends on how much I know, it won't take long."

Jasper leaned across the seat. "You probably know more than you think you do."

I could learn to dislike this Ron Howard look-alike. I turned and looked out of the window.

It was so eerie riding down the familiar streets knowing I was under arrest as a murder suspect. Knowing that the two men in the car with me were detectives with the Birmingham Police Department, men who were going to ask me questions about the murder of a man I had never met in my life. A Russian dancer. Weird. It would make more sense if they were arresting me for the murder of a fisherman on the Warrior River. At least I had known a few of them. Then a terrible thought occurred to me.

"Will I be able to post bail?" I asked Timmy. "My daughter's been in Warsaw, Poland, since last August, and she's coming home in a few days, and there are all sorts of things we need to do for her. She's four months pregnant."

"Can't see any reason why not. I expect all they'll do is question you and let you go home, anyway." Timmy said. He nodded his head toward Jasper. "His wife's four months pregnant, too."

Jasper leaned forward again. "We're having a girl. Going to name her Emily Claire."

"That's a beautiful name. Ours is Joanna. I don't think they've decided on a middle name yet. Is your wife showing?"

"Looks like she swallowed an eggplant."

"That's exciting."

"Yes, ma'am," he agreed. I had begun to like him a little. But not for long. As we pulled up to the downtown police station, he informed me that he was going to have to put the handcuffs on. Policy.

I looked at Timmy. He seemed embarrassed, but he nodded his head.

"Bunch of bullshit. Excuse the language, Mrs. Hollowell, but we've got to do it."

I held out my hands.

"We have to do them in the back," Jasper said. "It's too easy to get your hands out in front. Folks used to get loose that way all the time."

The click of the handcuffs around my wrists scared me. Until now, the whole thing had been unreal. I had a fever, I had a headache, one of my former students was arresting me for the murder of a man I had never seen in my life until he fell over dead in the orchestra pit at the Alabama. But the handcuffs holding my arms behind my back were real. And uncomfortable. Why on God's earth would I want to escape? I hadn't done anything.

I had been in the Birmingham Police Headquarters only once in my life, and that had been to pick up Henry Lamont's cousin, Trinity Buckalew, who had been charged with a misdemeanor. When we arrived, she had been playing cards with a man she had introduced as a narc who hung out under interstates, and she had been winning. I remembered the place as light and airy. Today, walking down the same hall between Tim Hawkins and Jasper Blankenship, it was much more grim. I was also very con-

scious of how uncomfortable it is to have your hands handcuffed behind you. It does something to your center of gravity
and forces you to walk carefully.

We came to a window like the windows in a doctor's reception area that you can't see through. A sign-in sheet was on the
counter in front of the window, and both Timmy and Jasper
signed in. I wouldn't have been surprised if the window had
opened and a receptionist had demanded my medical insurance
card. But nothing happened.

"This way, Mrs. Hollowell," Timmy said, pointing toward a
door that had a red light above it and code box on the side. He
punched in several numbers, there was a grinding noise, a green
light came on, and he opened the door into a narrow hall. "On
the left," he said.

We turned into a very pleasant room. There were two desks
and a round table with chairs around it. A long counter ran
down one wall with bookcases above it. In one bookcase,
African violets flourished under fluorescent grow-lights. In a
corner was a corn plant, tall, healthy, reaching toward the fluorescent bulbs in the ceiling. Bulbs that gave off a familiar slight
buzzing sound, familiar because Robert Anderson High was one
of the experimental schools built in the late sixties without windows. For thirty years that buzz had been part of my life.

A pretty young woman sitting at the front desk looked up. I
thought for a moment that she had very short blond hair, but
when she turned slightly, I saw that it was pulled back into one
long plait. She said, "Hey, Tim. Hey, Jasper," and looked at me
curiously.

"Charity, this is Mrs. Hollowell. She was my English teacher
at Robert Anderson."

"Wow."

Wow, indeed. The lovely Charity wouldn't have even been a
gleam in her father's eye at that point in time.

"We're booking her for suspicion of murder," Jasper added.

"Wow." Charity's eyes widened. "And she looks like a nice lady."

The three of them looked at me. I said, "I am a nice lady," and they all nodded.

"Well, I am," I insisted.

"She really is," Tim said, a little late, I thought. I frowned at him.

Charity reached into her desk and pulled out some forms. "Well, y'all fill these out." She leaned over and touched an intercom button.

"What?" an irritated loud voice answered.

"Need some fingerprints here, Jean."

"Snowed under back here. I'll get to you soon as I can."

"She'll get to us soon as she can," Charity announced as if we were deaf.

"I have to go to the ladies' room," I said. "Right now."

Charity stood up. "I'll walk you down there. It's right down the hall."

"There's a problem with the handcuffs."

Tim, on his way over to the table with the forms, said, "Jasper, get those damn handcuffs off. Excuse the language, Mrs. Hollowell."

"Who do they think you murdered, Mrs. Hollowell?" the lovely Charity asked as we walked down the hall.

"A Russian guy at the Alabama Theater."

"Oh, I heard about that. Somebody stabbed him on the stage while he was doing an Elvis dance."

"And I was in the audience." I pointed to the door with WOMEN on it. "Do you have to come in with me?"

"Oh, no, ma'am. There's no way to get out of there. I'll just wait here."

I thanked her and walked into the restroom to be confronted with the witch from hell. It took me a few seconds to realize that what I was facing was a full-length mirror.

Good Lord have mercy. The only thing I recognized was the navy suit. I was pale as a ghost except for my eyes, which looked like black holes. A sinus infection and getting arrested did not improve one's appearance. Or one's frame of mind. In my whole life I had gotten one speeding ticket, and here I was in the Birmingham jail under suspicion for murder of a Russian Elvis impersonator. Now what were the odds of that?

My head was pounding. When I came out of the stall, I wet a paper towel and held it against my face. Then I fished around in my purse (not the same one I had found the switchblade in) and located a couple of Extra Strength Tylenol. I cupped my hand under the faucet and managed to get enough water to wash them down. I should have brought my antibiotic, I realized. I was supposed to take it four times a day. Damn. I held the paper towel to my eyes.

"Mrs. Hollowell, you okay?" Charity called through the door.

"I'm coming," I said, throwing the towel in the wastebasket.

"We're going on down to the voice analyzer," she said as I came out. "She's not busy right now."

"How long does it take? I've got a splitting headache."

"Depends. You can wait on your lawyer if you want to."

I had no idea how long it would take Debbie to get my messages, and I couldn't think of any way that I could incriminate myself by answering some questions, so I said, "Let's get it over with."

Charity led me into a small but very pleasant office. A very pregnant woman in her early thirties stood and introduced herself as Margaret Sayres. Charity said she had to get back to work. Margaret invited me to sit down, which she and I both did. She reached in her desk drawer, pulled out a huge bottle of Maalox, and took a swig.

"You remember what the last month is like?" she asked.

I nodded. "I have three children."

"This will be my third." She turned a picture on her desk so I could see it. Two blond little girls in front of a Christmas tree.

"They're beautiful."

She studied the picture. "Yes, they are. We're having a boy this time." She placed it back on the desk and said, "Ready to get down to business?"

"How does the test work?"

"Nothing to it. We just talk. I ask you a few questions, and you answer. Give me a yes or no or say anything you want." She pointed to what I had thought was a small radio on her desk. "This picks up our voices, measures the amount of stress. Actually"—she reached over and patted the box—"this is better than a polygraph, believe it or not. They've found out that every person's voice is as distinctive as their fingerprint or their handwriting. You can take a tranquilizer or some other drug and fool a polygraph but not this baby." She leaned back. "Now I want you just to relax, Mrs. Hollowell."

Fat chance in hell. And I decided not to correct her grammar, too.

"Your name is Patricia Anne Tate Hollowell?"

"Yes."

"How old are you, Mrs. Hollowell?"

"Sixty-one."

"How long have you lived in Birmingham?"

"All my life." I began to relax a little.

"Have you taken any drugs today?"

"An antibiotic and two Extra Strength Tylenol. I've got a sinus infection. Splitting headache."

"But no narcotics? No cough syrup with codeine?"

I shook my head. "Makes me sick."

"Did you know Griffin Mooncloth?"

"No. I was sitting in the front row of the Alabama when he was stabbed. He came right toward us and fell in the orchestra pit. It upset my husband and me both so much that we left immediately."

Margaret leaned forward to adjust a knob on the voice analyzer, not an easy thing to do at eight months pregnant.

"Where are you having your baby?" I asked.

"Brookwood. I like their birthing room."

"My niece just had a baby there. She's a lawyer. Debbie Nachman. You may know her."

"Oh, sure, I know Debbie. She had a little boy, didn't she?"

I nodded. "David Anthony. They're calling him Brother."

Margaret patted her stomach. "I'll bet that's what happens to this one, too." How's Debbie doing? Is she back at work?"

"Part-time. I hope she'll be down here to get me out in a little while."

"Mrs. Hollowell, do you have any idea how the switchblade knife got in your purse?"

"I've narrowed down the number of people who could have done it to four."

"And you didn't kill Griffin Mooncloth?"

"Of course not. The extent of my killing is putting out Combat bait for roaches."

Margaret reached in her desk drawer and pulled out the Maalox bottle again. "I've got a little refrigerator. You want a Coke? Caffeine-free?"

"I'd love one." I pointed to the voice analyzer. "Are we through?"

"Oh, sure."

I breathed a sigh of relief. "This whole thing is ridiculous. They brought me in in handcuffs."

"Tacky. It's policy, though."

"So I've heard. Where's the refrigerator? I'll get the Cokes."

"Thanks, Mrs. Hollowell. It's over in the corner under that table."

I got the cans of Coke and handed one to Margaret. "My daughter's pregnant, too."

"When is she due?"

I felt better than I had all day. The Tylenol was taking effect, and I had obviously passed the voice-stress analyzer test. Or so I assumed. We had finished the pregnancy conversation, and I was listening to Margaret tell about her daredevil daughter Rosie's exploits when the phone rang.

"Debbie's here," she said when she hung up.

Chapter Twelve

It took Debbie more than an hour to get me out of the police station. I think she talked to everyone there before she came back to Margaret's office and told me I was free to leave. By that time, Margaret and I had gotten to be good friends.

"Your aunt's innocent as a baby," Margaret told Debbie when she finally showed up.

"Of course she is." Debbie eyed Margaret's girth. "Speaking of babies, are you going to make it through the day?"

Margaret sighed and reached for the Maalox. "Lord knows. I hear you had a boy this time. Me, too. Are they very different?"

"You have to be a lot more careful changing their diapers."

Margaret smiled, swigged the antacid, and tapped her chest with her fist. "I just want him out. We're running out of room here."

We all knew the feeling. During the last month of pregnancy

you get scared that nature has played a trick on you, that you will always be pregnant.

"Hang in there," Debbie said.

Margaret stuck out a white-coated tongue at her.

"Am I really free?" I asked Debbie as we went down the hall.

"They agreed that suspicion of murder was pretty far-fetched since half of Birmingham saw you were sitting in the front row when the Mooncloth guy was killed."

"Good."

"They still have some questions about the knife, though, Aunt Pat. About how it could have gotten in your purse. Tim Hawkins said he would be over this afternoon to talk to you. He said he knew you didn't feel like staying around here."

"They arrested me, Debbie. Read me my rights, handcuffed me."

"That's what I heard, Aunt Pat. I'm sorry."

We exited into a beautiful spring day. Debbie asked if I wanted to stop and get lunch somewhere, but I didn't feel like it. Not only did I have the sinus, but I was depressed. There's tacky, there's common, and there's common as pig tracks. Being arrested for suspicion of murder and handcuffed would have to rank in the latter category. Grandmama Alice was probably flipping over in her grave right this moment in spite of the fact that I was innocent. On her list of common as pig tracks were such things as chewing on a toothpick and, God forbid, smoking in public. Compared with those, being arrested would warrant the creation of a whole new category.

"What do you think could be more common than pig tracks?" I asked Debbie.

"Nothing."

That cheered me up some.

"I've been thinking," I said as we went up the entrance ramp to the Red Mountain Expressway. "This Griffin Mooncloth is Russian, he's defected, and he's been murdered. How come the state department isn't involved? Or the FBI or something?"

Debbie checked the oncoming traffic and pulled onto the expressway. "I guess they figure it's not a political thing. You take all of those illegal aliens who work in the poultry plants up in north Alabama. One of them gets stabbed to death, and it's up to the local police to find out who did it."

"That's true. But this Mooncloth guy was outstanding enough to be involved in a cultural exchange. And the Russians are still pretty strict about what they allow their citizens to do."

Debbie passed a truck loaded with huge steel coils that were bouncing ominously. I breathed a sigh of relief to be past it.

"I don't know, Aunt Pat. Just about all of the Russian ice skaters live here now. And I'll bet if you looked at the rosters of the largest ballet companies, half the names would be Russian. And I think that everyone's pretty sure that Griffin Mooncloth's murder wasn't a political one. Somebody had it in for him personally."

"You're right. I've seen too many Cold War movies."

I glanced up at Red Mountain and depression descended again. It looked bare without the statue of Vulcan raising his torch and mooning all points south. We needed him back. Vulcan Park was closed, but one night recently some teenagers had sneaked in and painted the dismantled statue's toenails red. If he wasn't back on his pedestal soon, there would surely be more vandalism. Whoever had had the bright idea to fill the largest iron statue in the world with concrete should have his head examined. Particularly when they left a hole in the statue's head that allowed water to get in and freeze.

I rubbed my forehead.

"Headache?" Debbie asked.

I nodded.

"He had a nice voice. Not much of an accent."

"Griffin Mooncloth?"

Debbie signaled and got into the turn lane. "He left word on my answering machine that he needed an appointment. When I called him back, I got his machine. I told him three o'clock the next day and if that wasn't okay to call me back. That was the day he was killed."

"He had an answering machine?"

Debbie nodded. "I'm sure it was one of those little portable ones you can stick on any phone. I called the police and told them when I heard what had happened to him. Gave them the number."

"So he wasn't staying at a hotel?"

"It was a direct line. Some of these business suite motels have them, though." Debbie took the exit. "I wish I knew what he wanted and how he got my name. He just said I'd been recommended."

"Hmm." I closed my eyes. I was almost home. I would put on my robe, open a can of chicken noodle soup, take another antibiotic. Muffin and I would watch the Rosie show or a movie on Lifetime.

"Mama's at your house," Debbie said.

I opened my eyes. Mary Alice and Tammy Sue Ludmiller were standing in my front yard talking to Mitzi.

"Where in the world have you been?" Sister asked as I got out of the car. "Mitzi said you left with two men in suits."

Tammy Sue said, "Wasn't that a movie title? *Two Men in Suits?*"

Sister shook her head. "I think it was *Two Men and a Baby.*"

"*Three Men and a Baby,*" Mitzi corrected her. "And she did leave with two men in suits. I saw her out of my kitchen window. She was all hunched over, and I came right out to see about her, but they were gone. I had to put on some clothes, so it took me a minute or two." Mitzi turned to me. "I was worried about you though, Patricia Anne."

All of them looked at me for an explanation as to why I had worried them.

"I was arrested for suspicion of murder. I've been at the police station."

"Have mercy," Mitzi exclaimed, clutching her chest. "And on top of the sinus."

"It was the knife," Debbie came around the car explaining. "But everything's cool now."

Cool? Everything was cool? Dear Lord. I hadn't heard that expression in ages.

Tammy Sue rolled her eyes. "They think she killed the Mooncloth guy? That's ridiculous. She was right in the front row."

"They've pretty much ruled out her murdering him," Debbie said.

"Well, I should hope so. And, besides," Tammy Sue continued, "Larry caught a glimpse of the person who did it just as they started toward the front doing their kick, so it couldn't have been Mrs. Hollowell."

"Patricia Anne's not strong enough to stick a switchblade knife in anybody anyway. She's always been weak as a kitten what with her eating problems," Sister said.

The way they were talking about me was beginning to make me feel invisible. I drew myself up to my full five feet and announced that I was going into the house to take some aspirin and antibiotics and open a can of soup.

"But we came to take you to lunch at Tannehill. I want to show Tammy Sue the church and see what she thinks about the reception."

Apparently Sister was making some headway with her soon-to-be stepdaughter by getting her involved with the wedding plans.

"I want to go with you," Debbie said, "Can I go? I'll have to stop by the house and feed Brother first. Can I meet you down there?"

"We'll just go by and pick him up. How about that?" Sister turned to Mitzi. "You want to go, Mitzi? I need all the input I can get. Like whether or not long dresses would be a problem."

"Just let me get my purse."

For a moment I considered climbing into the car and going with them. Then I remembered that Tim Hawkins was going to come by that afternoon to ask some questions. So I waved them off and went in to heat my soup.

There were three messages on my answering machine, two from Fred and one from Bernice Armstrong. Fred wanted to know how I was feeling, and Bernice was thanking me for calling to check on Dusk the night before. She was sorry they had missed the call. Dusk was feeling much better and would probably go back to New York in a couple of days. Give her a callback when I got a chance.

I called Fred and told him I was all right. I had decided that I would wait until he got home to tell him about being arrested. That would take more than a phone call. Bernice's line was busy, so I warmed my chicken noodle soup and sat down at the kitchen table. I was hungry, I realized, when I tasted my first spoonful. Here, at my kitchen table, was normality. The sun was shining through the skylight in the den, Woofer was marking his tree in the yard, and Muffin was stretched out on the sofa. I crumbled some crackers into the soup and relaxed for the first time that day. Handcuffs? Miranda rights? Voice-stress analyzer? The whole morning was becoming as unreal as a trip to Mars.

But someone had put a murder weapon in my purse. That was real. I could still feel it in my hand—cold, metallic—see the switch shaped like a crown, hear the *swoosh* of the blade. I shivered and forced myself to think pleasant thoughts. Haley. Joanna.

I was so lost in those thoughts that the phone's ringing startled me.

"Mrs. Hollowell?" a deep male voice said when I answered.

"This is Larry Ludmiller. Is Tammy Sue there by any chance? I know she's with Mrs. Crane, and I called her house and Tiffany said they were probably with you."

"They're on their way to Tannehill for lunch," I explained. I gave him Sister's car phone number. He thanked me and hung up. I didn't think any more about this conversation until hours later. At the time, it didn't seem important.

Tim Hawkins showed up alone around four o'clock. By then, I had had a short nap and the antibiotics seemed to be kicking in. I felt better.

"Do you have your handcuffs?" I asked him when I opened the door.

"No ma'am. I'm so damned sorry about that, Mrs. Hollowell." He actually blushed. "Excuse the language."

"I know. Policy."

"Yes, ma'am. My mama would have a fit. I'm sure you remember her. President of the PTA? Got the stage lights put up? The spots?"

"Little bitty? Space between her teeth?"

"That's her."

"Well, how's she doing?"

"Just fine."

"Give her my regards. Tell her they're still enjoying those lights at the school."

While this exchange was going on, I led Tim back to the den and motioned for him to sit on the sofa. He turned down the offer of coffee and got out his notebook.

"Mrs. Hollowell," he said, "I know you didn't have anything to do with the stabbing, but we need to find out how the knife got in your pocketbook."

"We sure do," I agreed.

"Do you have a theory?"

I told him all about the dinner party at Mary Alice's house and how the purse had sat on the table. I named the people who had had access to it and said how I hated to think that it was one of them because my sister was going to marry Virgil Stuckey and all of them were related to him.

Tim wrote down the names and allowed as to how Sheriff Stuckey was a good man. "I've worked with him on several cases," he said. "You know who he reminds me of? Willard Scott."

I allowed as to how he reminded me of both Willard and Norman Schwarzkopf, and he was, indeed, a good man.

"Timmy," I said, when I had told him all I knew about Virgil, Jr., Larry, Tammy Sue, and Olivia, which wasn't much. "Do you know what Griffin Mooncloth was doing in Birmingham?"

"No, ma'am."

He was lying. Thirty years of teaching is better than any polygraph or voice-stress analyzer for spotting a lie.

"He made an appointment with my niece, who's a lawyer, so he needed some legal advice."

"Yes, ma'am. Your niece called us. We're checking it out." He looked down at his notebook. "What we've got to figure out now is which one of these people could have had the knife. I think that would tell us a lot."

Tell us a lot? I looked at Timmy to see if he was serious. He was.

I said, "Any one of them could have had access to my purse, since it was right on the game table. But do you know what doesn't make sense to me? The fact that whoever it was carried a bloody switchblade around for a couple of days. Why didn't they just throw it away somewhere in a ditch or something? Why put it in my purse?"

"Trying to set you up?"

Again I checked him out. Yes, he was serious.

I shook my head. "They all knew I was in the audience."

"Trying to set someone else up?"

"By planting a knife on me?"

"Stranger things have happened."

I couldn't imagine what and decided not to ask. I rubbed my head, which was beginning to ache again. What a weird day this was turning out to be.

"Let's just go over again what you know about each of the people who were at the dinner party," Timmy suggested. "Maybe you're forgetting something."

I simply repeated what I had told him earlier. All I knew was that Virgil, Jr., was an Elvis impersonator; Larry Ludmiller was some kind of talent promoter; Olivia Ludmiller, his sister, seemed smitten by Virgil, Jr.; and Tammy Sue sold real estate. We had had a nice supper with steaks because my sister and Virgil were going to tell his kids that they were getting married, which they did, but Virgil, Sr., had had to leave early and Tiffany, the Magic Maid, had left to go on a date, but she didn't know anything about what was going on, I was sure.

Timmy looked at me as if he expected more.

I shrugged. "That's it."

Timmy closed his notebook and stood up. "Thanks, Mrs. Hollowell."

"I didn't tell you much, did I?" I said, following him to the door.

"Actually, you did."

"What?"

He leaned over and kissed my cheek. "Don't you tell my mama I arrested you." And then he was gone, turning halfway down the walk to wave.

What the hell had I told him?

The sun was low in the sky, but the weather was still pleasantly warm. The best thing for my headache, I decided, was a walk. I watched Timmy drive away and, still puzzled, went to get Woofer's leash.

The lights were on in Mitzi's sunroom, so the group was back from Tannehill. It looked, this time, as if Sister were really going to do it, get married. I paused for Woofer to sniff at a telephone pole, and let that fact sink in. There have always been men in Sister's life, other than her three husbands, whose time with her had been short. But sweet, she reminds me. Men love her, all two hundred fifty unpredictable pounds of her. And I can understand it. Yes, she has the nerve of a bad tooth, like Fred says, but she has a zest for life that's contagious and wonderful. I hoped that Virgil would appreciate that. Surely he would.

I walked along the sidewalk scuffing a few pinecones out of the way and thinking about the dinner party and the switch-blade knife. It was scary to think that one of those people so close to Virgil was probably responsible for putting the knife in my purse. For putting the knife in Griffin Mooncloth's back. I shivered. Tammy Sue had been sitting by me, so she was ruled out. Had Olivia been at the Alabama? Virgil, Jr., and Larry certainly had. Right next to Griffin.

But what motive could there have been? According to Virgil, Jr., and Larry, they had no idea who Griffin Mooncloth was. Did Olivia? Was there some connection there that Tim Hawkins knew about that I had verified when I talked to him? I thought about Olivia and how she had been clinging to Virgil, Jr.

"It makes no sense," I told Woofer, who looked around at me and nodded in agreement. "A man gets killed right in the middle of a thousand people and no one sees it happen." I paused. "Well, Larry Ludmiller got a glimpse, so he said, but Tammy Sue says he can't see anything without his glasses."

Woofer looked at me as if he were puzzling over it, too.

"And if Dusk Armstrong hadn't been in one of the Mooncloth

guy's dance classes, no one would have been able to identify him. At least right away."

Woofer sighed and sat down. It was indeed a mystery. But my thinking of Dusk Armstrong reminded me that I hadn't returned her mother's call. It was chillier outside than I had thought, too.

"I've got no business out in the cold, Woofer," I said. "I'm courting pneumonia."

He turned back toward the house agreeably. Some days you walk a mile. Some days you walk a block. But a treat was always waiting.

"Dusk is much better," Bernice said when I asked. "She wouldn't let me take her to the doctor, but she's been able to eat some today. It might have been a virus, but I think it was the shock of seeing that man that she knew killed at the Alabama. Lord knows it would upset my stomach seeing someone I knew stabbed like that, dead as a doornail, let alone falling into an orchestra pit."

I agreed that it would be unnerving to say the least and that I was glad she was feeling better.

"What I wanted to tell you, though, was that I've got the most wonderful rocking chair that you're welcome to. Mitzi told me that you were looking for one for Haley, and this is one that I bought for Dawn when she was pregnant the first time. It's one that a man made for Prime Time Treasures, you know the handicraft shop in Homewood where senior citizens sell their work? I was so excited when I found it. I swear to you, Patricia Anne, it's absolutely perfect for rocking a baby. Comfortable and even creaks just a little bit. Anyway, it was what I took to Dawn's shower. Even gift wrapped it, if you can believe. You've never seen so much paper and tape, and then I had to take Jerry's van because I couldn't get it in my car." Bernice paused to catch her breath. "And would you believe that was what Mary Lou Rider, Dawn's mother-in-law, brought her, too? Out of everything in Birmingham to buy for babies, we bought the same thing. Of course, Dawn felt like she had to keep the one Mary Lou brought. Didn't want to hurt her feelings, which I could understand. Not that I could tell an ounce of difference."

"You couldn't take it back?"

"No, but that's okay. I figured Day or Dusk would use it someday, but they tell me I might as well give up. Neither one of them is planning on having children. They're both totally into their careers."

"Maybe they'll change their minds."

"I doubt it. But if they do, Dawn can pass along her rocker. Her children are eight and twelve now. Can you believe?"

I could imagine Bernice shaking her head the way I do when I think about my two grandsons, Charlie and Sam, fast approaching teen age in Atlanta.

"Come over in the morning," Bernice continued. "It's up in the attic, and it won't hurt my feelings if you don't think it's as wonderful as I do. But I'd love to think of Haley rocking her little one in it. You wouldn't believe how wonderful she was to all of us when Jerry had his heart surgery, Patricia Anne. I hope she doesn't give up nursing."

There's nothing much better than hearing such nice things about one of your children. I thanked Bernice and told her that I would definitely be over the next morning, sinuses willing. I hung up smiling, got a can of Dinty Moore beef stew out of the pantry, popped open a can of biscuits for a topping, and had supper ready for Fred when he came in.

"Smells good in here," he said. He gave me a hug and went to the refrigerator for a beer.

"I got arrested today." I said.

"Really?" He popped open the can, took a long swig, and headed down the hall.

I waited.

In a minute he was back, a startled look on his face. "You what?"

"We'd better sit down for this one," I said.

Chapter Thirteen

arry Ludmiller didn't come home last night," Yul Brynner announced as she came into my kitchen the next morning. "Virgil just called me. Tammy Sue is having a fit."

I was sitting at the kitchen table and had just taken a bite of French toast. I chewed, swallowed, and looked at Sister as she sat down across from me.

"Did they have a fight or something?"

She shook her head. "Apparently not. Virgil said she had supper all ready for him, and he never showed up. And she'd told him she was going to cook a pot roast."

"He called here yesterday looking for her. Right after y'all left for Tannehill. I gave him your car phone number."

"We never heard from him." Sister got up and poured herself a cup of coffee. "Tammy Sue called Virgil about two o'clock this morning and said Larry hadn't shown up."

"Maybe he was with one of the acts that he handles at some club. Is that a possibility?"

Sister sat back down and reached for the sugar. "That's what I said, and Virgil said that it was highly unlikely and that he would have called anyway, that he never worries Tammy Sue like that. Besides, she was cooking a pot roast. I asked him if he wanted me to come up there, if there was anything I could do, and he said no, that he and Tammy Sue had called everywhere and they were going to go out looking." She stirred her coffee. "He said Larry's got a couple of apartments on Valley Avenue that his out-of-town acts stay in. They're going to go over there." She put her spoon down. "He didn't say they were going to look in ditches on the way, but I'm sure they are."

I pushed my French toast away. "This sure doesn't sound good, does it?"

"Sounds scary as hell. I told Virgil I was on my way to my martial arts class and he said to go on, that there wasn't anything I could do, but I just didn't have the heart for it."

"Well, maybe Larry's all right. Maybe he left a message that got erased or something." Little Miss Sunshine not believing a word of what she was saying.

"I hope so." Sister looked over at me. "You feeling better this morning?"

"I was."

"I know what you mean."

We were quiet for a few minutes, both of us lost in thought.

"There could be a girlfriend," I suggested.

"I don't think so."

"But it's possible."

"I doubt it." She eyed my French toast. "Any more of that left?"

I shook my head. "But there's some Sister Schubert's orange rolls in the refrigerator. Nuke them for about fifteen seconds."

"I like Tammy Sue," she said, wrapping a couple of the

orange rolls in paper towels and sticking them in the microwave. "Down to earth. Said she thought the long sunflower bridesmaids dresses would be great." The microwave dinged. She took the sweet rolls out and came back to the table.

So Sister wasn't the only one trying to get along here.

She blew on the sweet roll and then took a bite. "We walked down to the creek at Tannehill and there was a big old water moccasin slithering out of the water, and she grabbed a pistol out of her purse and shot at that snake before he could even blink." Sister swallowed and took a sip of coffee. "Missed him but scared the hell out of him and us, too. Just as well that Debbie was in the car feeding Brother. He'd still be yelling."

"She just snatched a gun out and shot it?"

Sister nodded. "She's had training. She said she'd have hit the snake if she'd wanted to. And I think she would have. It just wasn't that snake's time to go."

"A stepdaughter to appreciate."

"That's what I'm beginning to realize. She was going to take me to see a cabin up at Smith Lake this afternoon, but I guess since her husband's missing, that's off."

"You're buying some lake property?"

"Might as well." Sister popped the rest of the sweet roll into her mouth and wiped her hands on a paper towel. "You know what I forgot, though? Deena just slipped out of my mind totally."

"Who's Deena?"

"Virgil's other daughter. The one who lives in Texas. I just plain forgot he had three children, and he hasn't said a thing about it when I've talked about the wedding. I guess I'll have to ask her to be in it. And she's got a couple of little girls, and if Fay and May are going to be in it, I guess her girls will have to be, too, except Tammy Sue says that Deena has a tendency to have panic attacks and might not be interested. I'll have to ask her, though."

"Panic attacks?"

"Well, Tammy Sue says she's been known to faint dead away and twitch. Sounds awful, bless her heart. But she's on medication now and a lot better."

"Reckon she carries a gun, too?"

Sister narrowed her eyes and looked at me. "I don't know, Patricia Anne, but there's something to be said for a woman who can sell a piece of property, shoot a snake, and cook a pot roast in a Crock-Pot all at the same time. Neither of us could do it. Or our daughters, either."

She had me there. "You're marrying into rugged stock," I said.

"If you discount impersonating Elvis and panic attacks."

"Well, no family's perfect."

"True."

We grinned at each other.

"Speaking of which," Sister said, "Marilyn hasn't been in touch with you any more has she?"

"No, and there's nothing wrong with Marilyn."

"Of course there is. If she'd had any common sense, she'd have snatched Charlie Boudreau up years ago and had a bunch of kids by now."

"She said she couldn't live with him."

"That's just an excuse."

No way I could figure that one out. I got up and put my dishes in the dishwasher.

"You over being arrested yet?" Sister asked, handing me her coffee cup.

"Fred made me feel better. He said he was going to go down to the police station and beat them all up. And then he fixed me hot chocolate with marshmallows and we watched *Who Wants to Be a Millionaire*." I closed the dishwasher. "I'm going to go over to Bernice Armstrong's house this morning. She's got a rocking chair that she says would be perfect for Haley."

"You want me to take you? You couldn't get it in your car if you decided you wanted it."

"You're sure you don't want to go to your karate class?"

"I'm not in the mood. Go get dressed while I call and see if Larry's shown up." She reached for the phone. "I declare I hope he's in one piece somewhere."

I shared that wish fervently.

The Armstrongs live in a beautiful old part of Birmingham called Forest Park. Most of the homes here were built in the early 1900s, large homes on level lots and lush lawns with huge old trees. Many of the detached garages were probably built for carriages originally. There are sidewalks and small parks, and a ride through this neighborhood is a trip to a more gracious time. One can imagine the ladies sitting in wicker chairs on the large, cool porches visiting and drinking tea while the cooks cooked supper, the yardmen cut the grass, the cleaning ladies cleaned, and the nannies took the children to the park. Now the Magic Maids come in once a week, a yard service does the yard, and the kids are at Mother's Day Out or day care. Still no bad deal. And a few lucky ones still have a nanny. As for the cooking, the ladies go to the Piggly Wiggly or the Winn-Dixie like the rest of us. The houses are still treasured, though. And it shows.

The Armstrongs' house is a three-storied dark brick set well back from the sidewalk. When Mary Alice and I pulled into the driveway, Sandy's Lawn Service was hard at work. One young man was circling on a riding lawn mower, one was weed-eating around the trees, and one was planting red and white begonias in a triangular flower bed between the drive and the walkway.

"Those things are going to freeze," Mary Alice informed him as we walked by on our way to the front door. "North of Montgomery you don't plant flowers until the first Sunday after the first full moon after March twenty-first."

He looked up and smiled. "Sometimes you gotta take a chance, lady. And begonias are right hardy."

"They do look pretty," I assured him. And to Sister, "That first full moon thing is the date for Easter."

"Which is the right time to plant flowers. You miss blackberry winter."

She was confused but she had a point. Blackberry winter is the last cold snap we get in the deep South. It invariably falls at Easter and kills the blackberry blooms as well as a lot of other flowers.

We walked through the spring smell of newly cut grass and rang the doorbell. Sister looked around at the well-kept house and lawn. "The insurance business must be doing all right by Jerry Armstrong," she said. "But didn't I hear he was sick or something?"

"He had open-heart surgery. He's doing fine now. Haley was the scrub nurse and that's why Bernice wants her to have the rocker. She said Haley was wonderful."

"Hmm. You know, Mouse, we've got to decide no later than today what we're going to do to welcome she and Nephew home. It's just a couple of weeks away."

"*Her*. You don't welcome 'she.'"

Sister scowled. For a second I thought she was going to reach over and pinch my arm, something she learned how to do sixty years ago without leaving a bruise. It has something to do with the way she rolls her fingers. It hurts like hell, and you have no proof that Miss Innocent has done a thing.

Fortunately the front door opened.

"Hey, y'all," Bernice said. "Come in. Day and Dusk and I are just having coffee in the sunroom. Y'all come on back."

We stepped into the foyer and both of us shrieked. A monster stood there, arms raised to attack. Sister and I grabbed each other. (Later on we would both swear we were trying to protect the other.)

"Oh, I'm sorry, y'all," Bernice said calmly. "I forgot to warn you about Maurice. I know it's tacky having him here right at the front door, but we haven't decided where to put him, and this is as far as we got. You wouldn't believe how bunglesome he is, and how heavy."

I peeked around Mary Alice's arm and saw that Maurice was a grizzly bear, larger than any bear I had ever seen in a zoo. Standing on his hind legs, he was in an attack mode. Only the glass eyes gave away the fact that those six-inch-long claws weren't going to rip us open at any given moment.

"It's a stuffed bear," I said, peeling Sister off of me.

"My God," she said when she opened her eyes and looked. "What the hell?"

"I apologize." Bernice reached way up and patted Maurice's chest. A chunk of fur slid down and over his belly. "Bless his heart. He's molting and falling apart. But Jerry treasures him. His uncle left it to him when he died last month. He supposedly shot it in Alaska when he was a boy, the uncle that is, but knowing Uncle Hardy, I have an idea that the poor bear died a natural death, and Uncle Hardy just stumbled upon him. At least, I hope so."

Mary Alice and I looked at Maurice and he looked back, glassily. My heart was slowing down, and I hoped Sister's was, too.

"I know he's tacky here in the foyer," Bernice repeated. "I mean, how many people in Birmingham have a whole, stuffed grizzly bear in their house, and them an endangered species to boot. It's embarrassing. But what are you going to do when your husband thinks something is wonderful and it was a gift from his own dead uncle?"

Mary Alice reached over and touched Maurice. Fur drifted to the floor. "Dustbust him?"

Bernice shook her head. "Jerry would have another heart attack. I just don't understand men. Do y'all?"

"Fortunately it's not necessary." Sister paused to give Maurice another pat as we walked by on our way down the hall.

Day and Dusk were standing by the window in a deep conversation as we came into the sunroom, though Day seemed to be doing most of the talking. It was eerie the way they matched their names. Blond Day was dressed in a jade green suit; dark-haired Dusk had on a black leotard and tights. They both looked up.

"Heard you greeting Maurice," Dusk said, grinning. "Mama really needs to warn people."

"I'm going to send him back to New York with you," Bernice said. "He'd be better than all those chains and bolts you weight your door down with."

"That's for sure. Her door has so much metal on it you can hardly open it." Day motioned to a wicker love seat. "Y'all sit down, and I'll get you some coffee."

"I'll do it," Dusk offered. "You need to get back to work."

Day glanced at her watch. "I guess I'd better, but I hate to. Y'all come see me at the bank, ladies. We've got great CD rates."

Bernice gave her a hug. "Go peddle your wares somewhere else."

"Bye, ladies. I'll call you later, Mama." We heard her tell Maurice to behave himself as she went out the front door.

Tiny Dusk poured each of us a cup of coffee and offered us sugar and cream.

"Are you feeling okay now?" I asked, taking the napkin she offered.

"Much better, thanks."

"It was the shock of seeing that Griffin Mooncloth dead," Bernice said. "Y'all want some cookies or something?"

We both shook our heads.

"It shocked us, too," Sister said. "We were sitting in the front row and he nearly landed in our laps." She took a sip of her coffee and then put the cup on the table. "Which reminds me. You know Larry Ludmiller, Dusk?"

Dusk had curled up in a wicker chair in a position that only a dancer could accomplish. Her legs seemed to have disappeared.

"The one who books acts?" she wanted to know. "I've met him is all. Why?"

"He seems to have disappeared. He didn't come home last night."

Bernice looked up, alarmed. "They don't think it's connected to the Moonflower case, do they?"

"Mooncloth, Mama." Dusk said. Bernice shrugged

"I don't know what they think," Sister said. "I just know they're trying to find him and that they say this is totally unlike him. They're worried."

"Maybe he had a wreck," Dusk suggested. "His car could be down an embankment or something. Remember that lady who ran off the road in Shelby County and kudzu covered her car for weeks?"

"Oh, surely not." Bernice pushed her coffee away. "Do y'all know him?"

"He's Virgil Stuckey's son-in-law. Virgil and I are getting married in May." Sister turned to me. "Do you remember the exact date?"

I shrugged that I didn't.

"Virgil's the sheriff of St. Clair County until the end of this month," Sister explained, "and then he's retiring."

"Well, I declare, Mary Alice." Bernice beamed. "That's wonderful. When did all this happen?"

"Recently." It was the first thing I had said since we sat down. The other three looked at me in surprise as if they had forgotten I was there.

"You wouldn't believe, Bernice. He looks a lot like Cary Grant," Sister said. "And the wedding is going to be in the little church at Tannehill Park."

It's hard to believe that even as strong an emotion as love could turn a combination of Willard Scott and Norman Schwarzkopf into Cary Grant. Proof that it really is blind, I suppose.

"Well, tell me all about it," Bernice said.

So Sister did, including the wedding dress and the sunflower and magenta bridesmaids' dresses. Bernice seemed enthralled and even Dusk seemed excited. Too excited, I realized, when she clapped her hands as Fay and May tossed rose petals. Her face seemed flushed, too, I noticed. Was she still sick? Or was she on something? Some people were allergic to stomach medications. Maybe that was it.

Mary Alice and Bernice were engrossed in the talk about the wedding, and I watched Dusk. Surreptitiously, of course. To a casual observer, she would look relaxed, curled up in a chair. But I realized that she was in constant motion, pushing her hair back, patting the leg that was curled under her.

So I wasn't as surprised as the other two were when she suddenly jumped up, excused herself, and left the room.

"You okay?" Bernice called after her.

"Fine," echoed down the stairs.

"No, she's not," Bernice said sadly. "She's still in a dither about the murder. I wish she'd talk about it, but she won't. Not even to Day."

I put my coffee cup on the table. "I'm sure it shook her up terribly."

Bernice sighed. "I wish she wouldn't go back to New York just yet. But she says there's a new show that she wants to try out for. And when Dusk makes up her mind, she's adamant."

"How well did she know the Mooncloth guy?" Sister asked.

"Not all that well. She knew him in class, of course, but it was actually Day who knew him better than Dusk. Day met him when she was visiting Dusk in New York and went out with him some. She thought a lot of him. Said he was the last person in the world who she could imagine anyone murdering." Bernice shook her head. "So sad. They're going to have a memorial service for him in New York, so she's going back with Dusk. I'm glad she'll be with her for a few days." Bernice looked toward the steps. "I'm still worried about Dusk. To tell you the truth, I think she may have an eating disorder. Have you noticed how terribly thin she is? I can't get her to go to a doctor, though."

"Patricia Anne's always had one," Sister commiserated.

"I have not." I rubbed my forehead. I could use some aspirin. Sister looked at me sadly. "She plays the denial game."

"I'm afraid Dusk does, too," Bernice said. "Well, enough of that. You want to go see the chair?"

"I eat," I said as we went up the steps. "I eat a lot." But sometimes you're just plain talking into a vacuum.

Bernice led us up two flights of stairs. As we paused on the second landing to catch our breath, we could hear Dusk talking to someone. She sounded quite angry.

Her bedroom door was half open so Bernice stuck her head in. "You okay?"

"Just trying to get our plane tickets straight, Mama."

"You'll get more done with sugar than vinegar, Dusk." Bernice closed the door, and we continued on up the steps, leaving, I imagined, a young woman rolling her eyes at her mother's remark.

"Mama used to tell us that all the time," Mary Alice said. "Only I think she said we'd catch more flies with sugar than vinegar. Wasn't that what she said, Patricia Anne?"

I nodded.

"Mine did, too. I remember wondering why we wanted to catch flies." Bernice opened the attic door and we stepped inside. The house was grander than mine, but the attic was the same. An old sewing machine, a dressmaker's form, trunks. Bernice walked over and pulled a sheet from over what I knew immediately was the perfect chair. It wasn't at all what I had expected. I think what I had had in mind was a smaller version of President Kennedy's rocker. But this was a small, upholstered mahogany rocker. The arms were very low so Haley wouldn't have to worry about bumping Joanna's head. The upholstery was a delicate blue brocade patterned with pink and darker blue flowers.

"Oh, my," I said, sitting in it. "This is wonderful, Bernice."

"I think they call it a ladies' rocker or a boudoir rocker, something fancy like that," she said. "I just think it's a perfect rocking-the-baby chair."

"You're sure you want to part with it?"

"I'd love to think of Haley with it."

"She'll treasure it." And she would. I closed my eyes and rocked a minute until Sister said she wanted to try it out. "Test it for sturdiness."

I have seen the legs of chairs splay when Sister sat in them. This one didn't. It passed the sturdiness test.

"Mama?" Dusk called up the stairs. "I'm going down to the Alabama to pick up my bag I left there the other night. It's got all my stage makeup in it."

"Okay, honey. The keys are in my purse. Be careful." Bernice turned back to us, smiling at our obvious pleasure. "Do I have a taker here?"

I nodded and helped pull Sister up. "You have a very grateful taker. But if either Day or Dusk changes her mind and wants it back, just let me know."

"Don't I wish. Well, let's get it down the stairs."

The chair wasn't large, but maneuvering it down two flights of steps wasn't easy. I was in front, Sister behind, and Bernice cautioning us to be careful. After the first flight, I had discovered the law of physics that states that the person at the bottom of a load is carrying most of the weight.

"Maybe it would be better if you put the seat on top of your head and you could go frontward," Sister suggested.

I didn't answer that.

Dusk was standing in the foyer grinning at us as we tried to avoid banging into the banisters.

"I thought you'd left," her mother said, out of breath. Vicariously, I suppose, since her involvement in moving the chair had strictly been giving directions.

"Your car wouldn't start." Dusk reached over, took the chair from Sister and me, and placed it on the floor.

"Damn. Probably the battery. Or the computer." Bernice fanned her face with her hand. "I swear, y'all, I was driving down two hundred and eighty one afternoon at four-thirty and the car just went dead. Even the power steering was gone. God only knows how I managed it with all that traffic, but I coasted into a Hardee's. I figured it was the carburetor, but the woman who fixed me a peach milkshake, so I could take some aspirin, said she bet it was the computer, that they didn't make carburetors anymore. And sure enough it was. Had to tow me in. I just don't have any idea what happened to carburetors, do y'all?"

"They're gone?" I asked.

"Maybe not in your car." Sister turned to Dusk. "We'll take you to the Alabama. We've got to go right through town."

"Thanks, Mrs. Crane. I'm sure I can get a ride home."

"Call your daddy if you can't," Bernice said. "And don't go inside that theater if nobody else is there."

"Okay, Mama."

"We'll check it out." I hugged Bernice, thanked her again, and we took the chair out to Sister's van. The young man who had been planting begonias was now clipping shrubbery and came over to help us. Mary Alice was right. My car would never have held us and the chair.

"Who was the boy you were dancing with the other night, Dusk?" Mary Alice asked as she stopped at a light.

"His name's Bobby Miller, and he's a student at the Alabama School of Fine Arts. He's wonderful, isn't he? And he's only eighteen years old."

"Wonderful," Sister and I both agreed.

"I'm trying to talk him into coming to New York and putting

college off. But he probably won't. His father doesn't approve of him being a dancer. Thinks it's sissy."

I remembered how lightly he had lifted Dusk, the unbelievable leaps. Nothing sissy there. I felt the old familiar anger all teachers feel when parents insist that their gifted children follow in the path that they, the parents, have decided is the right one. And for the millionth time, I wished the arts were appreciated more.

"Y'all can just let me out at the side entrance," Dusk said, pointing to a door in the side of the Alabama that was almost lost in the shells and curlicues that adorned the outside of the building as well as the inside.

"We'll wait and see if anyone's here," Mary Alice said.

"Have you ever been backstage?" Dusk asked. "Would you like to see it? They've even got some of Tallulah Bankhead's old costumes back there. And the most wonderful old movie posters you've ever seen."

Mary Alice and I looked at each other. "You feel like it, Mouse?"

If I'd been half dead, I would have jumped at the chance. I'm totally addicted to old movies. And the Alabama has always been the most magical theater in the world.

"Park the car," I said.

This was no problem. As in most American cities, the large department stores and shops that once flourished in the downtown area have moved to the malls. Several plans have been proposed to bring the area back, including Birmingham Green, where a median of one of the principal downtown streets was planted with trees and flowers. Benches were placed strategically to welcome tired shoppers or to draw brown-bag lunchers from the office buildings to sit in the sun. It's beautiful, but usually deserted. Only recently have a few people begun to move back downtown into the loft apartments that are being created in the historic old buildings.

We parked across the street, jaywalked safely to the door in the side of the theater, and Dusk knocked on it. There was no answer, so she knocked again, louder. Still no answer. Mary Alice reached over and turned the doorknob. The door opened, and we stepped inside into a narrow hall. Dusk clicked on the light switch and a couple of sixty-watt bulbs dangling from the ceiling lit the concrete block wall and the cement floor. All pretensions of grandeur had been left at the door.

"It gets better," she promised. She walked to the end of the hall, opened another door, and called, "Hello? Anyone here?"

"Who is it?" a male voice called back.

"It's me, Dusk Armstrong. Is that you, Mr. Taylor?"

"What are you doing here, Dusk?" Mr. Taylor appeared out of the darkness. His thin, reddish hair was sticking up as if he had been sleeping on it. What riveted our attention, though, was the rag that he clasped in his hand. It looked like an old undershirt; it was covered in blood.

"What's the matter?" he asked, seeing the three of us as one begin to back up. I can only imagine how frightened we looked. It took him a second to catch on. "Oh, the rag. It's paint, ladies." He held it up for our inspection. "Just paint. I'm touching up the Wurlitzer, where that unfortunate young man fell on it the other night. Actually he did more than scratch it. He popped a corner right off. But somebody who knows woodwork is going to have to fix that. All I'm doing is fixing the scratches and polishing it." He stepped back. "Y'all come on in. I'm sorry I scared you."

We followed him in nervously. He was older than he had looked rising majestically on the Wurlitzer, makeup in place. Probably in his late sixties.

Dusk introduced us and said that she was there to get her makeup bag.

"You go right ahead. I was fixing to make sure the lift is okay on the Wurlitzer." He turned to Sister and me. "You ladies want to ride up on it?"

"Lord, yes," Sister said.

Dusk grinned at our enthusiasm. She hadn't spent her childhood at the Alabama watching the miracle of the Wurlitzer rise from the floor. "I'll go get my case," she said.

We were on the level where the orchestra pit was located. We followed Mr. Taylor down a hall that was carpeted in a gray indoor-outdoor carpeting, and which was painted the color I figured my bridesmaid dress was going to be, a magenta. I hoped that it was some paint left over from a production and not some that someone had chosen for the wall.

"I like your outfit," Mr. Taylor told Sister. "You trying out for *The King and I*?"

"Taking a martial arts class."

"That's good. A lady should be able to protect herself. My sister got a gun, but she shot her big toe off while she was taking a class on using it."

"Lord, I'll bet that affects the way she walks," I said.

"Not really. She has trouble wearing sandals, though."

Sister cut her eyes around at me. We had reached the orchestra pit, which I had never seen from this advantage. It was a mess with chairs turned over and several broken instruments.

"There's police tape up all around," Mr. Taylor said. "We can just duck under it, though. That's what everybody's been doing coming in here and getting their musical instruments. The bass fiddle was ruined, though."

"We know," I said. "We were here and sitting in the front row when the guy fell."

"Scared the hell out of me. Y'all watch the paint now. It's just on the very top, but be careful."

"You're grinning like a jackass eating briars," Mary Alice whispered to me. I didn't take offense because she was, too.

We settled on the bench, two ten-year-olds.

"You ready? I'm going to push the button."

"But we need music and neither of us plays," Mary Alice said. "Can't you get on here with us?"

"Not enough room. How about I whistle 'How Great Thou Art' and y'all sing?"

Not exactly majestic, but still exciting. Mr. Taylor pressed a button and began whistling. Sister and I felt the Wurlitzer leave the ground.

"Sing," Mr. Taylor commanded.

"Oh, Lord, my God," I began to sing tremulously as we rose past the other instruments, breaking the crime tape.

"Good." Mr. Taylor started whistling again.

I looked over at Sister, which was a mistake. She was twitching.

"What's the matter with you?" I asked.

She burst out laughing. "Oh, Mouse, look at us. This is one of the funniest things that I think has ever happened to us."

"Y'all sing," Mr. Taylor called and resumed his whistling.

But we were holding on to each other, laughing so hard by this time that we were crying. Two old ladies rising up to heaven on a Wurlitzer that reeked of wet paint while an old man whistled a hymn.

We were laughing so hard that for a moment the screams seemed simply white noise, a creak in the lifting mechanism of the organ.

The organ stopped its rise with a slight bump. For a second there was silence, and then we heard what we knew were screams. Sister and I both looked over the side of the bench.

Dusk was clutching Mr. Taylor's arm and pointing toward the dressing rooms. "Call nine-one-one. He's dead."

"Who's dead?"

They rushed off leaving us in the air.

"Larry? You reckon it's Larry?" In panic, Sister started punching every button on the console. "Damn."

Every button that she wasn't hitting, I was. One of us finally connected with the magic one and the organ began to descend. We were off and running before it even touched the floor.

"Oh, Lord, I know it's Larry," Sister said.

We ran down the hall in the direction that Dusk and Mr. Taylor had gone. An open door and a light told us where they were. They were kneeling on either side of Larry Ludmiller, who lay crumpled and bloody on the floor. Dusk was wringing her hands and sobbing, and Mr. Taylor was holding up a baseball bat.

"I think he's dead," he said.

Chapter Fourteen

"Oh, Lord." Dusk moaned, leaning over Larry. "Somebody call nine-one-one."

Mary Alice reached into her purse, pulled out her cell phone, and hit the 911 button. Then she handed the phone to me and rushed out of the room. I understood this. Sister's stomach and the sight of blood have never been compatible.

Unfortunately we have had so many emergencies since I retired from teaching that, I swear, I'm on a first-name basis with most of the 911 operators. They even recognize my voice, which is embarrassing. Today a new person answered though, for which I was grateful. I explained that there was a badly injured man at the Alabama Theater and that we needed help immediately. No use telling them that he was dead as a doornail.

I closed the phone, stepped out into the hall, and sat down on the floor. I could hear Dusk and Mr. Taylor talking excitedly.

Down the hall I heard a toilet flush. Hopefully Sister was feeling better; I wasn't.

I shut my eyes and tried to concentrate on my mantra. Omm. The cute white wicker wastebaskets with pink shells on them at Bed Bath & Beyond. Omm. New shower curtains for the guest bathroom. Omm. White battenburg. Omm. Would probably just wilt in the humidity of a bathroom. Omm. Didn't want to have to spend time starching and ironing shower curtains. Omm. Omm. Some new towels would be nice. And some of those thin washrags that Fred favored. Felt like almost nothing in your hand. Cheap. Omm.

"Where are you?" Sister asked. "Bed Bath & Beyond? Rich's?" I had made the mistake once of telling her about my white-sale fugues.

"Bed Bath & Beyond," I answered truthfully. "I got a five dollar coupon yesterday in the mail. They're having a sale this weekend."

She sat down beside me on the floor. No easy feat for a two-hundred-fifty-pound sixty-six-year-old woman. What she did was lean against the wall and just sort of slide down. She was sucking on an Altoid; I could smell peppermint.

"Lord," she said. "I just can't believe this. Hand me the phone. I guess I'd better call Virgil. Poor Tammy Sue. I can't imagine how she's going to take this."

I really needed some new hot pads, too. I had seen some cute ones, a little muffin man wearing a chef's hat and holding up a plate. They had some with cows on them, too, sort of like the Gateway cow.

"The phone?"

I handed it to Sister. I had never quite understood that Gateway cow.

There was a shriek from inside the dressing room. "He moved. He moved his hand!"

Sister dropped the phone. I looked around the door. Dusk

had her fingers against the side of Larry's throat. Mr. Taylor was kneeling, wringing his hands.

"I feel a pulse," Dusk exclaimed. "He's alive. Call nine-one-one!"

"I just did." I got up and walked slowly toward the prone figure. "You're sure he's alive?"

"Feel." I leaned down and Dusk placed my fingertips against Larry's throat. A slight, thready pulsing. Oh, God.

"I'll go meet them at the side door," Mr. Taylor said. "Lord, I thought he was done for for sure." He dashed out, nearly crashing into Sister, who had just appeared in the doorway.

"He's really alive?" she asked. "Not just some dead muscles jumping like frog's legs or a chicken with its head chopped off?"

I said, "Not very alive, I don't think. But he's got a pulse."

Sister stepped into the room. "Maybe we should give him CPR or something."

Dusk looked up at her and scowled. "We're leaving him alone until the paramedics get here."

"Good idea," Sister agreed.

It was only a few minutes before the paramedics arrived, but it seemed forever. The three of us watched Larry, who never moved again. Occasionally Dusk or I would reach over to feel the pulse that was still there but faint. If he was breathing, and he had to be, surely, his breath was so light that there was no discernible movement of his chest.

"Somebody hit him right above the ear. See?" Dusk said. "Probably with that baseball bat."

Sister disappeared down the hall again.

I took Dusk's word for it. I picked up Larry's hand and rubbed it. Surely that wouldn't hurt anything. The hand was cold. But the pulse beat in his throat.

And then the room was full of paramedics, of equipment, of commands. We were told to wait in the hall. Mr. Taylor and Sister joined us there.

"Damn," he said. "Damn. He was lying back here the whole time I was working on the organ."

"He might have been here since last night," Sister said.

I noticed her phone lying on the floor and picked it up. "You going to call Virgil?"

She reached for it hesitantly. "I guess I'd better. Reckon where they'll take Larry?"

"University Hospital," Mr. Taylor said. "It's the closest trauma center."

Dusk suddenly began to cry deep sobs that shook her tiny body. She put her hands to her face, and I saw that they were blood spattered. I looked down. Mine were, too.

"Come on," I said, putting my arm around her. "Let's go get cleaned up."

Sister volunteered the information that the restroom was right down the hall on the left.

Dusk and I washed our hands and arms, and I wet a paper towel and wiped her face, which was as flushed and hot as if she had a fever.

"You were very brave back there," I said. Tears ran down her cheeks. I wiped them away.

"It's all my fault," she whispered.

"No, it's not. It's not your fault at all."

"But Griffin wouldn't have been here if it weren't for me." She sobbed into the wet paper towel.

"That doesn't make what happened your fault."

She sighed and wiped her face. "But I feel so guilty."

"The curse of the Southern woman. I feel guilty when it rains on our picnic."

Dusk tried to smile. "No, Mrs. Hollowell. I feel that guilt, too. But Griffin is dead because of me. I was married to him."

"You what?" There was a small bench in the restroom, and I sat down heavily. "What?"

Dusk sat down beside me and held the paper towel to her

eyes again. "It's true. No one knows it but Day and probably the police by now. They're going to think I killed him, I know." She leaned over and placed her head against her knees, sobbing.

I was having trouble absorbing this. The red velvet cushion on the bench was worn, and in several places yellowish-brown foam rubber was visible. Bed Bath & Beyond would have some cushions to fit; they were beckoning. But Dusk's voice brought me back.

"It was so simple," she said, sitting up and wiping her face. "He wanted to become a United States citizen, and I admired him so much." She looked at me. "It's all my fault."

"Your parents don't know about this?"

She shook her head. "Day does, but I didn't think I would ever have to tell Mama and Daddy. As soon as Griffin became a citizen, we were going to get a divorce." She leaned her head back against the wall. "We never even lived together, Mrs. Hollowell."

I was trying to put two and two together here. "Is that what he was doing in Birmingham, then? Seeing about a divorce?"

"Oh, Lord, I wish it had been." Dusk got up, got another paper towel, and wet it. Outside we heard several pairs of footsteps hurrying down the hall. Suddenly I wanted to know if Larry was still alive, what his chances were.

"Wait right here," I said in my best schoolteacher voice, pointing to the bench. "I want to hear the rest of this, but I want to see how Larry's doing."

"Not too good," Mary Alice said when I asked. She was standing at the end of the hall with Mr. Taylor. "They've put his head in one of those foam things, and they're hooking him up to everything on God's earth. I called Virgil. He's going to meet us at UAB with Tammy Sue. They're trying to stabilize him some before they can move him, though."

Mr. Taylor was wringing his hands again. "I just can't believe it. I just can't." He looked around me and down the hall. "Where's Dusk? Is she all right?"

"She's been better. I'm going to stay in the bathroom with her until she calms down some."

"I'm going to call Debbie," Mary Alice said, opening her phone. "Tell her what's happening."

Debbie. Griffin Mooncloth had had an appointment with Debbie. I hurried back to the restroom where Dusk was sitting on the bench just as I had ordered. She looked up, waiting for information.

"They're trying to stabilize him enough to move him," I said. "That's all I know."

She nodded and bit her bottom lip like a child. She looked about ten years old, I realized, tiny and with a tear-stained face.

"Griffin Mooncloth had an appointment with my niece Debbie," I said. "And it wasn't about a divorce?"

"Day recommended her. She and Debbie were in school together."

I nodded that I had known that.

"Anyway, what he wanted was to find out if he could keep me from divorcing him. He said he loved me and wanted us to be married, really married."

"And what about you?"

"I was fond of him, Mrs. Hollowell. I really was. But I went through the ceremony as a favor to him, not because I wanted to be his wife." More tears and the wet paper towel. "And when I said I was getting a divorce, he started threatening me, saying that I had broken a federal law by marrying him so he could become a citizen. And I had. Day and I looked it up." Dusk looked up. "I could have been put in prison, Mrs. Hollowell."

"But he was still seeing Debbie? He still thought you might divorce him?"

She sighed. "I think he was trying to find out if there was some simple, legal way that he could prevent the divorce. I honestly don't think he wanted to have me arrested. He wasn't a vicious man, Mrs. Hollowell."

"But he wasn't above threatening you."

"True."

We were quiet for a few minutes, each of us lost in our thoughts. Outside there were calls down the hall, and the sounds of people scurrying by, even some equipment being rolled past.

"They're going to think I killed him, aren't they? But I didn't, Mrs. Hollowell," Dusk finally said. "I don't know why I didn't just admit to this to start with."

"The switchblade knife wasn't yours, was it?"

"Good heavens, no." Dusk looked astonished that I had even asked her this. "I didn't know a thing about it. I didn't even know Griffin was going to be in the Elvis line. It sounds like something he'd do, though. He'd think it was fun to come out on the stage and improvise." Dusk began to cry again. "He could be a lot of fun, Mrs. Hollowell. I just wasn't in love with him. Not like Day was."

"Day was in love with Griffin Mooncloth?"

The sobs stopped. Dusk realized that she had revealed more than she had meant to.

"She was fond of him," she said carefully, trying to cover her mistake. "She met him when she came to New York to visit me. That's what I meant. She admired his dancing."

The door opened and Sister stuck her head in. "They've done all they can. They've got him loaded up and are fixing to take him to the ambulance. I'm going to follow them to UAB. Do you want to go, Mouse? Mr. Taylor said he would take you and Dusk home if you don't."

"I'll go with Mr. Taylor unless you want me to go with you."

"What I want is a Valium and some Maalox, and I know you don't have any." The door closed and then reopened immediately. "Oh, I forgot. The police are here. A man named Tim Hawkins said he wanted to talk to you."

Oh, Lord. We'd be here forever.

But we weren't. We waited until we heard the gurney being

rolled down the hall before we came out of the restroom. Tim Hawkins and Mr. Taylor were standing in the hall talking. Behind them, in the dressing room, several policemen were busy working, measuring, dusting for fingerprints. A lot of good that was going to do them. Sister, Dusk, Mr. Taylor, and I had done a pretty thorough job of trashing the crime scene, including examining the bat and kneeling beside Larry.

"Hello, Mrs. Hollowell. We meet again." Tim grinned.

I gave him my schoolteacher look. "Hello, Timmy."

He turned to Dusk. "And you're Dusk Armstrong. You found Larry Ludmiller."

"I came to get my makeup bag." Dusk's voice was shaking. "When I went in the dressing room, I fell over him." She pointed to her knees. "Really fell over him. I flipped the light switch and turned around and there he was. I thought he was dead."

"We all did," Mr. Taylor said.

"Yes, we did," I agreed. "And then Dusk saw him move his hand."

"His finger." Dusk held her hand up. "He moved his finger like this."

Tim Hawkins nodded. "Tell you what, Miss Armstrong. I'm going to need to talk to you, but we've sort of got our hands full here. Mr. Taylor's said he'll take you home." He turned to me. "You too, Mrs. Hollowell. Then he's going to come back and help us out some. Show us around. Okay?"

"You don't want to talk to me again, do you?" I asked.

Tim shrugged. "Maybe."

"Can I get my makeup bag?" Dusk asked.

"Sorry. Later. We've got the room blocked off."

"Well, y'all don't get near the Wurlitzer, you hear? I just touched it up where that guy fell on it the other night, and the paint's not dry." Mr. Taylor looked at the busy policemen. "I swear, eighty years and the most we've ever had happen here at the Alabama is an occasional heart attack. And they say that during the opening of *Gone With the Wind,* somebody threw a stink bomb. Can you believe that? Just goes to show."

What it went to show wasn't clear, but none of us questioned him. He told Tim Hawkins that he would be back as soon as he delivered the ladies to their homes. We followed him out to his once-black Chevrolet, which was older than mine, and had been, as Fred would say, rode hard.

"Don't look down at the floor if you tend to get carsick," he said, opening the back door for me. "I ran over a concrete block one day and it came right through. I tried to hammer it down, but it's too rusty. I've been meaning to get a carpet piece, but you might want to put your feet over the hole, so rocks won't come up and hit you.

"The front's okay," he assured Dusk.

So much for age over beauty.

I moved over to the far side of the backseat away from the hole in the floorboard, but a spring that had worked its way through the upholstery looked too threatening for my good gray pants. I moved back to the other side and placed my feet over the hole, which reared up like a tumor.

In the meantime, Mr. Taylor had settled Dusk on the front seat. "Comfortable?" he asked her. If I had been a mean person, I would have reached over and snatched him bald headed, which would have been easy to do. Instead, I sank back among candy bar wrappers and potato chip bags (Mr. Taylor favored sour cream and chives) and forced myself to relax.

As we pulled out of the parking lot, Dusk reached in her purse for a Kleenex.

"Mrs. Hollowell," Mr. Taylor said, "look on the floor on the other side and hand Dusk her makeup bag."

Sure enough, there was a black bag that looked like a Norman Rockwell doctor's bag on the floor. I hadn't even noticed it. I picked it up and handed it over the seat to Dusk. It was so heavy, Estée Lauder herself could be hiding in there.

"Oh, Mr. Taylor," Dusk said. "How did you get this out?"

"Just walked out with it before the police came. I figured they'd close everything down."

"How did you know it was mine?"

"Recognized it from those summers when you did the Summerfest plays. You were so little, that bag was bigger than you were."

Dusk opened the bag and looked inside. "Everything's here," she said. "Thank you, Mr. Taylor."

"You're welcome, Dusk." Mr. Taylor cleared his throat. "Where do you live, Mrs. Hollowell?"

I told him, and he turned right onto Twentieth Street. We passed University Hospital. An ambulance was parked at the emergency room and a patient was being unloaded. Larry? I thought of Tammy Sue and felt my chest tighten. The day that Haley had been called to University Hospital when her husband, Tom, had been hit by a drunk driver was still a raw wound. Please, God, let Tammy Sue be luckier.

"Say you're a retired schoolteacher, Mrs. Hollowell?" Mr. Taylor's voice startled me.

"Last year," I said. "I taught English at Robert Alexander."

"Me, too. I taught music at North Jefferson County. I've been filling in down at the Alabama for years, though. They call me the Wurlitzer substitute." He laughed slightly. "You know, like a teacher substitute."

"I'd rather substitute at the organ than in a classroom."

"God's truth. I love that old organ."

"You're good at it, Mr. Taylor."

Mr. Taylor beamed at Dusk's compliment.

We went over the mountain, past Vulcan's empty pedestal, past the entrance to the Club where Mitzi and I had had lunch a few days before, where we had run into Bernice and Day Armstrong.

"Oh, my God!" I exclaimed.

Mr. Taylor and Dusk both jumped.

"What?" Dusk asked, twisting around. "What's the matter?"

"You gonna throw up?" Mr. Taylor eased the car over to the curb. "I told you not to look at the floorboard."

"No. I'm not sick. I'm all right." I had just suddenly remembered my purse hanging on the chair while Mitzi and I had lunch, how Bernice had sat down with us and Day had come to tell her that Dusk was sick. How Day had stood by my chair, by my open purse, leaned over to pat Mitzi's arm. That's where the switchblade had come from. I knew it in my bones.

"I'm all right," I said again. I wasn't. Pieces of the puzzle were coming together. Terrible pieces. Day in love with Griffin Mooncloth, who was married to Dusk and wanted to stay married to her, who wanted to stay married to her so badly that he was threatening to turn her over to the federal authorities rather than lose her. Day coming up behind the line of dancing Elvises, plunging the switchblade knife into Griffin's back and turning it, twisting it.

And there was more. Larry Ludmiller had said he had seen someone behind the line. He couldn't identify her, but how could Day be sure if she saw him glance around. She couldn't take any chances.

I began to shake. "I need to get home," I said.

Fortunately it wasn't far and Mr. Taylor didn't waste time.

Chapter Fifteen

When I got in my kitchen, I sat down at the table without even pulling off my jacket. I was shaking, but I couldn't tell if I was really chilled or if it was nerves. Or maybe my fever was coming back. God forbid.

I got up, gulped down an antibiotic and an aspirin with a whole glass of water, and sat back down. Muffin jumped up on the table and rubbed against my propped arms.

"A cat on a table is totally unsanitary," I told her, scratching behind her ears, listening to her purr. "You remember the switchblade knife that I thought one of Virgil's family had put in my purse at Sister's dinner party?" Muffin nodded. "Well, I was totally wrong. I know exactly when it was put in there and who did it. She had killed a man with it, and there was my open purse, just a perfect place to dump it." I looked at Muffin. "Do you understand why women's purses are such good places to hide things? Stuff gets lost in there with all the lipsticks and loose change and receipts. At the grocery store they hand you your receipt with the change on top of it, and you dump it all in your purse, and you tell yourself that someday you'll clean it all out, but you never do, and the shelves in your closet get heavier and heavier with different-colored purses."

Muffin lay down and closed her eyes. If she had been Mary Alice, she would have said, "What the hell are you babbling about?"

What the hell *was* I babbling about? What proof did I have that Day Armstrong was involved in Griffin Mooncloth's murder? I could imagine Timmy Hawkins's reaction if I called him and told him that my purse was open when Day just happened to be standing by the table for a second. And that I knew she had dropped the switchblade in it.

"What makes you think so?" he'd ask.

And I'd have to answer, "I just know." At least I'd know better than to claim women's intuition. Men have been known to die laughing over women's intuition. I mean, really die. My great-aunt Sophie had a feeling one day that the hundred-year-old oak tree in their front yard was going to fall. Uncle Joe and his neighbor were standing in the yard laughing about women's crazy intuition when the tree smashed them. Aunt Sophie had "Never Underestimate the Power of a Woman" inscribed on his tombstone and moved to the beach where she could fish every day and didn't have to cut the grass.

Timmy Hawkins wouldn't believe a word of that.

I put my head on the table, cradling it in my arms. Even with my ears covered, I could still hear Muffin purring. Ice tumbled down in the ice maker in the refrigerator. Outside, Woofer decided to come out and bark at something. Afternoon sun sliced across the white kitchen floor. This was my world, safe, comfortable. In this world, vice presidents of banks didn't cut out people's gizzards with switchblades or hit people over the head with baseball bats. Especially if their mothers were friends of mine who gave me chairs to rock my granddaughter.

The ringing of the phone brought me straight up. If it was Mary Alice calling this soon, it meant that Larry was dead when they got him to the hospital. I reached for the phone on the counter. My hello came out not much louder than a whisper.

"Aunt Pat? Is that you?"

I was so relieved that for a moment I couldn't answer Marilyn.

"Aunt Pat?"

I took a couple of deep breaths. "It's me, honey."

"Are you all right?"

No way I could go into everything that had happened. "Sinus," I said.

"Bad?"

"I've been to the doctor. I've got some antibiotics."

"Well, my news is going to cheer you up. Charles and I got married this morning. We just went down to the courthouse and did it."

There was such a long pause here that Marilyn said, "Aunt Pat?" again.

"You and Charles Boudreau got married this morning?"

"We did. At the courthouse."

"Well, congratulations, honey." I hoped Marilyn would think my lack of enthusiasm was due to clogged sinuses.

"Thanks, Aunt Pat. I know you're surprised because I said I couldn't live with him, but we've worked that out. And he does have excellent genes."

"That's nice. Excellent genes are important." If damp dishrags could talk, they would sound like I did. But Marilyn didn't seem to notice.

"I'm not changing my name, and the children will have hyphenated names. Sullivan-Boudreau or Boudreau-Sullivan. We've got a few more details to work out. But the most important thing is that Charlie has bought the condo right next to mine. That way we can live together when we want to and then go home when we want to."

I wanted to ask, "What about love?" Instead, I said that it sounded practical and asked if she had told her mother yet.

"Left word on her machine." Marilyn giggled. "Charlie and I have business to attend to, Aunt Pat. He hasn't signed the papers on his apartment yet. We'll see you soon."

"Okay, sweetheart. Tell Charles I'm happy for you both."

Astonished for them both was more like it. And to leave word on your mother's answering machine that you were married? That was downright tacky.

At least I had something to think about other than Day Armstrong as a murderer and Larry Ludmiller on the verge of death. Marilyn had sounded happy. I got up and stuck a cup of water in the microwave. Some spiced tea would be good. I was warm enough to pull off my jacket, too. The shivering had stopped.

Maybe Marilyn would be happy. In cultures all over the world there were arranged, loveless marriages that turned out very well. And Marilyn was no spring chicken like I had been when Fred and I got married. I'd been so much in love that the first time I washed a tub of our clothes together at the Laundromat, I thought I would die of happiness. I've never told anyone that, not even Sister. Especially not Sister.

I was taking the water out of the microwave when there was a tap on the kitchen door. I looked up and saw Bonnie Blue Butler standing there, a couple of large books propped on her hip.

"Hey," I said, opening the door, grateful to see one of my favorite people in the world. "What are you doing off from work?"

Bonnie Blue nodded toward the books. "I'm working. These designs just came in, and I wanted Mary Alice to see them. She was supposed to meet me at her house, but she's not there."

"Come in." One of the books was sliding sideways. I caught it just in time. "She's at University Hospital. Larry Ludmiller, Virgil's son-in-law, was hurt at the Alabama Theater. Hurt real bad."

"What happened?" Bonnie Blue came in, and we put the books on the table.

"Somebody tried to kill him, Bonnie Blue. Hit him on the head with a baseball bat."

"Well, do, Jesus. What would they go and do that for?"

I wanted to say, "Because he saw her kill Griffin Mooncloth." Instead, I shrugged. "Sit down, and I'll fix you some spiced tea."

"Is he going to make it? That's the husband of the cute little girl who was in the shop with you. Right?"

I nodded. "It's her husband. And I don't know if he's going to make it or not. He looked pretty awful." I felt the shivering beginning again.

Bonnie Blue didn't pick up on the fact that I had seen Larry Ludmiller, which suited me. I didn't want to have to go through the events at the Alabama again.

"Marilyn just called," I said, putting another cup in the microwave. "She and Charles Boudreau got married this morning."

Bonnie Blue was the person Marilyn should have talked to instead of me. She clapped her hands and said, "Well, do, Jesus" again. And then, "Now isn't that wonderful?" And I began to think that, yes, maybe it was.

"Mary Alice is going to be pleased." I turned on the microwave and got out another envelope of tea. "Marilyn was considering the UAB fertility clinic. She really wants a baby."

"Well, a turkey baster can do the job, but the old-fashioned way has got to be more fun."

I couldn't argue with that. I fixed the tea and took it to the table. "They're going to live in condos right next to each other. Marilyn says she doesn't think they could live together."

"Sounds like a perfect arrangement. You have a fuss, you send him next door. Invite him to dinner when you want to. Send the kids over next door to play at Daddy's apartment."

"Oh, Bonnie Blue. You don't believe that."

"I know it." She stirred her tea. "What do you want to bet that a wall gets knocked out in two months' time?"

"We'll see."

Bonnie Blue was looking out at the yard. "Woofer okay?"

"He's fine. That arthritis medicine has made him a happy dog. He even digs holes in the yard again. Chases chipmunks."

"That's great. I need to get some for Daddy."

"Don't tell me he's quit chasing chipmunks."

She and I smiled at each other. Her father, now in his eighties, is a renowned Alabama folk artist. He's also a renowned ladies' man.

"Not hardly. Just slowed down his catting a little." She moved her tea to the side. "Let's let that cool a minute. I want to show you what I've got picked out in these books. See what you think."

I pulled my chair around. "What kind of books are they?"

"There's a lady in Atlanta who designs wedding dresses for big, bold, and beautiful ladies like Mary Alice. These are some of her designs. She'll also do the whole wedding party, but she specializes in larger sizes."

Bonnie Blue had several pages marked. She opened one to a picture of a girl in her early twenties dressed in a white, strapless bridal gown that was probably a size four. "You have to use your imagination a little."

I tried to imagine Sister in this dress and failed miserably.

"And then there's this one." Bonnie Blue turned to another page where the model was dressed in a clingy jersey number. Flat stomach. Perky breasts that would pass the pencil test.

"What do you do about underwear in this dress?" I asked.

"Don't wear any. Get waxed."

I cringed at the thought. I had an idea that Sister would, too.

We looked at several more pictures. Some of them actually had possibilities.

"We'll need to get right on it," Bonnie Blue said. "A couple of months is pushing it." She pulled the other book over. "This is bridesmaids and mothers of the brides." She looked at me and frowned. "I guess they could make one to fit you."

Damned if I was going to feel guilty for being small.

Bonnie Blue glanced up at the clock. "I really need to get back to the store. Tell you what. How about I leave these books with you? You can look through them, and you'll see Mary Alice before I will." She drank her tea in one long gulp. "Be sure and point the jersey one out to her."

"I will," I said truthfully.

On the way out of the door, she stopped and turned. "If Larry Ludmiller dies, it won't have any effect on the wedding, will it?"

"I guess everybody would still be sad."

"But they'd still have it?"

"I'm sure they would."

"Good." She waved and went down the steps. I swear she and Sister were cut from the same pattern.

I put on some jeans and a sweatshirt to take Woofer for a walk and then decided that I'd better wait as long as I could in case Sister called. I made a salmon loaf, stuck it in the oven, and cut up some squash to boil. There was a package of angel-hair slaw in the refrigerator. I dumped it in a bowl, drizzled John's slaw dressing on it, and put it back in the refrigerator.

For a little while, between Marilyn's news, the bridal gowns, and fixing supper, I had managed to keep Day Armstrong at the back of my thoughts. But as soon as I sat down in the den, she came whirling back. I couldn't even concentrate on the new Oprah Book Club selection. When the phone rang, I grabbed for it. Her second victim was dead, I knew it.

But it was Debbie. Had Marilyn called me? What did I think about it? Was I as shocked as she was? Marilyn had said that the last thing she would ever do was marry Charles Boudreau, and what on God's earth were they thinking about living next door to each other? Had I ever heard of such a thing? Did I think it would work out? Did I think Marilyn had lost her mind?

I admitted that I was surprised. And then I told her what Bonnie Blue had said about the wall coming down.

"I hope so. I know I wouldn't want Henry living next door."

We were both quiet for a moment, thinking. Then we burst out laughing. There's not a woman alive who wouldn't move her husband out sometimes. Just next door.

Then I asked her if she had heard about Larry Ludmiller.

"That he didn't come home last night? Yes. Mama told me Tammy Sue was beside herself with worry."

"No. That we found him at the Alabama Theater almost dead. Your mama didn't call you? Somebody had hit him on the head with a baseball bat."

"Oh, my God, Aunt Pat. Where is he? Is he going to be all right?"

"I don't know, Debbie. He's at University Hospital. I'm waiting for your mama to call."

"Oh, that's awful. And poor Tammy Sue."

There was a moment's silence. Then I said, "Debbie, I think I know who did it. Who hit him. Who killed Griffin Mooncloth, too."

"Who?"

"Day Armstrong."

"Day?"

"I know it sounds crazy, but I'm sure." The shakes were back. "I just don't know what to do about it. Nobody's going to believe me."

There was a mumbled conversation at the other end of the phone. Then Debbie said, "Aunt Pat? Richardena's here with the children. I'm coming over there."

Ordinarily I would have insisted that I was okay and that she needn't bother. Today I said, "Hurry."

"You could be right." Debbie was curled up in the corner of my sofa. "I'd hate to think it, though."

"And it is illegal to marry someone so they can become a citizen?"

Debbie nodded. "I'll have to look it up to see what the law is exactly, but it's illegal. Dusk would have been in trouble if Griffin Mooncloth had decided to report her." She paused. "Of course, he'd have been cutting off his nose to spite his face because he never would have gotten back in the country again. But, you know, I can't imagine what he thought I could do for him."

"Dusk said he didn't want a divorce. Maybe it was about some kind of legal separation hoping Dusk would change her mind, or maybe he thought you might know some kind of loophole that he could use to stay here."

Debbie frowned and rubbed a spot on her sweater that looked suspiciously like dried milk. "But if Day recommended that he come to see me and thought he could work something out legally, why would she kill him? There's something missing there, Aunt Pat."

"I know. But I'm still sure as anything that she put the knife in my purse."

Debbie gave up on the spot, which was going to take more than rubbing, and frowned. "You know, maybe she was protecting somebody else. Maybe she saw Dusk with the knife, and got rid of it for her. That would makes sense."

"I guess so."

"Or she could have seen it on the floor at the theater and assumed Dusk was responsible and picked it up."

"That's a possibility, too."

The phone on the table beside Debbie rang. She picked it up and said hello.

Mama, she mouthed to me. Then, "Just visiting. Yes, ma'am. She told me about it. How is he?" A pause. "What do they say?"

So Larry was still alive. I went in the kitchen, took the salmon loaf from the oven, and glanced at the clock. I opened the door and called Woofer. If I couldn't take him for a walk, he could at least come in for a visit. But he was sitting by the fence eyeing a little white poodle who had wandered into Mitzi's yard. No way he wanted to come in.

"Mama wants to talk to you, Aunt Pat," Debbie called.

I picked up the phone. "What do the doctors say?"

"They're still running tests. They're going to have to do surgery."

"What are his chances?"

"Not good, I don't think."

"Are you going to stay there?"

"No. His whole family is here. And Tammy Sue needs Virgil to herself. I'm going to leave in a few minutes."

"Well, come have supper with us."

"What are you having?"

"Salmon loaf."

"Dill sauce?"

"I can make some."

"Then I'll be there in a little while. I need to bring your chair anyway."

I hung up and went back into the den.

"Did she say anything about Marilyn?" Debbie asked.

I shook my head.

"I guess she hasn't checked her messages yet. I can't believe Marilyn did that, can you?"

I shrugged. Worrying about Marilyn could wait. "Your mama's bringing the chair Bernice Armstrong gave me for Haley. The rocker." I sat down and looked at Debbie. "How can

I tell the police that Bernice's daughter probably dumped a murder weapon in my purse and chances are that she's the murderer? I wonder what Miss Manners's advice would be on that?"

"Does Mrs. Armstrong know anything about Dusk and Griffin Mooncloth?"

"No. She doesn't even know that they were married. She thinks Dusk knew him in dance class." The mention of Bernice and the chair had reminded me, though. "They have a grizzly bear in their house named Maurice."

"What?"

"The Armstrongs. A real grizzly bear in their foyer. Stuffed. Got his arms up like this." I held my arms up Maurice style. "Scared the hell out of your mother and me."

"What?"

"Mr. Armstrong's uncle shot him years ago. He's molting, and it's really sort of pitiful because Bernice is embarrassed by him, you can tell. I mean he's standing right there in their foyer. But she says her husband treasures him. And he's already had open heart surgery, the husband has, and damn it, I know it was Day who put that switchblade in my purse, and I don't know what to do."

Debbie handed me the phone. "Call Detective Hawkins, Aunt Pat."

"But what if I'm wrong?"

"What if you're right?"

"Hand me the phone book." I dialed and left word for Tim Hawkins to return my call. No, it was not an emergency.

I gave the phone back to Debbie to put on the table. "Now," I said, "let's talk about something else. How about I show you the books of wedding designs that Bonnie Blue brought over."

"I'm not wearing yellow."

I got the books and sat down by Debbie on the sofa. I turned to the first one that Bonnie Blue had marked, the strapless one. Debbie sighed.

"And Bonnie Blue liked this one, too." I turned to the jersey, the one that you couldn't wear anything underneath. Debbie sighed again.

I glanced up. Her chin was on her chest, and her eyes were closed. Bless her heart. I'd forgotten what it was like to have a two-month-old baby.

I straightened her, put a pillow under her head, and covered her with the afghan. She woke up enough to smile slightly.

When Fred came in, she was still sleeping, and Tim Hawkins hadn't returned my call. When Mary Alice came in, Debbie was still sleeping, Fred was taking a shower, and Tim Hawkins still hadn't returned my call.

"Well?" I asked as Mary Alice came through the kitchen door.

"He's still alive. That's about all they know."

I nodded toward the den. "Debbie's in there asleep."

She looked around the door. "Worn out, bless her heart."

"You want something to drink?"

"I'll get me a beer after I check my messages."

I stirred the dill sauce and waited for her reaction to Marilyn's message.

"How about that," she exclaimed happily as she hung up the phone. "Marilyn's finally married Charlie Boudreau, Mouse. I knew she had good sense."

Chapter Sixteen

Supper was a quiet affair. Before Fred came in, I had told Sister I knew that it was Day Armstrong who had put the knife in my purse. I also told her that Tim Hawkins was going to call, but if the call came while we were eating, she was to take it on the bedroom phone and tell him what had happened, that Fred was going to have a nice quiet meal. "He's still upset about my being arrested, and I don't want to worry him anymore," I added.

Sister rolled her eyes. "God forbid that Fred should be worried."

"And don't mention Larry Ludmiller, how bad he's hurt, or that we found him. I'll tell him later on."

"Hey, the world's going around, Mouse. Don't you think he's going to find out?"

I gave the dill sauce one last stir, put it on the back burner, and turned off the front. "I told you I was going to tell him. It's just that he worries about how we keep finding bodies. He says it's not normal."

"Well, it's not my fault that people keep getting killed around here. It never happened before you retired." Sister opened the refrigerator and got out a beer. I offered her a glass, but she shook her head. "The other day at the Angel-sighting Society meeting a tacky woman said, 'Oh, you're the one who keeps finding bodies.' I think I'd have slapped her, if I hadn't been a lady." She held the top of the beer bottle by the knuckles of two fingers, tipped it up, and drank half of it in one gulp. "Besides"—she burped lightly—"Mama would have turned over in her grave."

I was too tired to fuss with her or point out the obvious, the fact that she was the one who had gotten us involved in most of the murders with her harebrained schemes like the country-western bar and the investment club.

"Anyway," I said, "just don't mention Larry."

"Okay. I guess we can talk about Marilyn and Charlie. I wonder what she wore. I'll bet they just went down to City Hall like Philip and I did."

"That was Roger. You and Philip were married by a rabbi and you wore an off-white chiffon dress."

"Did I say Philip? I meant Roger, my old teddy bear." Sister, I swear, has her husbands categorized as the lantern-jawed but sweet (Will Alec), the intellectual (Philip, because he read books), and Roger the teddy bear (I'm not sure why; maybe he was hairy).

Which reminded me. "Bonnie Blue left you some wedding dress books. They're on the coffee table."

"Great. Have you looked at them?"

"Some."

"What do you think?"

"Some of them are beautiful."

Debbie woke up when her mother sat down on the sofa. "I'm not wearing yellow, Mama," she mumbled when she saw her mother pick up one of the books.

"Of course you are. It's your color."

Debbie groaned and sat up. "I've got to go feed Brother."

"You want to stay for supper?" I asked.

"I can't, Aunt Pat. I'm hurting."

That was another thing I had forgotten about having a two-month-old baby. Some things just can't wait.

"Tell the twins that Teeny sends kisses." Mary Alice had already opened the first book and now she said, "Wow."

"How's Larry Ludmiller, Mama?" Debbie was putting on her coat.

"Not good. But isn't it great about your sister getting married?" She turned the page. "Look at this strapless one. Do you think I could get away with that?"

Fred came into the room just then. Mary Alice held the book up for him to see. "Do you think I could get away with that, Fred?"

"Well, it sure wouldn't fall off you like it's about to do that girl."

"True."

I walked Debbie to the back door and promised to call her if I heard anything about Larry. "Or anything else for that matter," I added. I also added my kisses for the children to those that "Teeny" had sent. One of the joys of Sister's life is being called "Teeny" by Fay and May, something that we've never figured out. Richardena, the nanny, is "Deeny" so maybe there's some connection there. Who knows. For a second I wondered what Joanna would call me and felt a little flutter in my belly.

When I looked back into the den, I saw something that I never thought I would see. Fred and Sister were sitting on the sofa looking at the bridal gowns, discussing the pros and cons of each one.

"Look at this one," Fred was saying. "That woman's skinny, and she looks like a lard-ass with all that material in the back."

"But if she really had a lard-ass, nobody would know. They'd think it was the material."

"True."

I left the amazingly congenial duo to their fashion perusal and set the table and put supper out.

"This one is amazing," Fred was saying when I called them to supper. "Look, honey." He showed me the book. "Isn't that amazing?"

The dress consisted of about a hundred yards of material covered with net that was caught up in places by bouquets of white roses and lace. Ribbons fluttered from the bouquets. I checked to see if Fred was serious. He was.

"Amazing," I said. I went into the kitchen thinking that no matter how long you're married to a man, he can still surprise you. And that's not bad.

Like I said, supper was quiet. We talked about Marilyn and Charlie Boudreau and how we hoped they would be happy. "A proper conduit, anyway," Fred said, grinning. Then he asked what we had been doing today. I explained about the rocking chair, told him it was outside in Sister's car. Sister described Maurice, the grizzly bear, which got a chuckle out of Fred. While we were eating chocolate Popsicles, the only dessert I could find, the phone rang. Sister jumped up, claimed it was for her, and disappeared down the hall. Fred didn't think this was at all unusual. I had trouble swallowing my Popsicle, though, until she came back and said that it was the Hannah Home and their truck would be on our street picking up discards on Wednesday. She had told them we didn't have anything to discard.

I thought she was telling the truth until Fred went into the den to watch *Who Wants to Be a Millionaire*. She leaned over and whispered loudly that the caller had been Tim Hawkins and that he would talk to me in the morning. She had told him I suspected Day, though.

Suspected, hell. I *knew* she had done it. And *I* had gotten arrested for it.

"Here's a pretty one, Mary Alice," Fred called from the den. I glanced around the door and saw that he was looking at the bridal designs again. The man had lost his mind. Sister went galloping in to see what he had found, and they spent another hour engrossed in the dresses. Amazing.

It was drizzling rain when Sister left, a book propped on each hip. She said that she would keep the chair in her car, and we could take it over to Philip's house the next day. "And I'll call you if I hear anything about you know who."

"Who?" Fred asked as the door closed.

There's a big difference in keeping something from your husband and straight out lying to him. "Larry Ludmiller," I confessed. Which meant that I had to tell him the whole story.

"Damn, Patricia Anne," he said. "Damn. Why didn't you tell me?"

"I didn't want to worry you."

He frowned at me.

"Besides, I just did. I told you everything."

He picked up the newspaper. "I'm going to bed."

"You're mad at me, aren't you."

"I'm just put out." He disappeared down the hall.

Fred seldom gets mad at me, so seldom that I fall apart when he does. I finished straightening up the kitchen, watched the ten o'clock news, took another antibiotic and aspirin, and kept hoping that he would come back in and say he was sorry. He didn't. Around eleven I tiptoed into the bathroom, put on my nightgown, and slid into bed beside him. I'm not sure if he was asleep or not, but he didn't turn over or tell me good night.

There was no way I could sleep. I finally went into the den, picked up Carolyn Hart's *Sugarplum Dead*, and tried to lose myself in the Christmas adventures of the Darlings. But not even Max and Annie Darling could keep my mind off the day's events. Larry Ludmiller, crumpled and bloody, kept getting between me and the pages. Surely he would be out of surgery by now, or they would know something. I finally got the phone book, looked up University Hospital, and reached the intensive care waiting room's number from the operator by telling her I had a family member in intensive care. Well, it wasn't much of a lie.

Hoping that I wasn't waking anyone up, I dialed the number. A woman answered, and I asked if Virgil Stuckey was there. When he came to the phone, I apologized for calling in the middle of the night but told him I couldn't sleep because I was worried about Larry.

"He's still in surgery, Patricia Anne," he said. "They just don't know." There was a long pause before he said, "They've given Tammy Sue a sedative. She's dozing a little."

"I hope I didn't wake her up."

"No. It's fine. I appreciate your calling. Mary Alice has already checked in a couple of times."

So Sister was having trouble sleeping, too.

Virgil's voice was shaking when he said, "Keep us in your prayers, Patricia Anne."

I promised that I would, and I meant it. After I hung up, I went back to bed and whispered to Fred's back that I loved him and had just been trying not to worry him. Finally I slept.

Fred was gone when I woke up. In spite of so little sleep, I realized that I felt okay. The antibiotics had kicked in. I opened the blinds and looked out. It was a perfect spring day, sun gleaming on leaves wet from the night's drizzle.

I dialed Sister's number, and she answered on the first ring.

Larry had made it through surgery. Virgil had just come in and was drinking some coffee. Tammy Sue wouldn't leave the hospital.

"The prognosis?" I asked.

"Still questionable. But he at least made it through surgery. Wait a minute." I could hear a man's voice. "Virgil says to thank you for calling last night."

"Tell him he's welcome. Does one of us need to go stay with Tammy Sue?"

"Olivia's there. You know, Larry's sister. And Buddy—Virgil, Jr."

"Okay. Call me if you need me. I guess I'll have to stick around here for Timmy Hawkins."

I got a cup of coffee and checked my e-mail, hoping to hear from Haley. I had three messages. One said SEX SEX SEX, another asked if I was interested in working at home, and the third was from Martha Stewart. *Dear Patricia Anne* wasn't interested in those giant cookie cutters today. Instead, I typed in Haley's e-mail address and told her there was no news and that we were fine. She was in Warsaw and pregnant. What could she do about our latest escapades but worry? I had turned off the computer before I remembered that neither Marilyn nor Debbie might have e-mailed her about Marilyn's marriage. Maybe when Fred got home we'd call her.

I waited for an hour for Timmy's call. Nothing. And it was a beautiful day outside. I finally got Woofer's leash and left for a walk. Sister had told him basically all I could tell him the night before. I certainly had no proof that Day was the culprit. He could leave a message.

It was so good to be feeling better, so good to feel the freshness of a morning after rain. Woofer felt the same way, scampering from tree to tree, barking wildly at a squirrel. We walked all the way to Homewood Park, where I sat on a bench in the sun and Woofer lay on the ground beside me, wagging his tail at the few people who walked by pushing strollers or jogged by, everyone saying, "Good morning."

I closed my eyes. I could sleep here in this peaceful park with its huge old shade trees sprouting new green. For a few moments, Larry Ludmiller wouldn't be fighting for his life, Day Armstrong wouldn't be dropping knives in my purse, Fred wouldn't be angry with me. Sunlight, dappled by new leaves, made shadows across my closed eyes. I sighed and relaxed.

"Good morning, Mrs. Hollowell."

I must have dozed off because I jumped.

"Sorry I scared you." Timmy Hawkins sat down on the bench beside me. "I was driving past the park and saw you."

I rubbed my hand across my mouth, hoping it hadn't been open, and I hadn't been drooling—a bad habit of mine when I doze.

"Morning, Timmy," I said, wondering if he was on duty. He had on jeans and a University of Alabama sweatshirt with a red elephant holding a megaphone and declaring ROLL TIDE on it. On his feet were brown boots that had seen much, much better days.

"I was on my way to your house. Actually I was on my way to the Piggly Wiggly. It's my day off, and I thought I'd stop by if you were home."

"Sister said you were going to call."

"I was." He reached down and patted Woofer, who rolled over in delight. Good thing Timmy wasn't some mugger. "But I was going by anyway."

"Well, she told you about Day Armstrong, that she had the opportunity to drop the knife in my purse."

Timmy nodded. "Tell me about it."

So I did, adding that I didn't want to believe it, but I did.

"How do you suppose she got the knife?" Timmy asked.

I looked into his guileless blue eyes. "Don't hand me that,

Timmy. The same way you think she did. Picked it up off the floor of the stage. Or walked out on the stage with it. God knows. But I'm telling you this. Larry Ludmiller's in the hospital maybe dying because whoever killed the guy at the Alabama thinks Larry saw him. Or her," I added.

The eyes weren't guileless now. "What makes you think that?"

"He told us. Larry did. He said he turned around and got a glimpse of someone behind the line of Elvises just as Griffin Mooncloth began to sag. It was just a glimpse, mainly because Larry's blind as a bat without his glasses, but the person back there couldn't know that. For all she knew, Larry could identify her. Or him."

Timmy nodded. "Makes sense." He reached over and patted Woofer again. "Anything else you can tell me, Mrs. Hollowell?"

"I wish you could question Day about the knife without mentioning me. I don't want her mother to know I'm the one who told you. She's a friend of mine."

Timmy stood up. "Now how am I going to do that, Mrs. Hollowell?"

"You'll figure something out. Just like you figured out how to get someone to write your research paper on Chaucer for you."

I swear Timmy blanched. "You knew about that?"

"Of course. Just do the best you can, Timmy, to keep me out of it."

"Yes, ma'am. I will."

I watched him walk toward his car, his shoulders slumped. "Woofer," I said, "it's incredible how often that works."

Mitzi was spreading bonemeal on her iris bed when we walked past. I opened my gate, gave Woofer a treat, and let him in. Then I walked over to tell Mitzi about Larry Ludmiller.

She was kneeling on a plastic bag and had on gardening gloves. Mitzi is in her early sixties but has had gray hair as long as I can remember. More white now than gray, I realized, looking down at her as she pushed her bangs up with her arm. I would never be that lucky. Strawberry-blond hair, streaked with gray, looks orange.

"Your hair is beautiful," I said.

"Thanks." She smiled and pulled a plastic bag out of a box for me to sit on. "What's going on? You look like you're feeling better this morning."

"I am. But I just squealed on Day Armstrong, somebody nearly killed Virgil Stuckey's son-in-law yesterday, and Fred's mad at me."

"I believe the first two things. Not the third." She stuck her trowel into the sack of bonemeal and worked it lightly into the ground around an iris that I knew would be blooming within a month and that I would enjoy from my kitchen window.

"Believe it."

"Tell me."

Mitzi worked as I talked. Woofer came over and lay down by the chain-link fence, watching us, half-dozing.

"I'm right, aren't I?" I asked. "Day did have the opportunity to put the knife in my purse, didn't she?"

Mitzi nodded. "I guess she did. She wasn't there but a minute, though, Patricia Anne."

"That's all it would take."

Mitzi pushed herself up from her knees, groaned, and moved the plastic bag farther down the flower bed. "Lord, I'm stiff as a board," she said, kneeling again. She stuck her trowel into the dirt and frowned. "Tell me again about the divorce bit, about Dusk being in trouble."

I told her what Debbie had said, that it was illegal to marry someone just so they could become an American citizen.

"But would Day have killed someone to protect her little sister?"

"I don't know. But I think she may know who did."

A car pulled into my driveway. I looked up and saw it was Fred.

"I think that's the end of your third problem," Mitzi said.

Fred got out of the car and came over to where we were sitting. "I just thought I'd come home for lunch today," he said.

Mitzi grinned as I got up. "Bon appétit."

Making up was nice. I explained that I was trying not to worry him, and he explained that it worried him more to know that I was trying not to worry him. I promised not to do it again. At the time I meant it.

Later, we had tuna fish sandwiches for lunch.

Chapter Seventeen

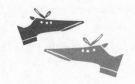

E-mail from: Haley
To: Mama and Papa
Subject: Occupant

Guess what! Joanna's moving. I've been feeling some flutters for a few days that I was suspicious of, but today, there was a definite bump. Philip is sitting right by me waiting for me to say, "Now," so he can feel it. But tonight she's quiet. We're starting to read to her, though, and to play music. Tonight he's going to read *Goodnight Moon*. Isn't it incredible?

Love from the three of us,
Haley

"Mouse?" Sister called from the kitchen.
"At the computer. Come on back."

She walked into the room saying, "I'm scared to come into your house anymore since that husband of yours had such a hissy fit about his privacy."

What she was referring to was a day a couple of months ago. Fred had just gotten out of the shower and, holding a towel around him, walked into the kitchen. Mary Alice and Miss Bessie were sitting at the table eating Keebler chocolate chip cookies and drinking Cokes, very much at home.

Fred, totally startled, dropped the towel and fled. All he remembered, he said later, were the Keebler chocolate chip cookie bag and a pink crocheted hat, and those two images were burned onto his retina. "Take the damn key away from her, Patricia Anne."

I didn't, of course, but I did ask her to be a little more discreet.

"I don't know why," she said. "Wasn't like he had anything to hide."

"Pitiful," Miss Bessie agreed.

Needless to say, I didn't pass their opinions on to Fred. No use pouring salt onto wounds. I did, however, remind them that he had just gotten out of the shower and they had scared him.

Both of them said, "Huh."

"What have you got?" Sister asked now, looking over my shoulder.

I moved so she could sit down. "Look at this. It's wonderful."

She read the e-mail and said, "How about that. Let's see. Haley's four months pregnant now. How big do you suppose Joanna is? Big as a cantaloupe?"

"I doubt it. They do most of their growing in the last two months."

"You always looked like a stick with a knot on it when you were pregnant, and I looked like I'd swallowed a pumpkin."

"Mama said you just carried yours high."

Sister nodded and tapped the screen with her fingernail.

"Pregnant's nice, you know, Mouse? If it hadn't been for my husbands all dying and stretch marks, I might have had some more. I hope Marilyn gets pregnant soon."

"So do I. And I wish Freddie would get married and settle down."

"He's happy. You want to print this?"

"Absolutely. I'm going to make her a scrapbook."

Sister clicked the mouse, and the printer came on. "I'm going to the hospital. I thought you might like to go with me."

"Is there any news?"

"Not really. Virgil's hoping I can talk Tammy Sue into coming to my house for a while and resting some. He's worried about her." She reached over and got the piece of paper that the printer had spit out. "I figured maybe you could help me."

"Larry's the same?"

"Hanging in there. Here." She handed me the letter. "What did your policeman say when you told him about Day Armstrong?"

"My policeman said he would look into it." I folded the letter and put it into a box in the corner that had "Haley" written on it. "I told him to keep me out of it."

"That's going to be hard to do."

"I know." I closed the box. "Give me a few minutes, and I'll go with you."

"Virgil says she hasn't eaten a bite since yesterday."

I took a quick shower and slipped on some light gray wool pants and a sweater.

"You look like you're already in mourning," Sister said when I came into the den. "You should wear bright clothes to a hospital."

"You want me to go with you or not?"

Sister nodded and stood up. She was bright enough for the two of us in a flowered broomstick skirt and her purple boots. "It's just that color cheers people up."

"You're right," I admitted. "And you look very nice."

"Well, you can't help it if you don't have my flair."

She was telling the truth.

"I left Haley's chair at their house on my way over here," she explained as we walked to the car. "Just stuck it in the hall."

"I didn't know you had a key."

Sister patted her purse. "Visa card. It's a wonder somebody hasn't robbed them blind. You'd think Philip would have better sense."

"They have the alarm system."

"With the code numbers punched so much they're worn off. Besides, I saw what you hit the other day to set it."

We climbed up into Sister's Mercedes. "I miss my Jag," she said. "I'm going to get me another one, I swear."

And with that, she backed out of my driveway, and we hauled ass to University Hospital.

"I think I've decided on my dress," she said, nodding toward the books Bonnie Blue had brought, which were bouncing on the backseat as we hit a few potholes.

"Is it one I'd remember? One of the ones you and Fred were looking at?"

"No. It's farther back in the book. It's called the Rubenesque design. No frills or froufrou. Princess style. But it's got a round neckline cut real low." She drew a circle almost to her waist. "I mean real low."

"The bridesmaids' dresses aren't going to match it, are they?" I asked, alarmed.

"Of course not. You don't have anything to hold it up."

I couldn't argue with her there.

"Look. There's a woman coming out of a parking place." Sister crossed two lanes of traffic on Nineteenth Street and grabbed it. A man in a Nissan, who had been slowing down, planning on parking there, shot her a bird.

"Rude," Sister said. "I swear folks get ruder every day. Don't make eye contact with him, Mouse. It's folks like that who cause road rage, and they say not to look them in the eye. You don't want them to think you're challenging them."

There was no way that I was going to look the man in the eye. I was concentrating on catching my breath. I had almost suc- ceeded in breathing normally by the time we got to the hospital elevator.

An attempt had been made to make the intensive care waiting room at University a soothing room. The walls were painted an attractive shade of pink, almost a peach, and a flowered wall- paper border at the top picked up the pink and added several other colors including the dark green of leaves, which a couple of the sofas matched. The other sofa and chairs were an indus- trial gray. On the TV mounted on the wall, Oprah and Deepak Chopra were discussing how important it was for people to renew the power of spirit in their lives. The message seemed to be missing its target here. Only one woman was looking at the TV, and she didn't look too hopeful.

Tammy Sue, Olivia, and an older small woman with gray hair, who was introduced to us as Larry's aunt Maude were sitting on one of the sofas. Aunt Maude sat between the two girls. I liked her immediately.

"I love your boots," she told Mary Alice, "and I hope you've come to get Tammy Sue out of here some. If she doesn't get a decent meal in her body and some sleep, she's going to fall over, and we're going to have two patients on our hands."

"That's what we've come for," Sister said. "Any news?"

Tammy Sue shook her head no. Her eyes were so swollen that I wondered if she were seeing clearly. "They say there's nothing to do but wait. We get to go in to see him five minutes every hour." She caught her breath. "He doesn't even look like himself."

"Well, Aunt Maude's right, Tammy Sue," Olivia said. "You need to get out of here for a while. Larry doesn't know you're here anyway."

Tammy Sue bristled at her sister-in-law. "Yes, he does. He does so know I'm here."

"No, he doesn't. He doesn't know a thing."

"Yes, he does."

The other people in the waiting room looked up with interest. Aunt Maude turned to Olivia and informed her quietly that she was acting like a Simpson. The Simpsons, I assumed, were the common-as-pig-tracks branch of the Ludmiller family. Every Southern family has one. At any rate, Olivia slid back into her corner of the sofa, thoroughly chastised.

"You go, honey," Aunt Maude said to Tammy Sue. "I'll be right here. Get yourself some rest and some food."

Tammy Sue looked at her watch. "We get to see him in ten more minutes. Then I'll go."

So we sat down and waited. And not even the pleasant decor of the room could make it anything but depressing.

"What are we going to feed her?" Sister asked while the three women went in to see Larry.

"She needs comfort food. Some homemade vegetable soup maybe, and some cornbread."

Sister nodded. "That sounds good. Do you have any?"

"In my freezer."

"Then we'll take her by your house to eat." She picked up a *People* magazine and glanced through it. I have no idea what she saw in the magazine that made her inform me and the other people sitting around us that, Lord, she was grateful that she was heterosexual.

An elderly woman got up, poured herself some coffee, and motioned for us to make room for her to sit on the sofa. Sister and I scooted down. The woman looked around the waiting room to make sure everyone had gone back to their sleep or returned to their magazines and then leaned over and whispered, "Elvis was here last night. I know everybody thinks he's dead, but he's not." She paused to see what kind of reaction she was going to get from Sister and me. "He had on his white satin jumpsuit, and he sat right on this couch."

"That was Buddy Stuckey," Sister explained. "He's an Elvis impersonator."

"No, this was Elvis. He looked good, too. Lost a lot of that puffy weight he'd put on. I just thought I'd tell you so you'd know that your loved one's going to be all right."

"Thank you," we both said.

"You're welcome." She glanced at the other occupants of the room again. "There's some here don't believe it."

Sister nodded. "I can understand that."

"Lost a lot of weight, he had. Wasn't good for him anyway. Just asking for diabetes, you ask me. That's what's wrong with my sister in yonder."

"I'm sorry," Sister said.

The woman sipped her coffee. "She's going to be all right."

We agreed that we were sure that she was.

Tammy Sue looked more woebegone when she came out than she had when she went in. "He's so pitiful," she said. "Black and blue." She wiped tears from her eyes with the back of her hand. "Who would have done this?"

"We'll find out," Aunt Maude said soothingly. "And he moved his leg. That's a great sign."

I caught my breath. I hadn't thought of the possibility of paralysis, which, of course, existed.

"Come on, Tammy Sue," Mary Alice said. "We got a great parking place almost at the front door." She put her arms around the girl's shoulders. "And how does some homemade vegetable soup sound to you?"

"Okay. And a shower would be wonderful."

I looked back as we left the waiting room. Olivia Ludmiller was standing by the window, her small face awash with tears.

*   *   *

An hour later, Tammy Sue, Sister, and I were sitting at my kitchen table. Tammy Sue and Sister were eating vegetable soup and corn muffins. I always double the recipe when I make corn muffins and put the extra in the freezer. A minute or less in the microwave, and it's like fresh-baked muffins. I wasn't hungry since I had had lunch with Fred, but I couldn't resist a muffin.

"This is good," Tammy Sue said, tasting the soup. She had taken a shower, washed her hair, and had on the navy velour bathrobe I had bought Fred for his birthday, which he didn't say he didn't like, but which he'd never worn. Draw your own conclusions.

"Patricia Anne's a good cook," Sister said.

I was pleased at the compliment.

"She spends a lot of time in the kitchen."

I wasn't as pleased with that remark. It sounded like I didn't have much of a life. I gave her a little kick on the ankle. "So does Martha Stewart."

"When Larry gets out of the hospital, I'm going to subscribe to *Martha Stewart Living* and do all of the things she does. Like make my own Christmas decorations instead of buying them at Wal-Mart. And I'm going to bone my own chicken and cook it with rosemary stuffed under the skin. I saw her do that one day on TV." Tears came into Tammy Sue's eyes. "Do you know I've never boned a chicken, and I don't even know what rosemary is?"

"It's an herb like parsley, sage, and thyme," Sister said. You could hear the three beats between sage and thyme.

"My mother was a wonderful cook. Not fancy food but good stuff like chicken and dumplings. I wish I'd paid more attention to how she did things, gotten her recipe for turkey and dressing, for instance. Things like that." Tammy Sue sighed. "She kept our house so clean you could eat off the floor."

"Really?" Sister cut her eyes around at me.

"And she'd even iron Daddy's underwear." The tears spilled over. "I've never ironed Larry's underwear."

Sister put her spoon down. She was beginning to look panicked.

"I've never ironed Fred's, either," I said. "I don't believe in ironing what doesn't show."

Tammy Sue gave me a weak smile.

"You could eat off her floor?" Sister asked.

"Yes, ma'am. She loved a clean house."

I could hear Muffin scratching in the litter box in the pantry. So much for eating off of my floor.

Tammy Sue heard the sound, too. "I love cats," she said. "Larry and I have two of them now. But when I was little, every year I'd ask Santa Claus for a kitten, and I never got one. Daddy hates cats."

Visions of Bubba Cat, asleep on his heating pad on Sister's kitchen counter, danced through my head. Through Sister's, too, I'm sure. I glanced at Tammy Sue to see if she was putting us on. But her face as she leaned over her soup was guileless. Sister, on the other hand, was frowning as she broke open a muffin and buttered it. She had been, I knew, considering taking Bubba Cat with them on their honeymoon in the RV, rationalizing that if she put him on a counter on his heating pad, he wouldn't know the difference.

I decided I'd better change the subject. "Something nice happened while you were in seeing Larry," I said. "A lady came over and told us that Elvis had visited them in the waiting room last night. Mary Alice told her that it was Buddy, but she didn't believe it. Tell him he's very convincing."

Tammy Sue looked up, puzzled. "Buddy wasn't there last night. He had to do a show at a VFW hall, and I told him to go ahead. There wasn't anything he could do at the hospital."

"Oh." I leaned over and concentrated on buttering my muffin. The rest of the meal was very quiet, each of us concentrating on her own thoughts.

"Maybe he left and came back while Tammy Sue was dozing

or was in visiting Larry," Sister said later. Tammy Sue was asleep in my guest room. Sister and I had cleared off the kitchen table and she had brought Bonnie Blue's books in.

"Probably," I said.

She opened one of the books to a place she had marked with a folded page from the *Birmingham News* that had a picture on it of spring shoe fashions. "Here's the Rubenesque."

It was beautiful, very simple, and certainly not cut as low as she had drawn it.

"Perfect." And it was true.

She sat down and studied the dress. "I don't know, Mouse. You heard all that stuff about Virgil's first wife. He's not going to get a spotless house or ironed shorts from me. He's not even going to get the body that all my other husbands married me for."

"Don't be silly. They didn't marry you for your body. They married you because they loved you. And so does Virgil."

"Well, I know that. But the first three never expected to have their shorts ironed, and they all loved cats. That really worries me. Virgil never mentioned that he didn't like Bubba."

"Maybe he's changed. Mellowed."

"I'm going to find out. That's for sure."

The phone rang and I grabbed it, hoping it hadn't awakened Tammy Sue.

"Patricia Anne?" It was Bernice Armstrong's voice. My stomach knotted, but I didn't get the anger from her that I had expected. Instead, she said that she wanted to apologize for Day's putting a knife in my purse and causing me so much trouble.

"I swear I can't imagine what came over that child," she continued. "She says it was on the floor of the stage, and she picked it up, not thinking, and then when she saw in the paper that it might be a murder weapon, she panicked. And your purse was there. She says she hardly remembers dropping it in."

"Has she told the police this?"

"She's still down there. I went down there with her, but they're going to do a bunch of stuff, make sure she's telling the truth."

"A voice-stress analyzer," I said.

"That sounds about right. Anyway, they said I might as well come on home, and it's a good thing I did because poor Maurice had fallen right over on his face in the foyer. It's the strangest thing. Looks like some kind of animal attacked him. There's fur everywhere."

It took me a second to put the name Maurice and the stuffed grizzly bear together.

"He's heavy as lead, so the best I can do is vacuum around him until I can get someone here to help me stand him up to see if he's all together." She paused. "I don't know where Dusk is."

"I'm sorry, Bernice," I said. What else could I say?

"No, I'm the one who's sorry, and Day is going to call you herself and apologize as soon as she sets foot out of that jail. I promise you that. I didn't raise my girls to act like that."

Apparently it had never occurred to Bernice that there might be more to the knife incident than Day just happening to see it on the floor and pick it up. I wondered if Dusk had told her mother about her marriage to Griffin Mooncloth and the fact that he was blackmailing her. I doubted it, or she would have sounded more upset about the consequences of the questioning that Day was going through at the police station.

"Well, let me go vacuum, Patricia Anne. And you can be expecting that call."

"Bernice," I said to Sister when I hung up. "Day admitted putting the knife in my purse. She's down at the police station now. Bernice was apologizing for her."

Sister closed the books and stood up. "You know, I just can't see Day Armstrong getting so mad at Griffin Mooncloth for trying to stay married to Dusk that she kills him. Unless she's in love with him herself. There are four things people kill for,

Mouse. Money, revenge, jealousy, and hatred. And, of course, sometimes they're just plain nuts. But, think about it. Would you kill a man because he wanted to stay married to me?"

"No. I'd let you kill him."

"Exactly. So, unless Day was madly in love with Griffin herself, Dusk was the one who killed him." There was some sense lurking around in here somewhere. Sister picked up the books and said she was going to the Big, Bold, and Beautiful Shoppe to talk to Bonnie Blue but that she would be back to take Tammy Sue to the hospital. "Let her sleep a couple of hours. Lord knows she needs it."

So the rest of the afternoon was very quiet. I pulled off my good gray outfit, put on some jeans, and cleaned the house. It was the first time I had felt like it in several days. I couldn't vacuum, but I mopped the kitchen floor and dusted, even in the living room, where we never go. I cleaned the toilets and scrubbed the sinks. By the time Tammy Sue woke up and came out of the guestroom, the whole house smelled as if a lemon tree had been grafted onto a pine.

The first thing she did was call the intensive care waiting room and talk to Aunt Maude. "Yes, ma'am," I heard her say. "Okay." And then, "Is Olivia still there?" When she hung up, she leaned over the counter as if she were too tired to stand up.

"Any change?" I asked.

She shook her head. "He's still unconscious. Where's Mrs. Crane?"

"She had a couple of errands to run. She should be back in a few minutes. You want some tea with a lot of ice in it?"

"That would be great."

"Then why don't you go sit down in the den, and I'll bring you some."

"Thanks. Do you have any Tylenol or aspirin?"

I opened the kitchen cabinet and handed her the Extra Strength Tylenol bottle. She took two and walked into the den as if all of her muscles were stiff. When I came into the den, she was stretched out in Fred's recliner.

"I didn't know it was possible to get this tired," she said, taking the tea. "This should help, though. Thanks, Mrs. Hollowell."

"You're welcome, Tammy Sue. You want a snack of some kind?"

"No, thanks." She took her Tylenol and drank some of the tea. "At least Olivia's gone from the hospital. Maybe she'll stay gone for a while." Tammy Sue stared into her glass as if it were a crystal ball. "I know she means well, but she's driving me crazy. She's not the easiest person to get along with at the best of times, and God knows this isn't the best of times."

"I'm sorry," I said.

"I am, too. She's so crazy about my brother, Buddy, that sometimes I think she's going to get him. Which is fine with me." Tammy Sue put her glass on the table and shrugged. "What do I know? They might be the happiest couple in the world. But right now she keeps saying that it's her fault that Larry was hurt, and that there's something she has to tell him. I keep asking her what, but she says she has to tell Larry."

"If she knows something about who attacked him, she needs to tell the police, not wait around."

"Of course she does. I can't imagine what she thinks she knows anyway. Probably nothing." Tammy Sue rubbed her hands down the side of Fred's robe. "On the other hand, she and Larry own two apartments on Valley Avenue that he rents out to acts that come into town. She handles them, and I know that that Russian guy was staying there. She told the police, but I think they already knew. So I keep thinking maybe she does know something."

"Maybe she'll talk to Buddy."

Tammy Sue shrugged again. "Maybe. I doubt she really knows anything, though. Olivia gets melodramatic if she stubs her toe."

The back door opened, and Sister called hello. "Well, aren't you looking better," she said to Tammy Sue.

"No. I look like hell, but I do feel a little better."

"Well, that's good. Are you ready to go back to the hospital?"

"Just let me get dressed." Tammy Sue headed down the hall.

"She does look like hell," Sister whispered.

"I heard that," Tammy Sue called.

It didn't bother Sister at all. "What big ears you have, child," she said.

"The better to hear you with."

These two were going to be all right.

Chapter Eighteen

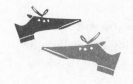

Two things happened the next morning. Larry Ludmiller regained consciousness and Dusk Armstrong went missing. I heard about Dusk from Mitzi, who came running over as soon as she saw that I was home from walking Woofer.

"She's been gone since yesterday," Mitzi said, slightly out of breath. "Flora Gibbons just called and told me. They've called in the police and everything, and Flora says that Bernice is beside herself with worry."

"Well, Lord, I guess so. I talked to Bernice yesterday afternoon, and she said then that she didn't know where Dusk was. She wasn't worried about her, though, just thought she was out somewhere. She was upset because the big grizzly bear they keep in their foyer had been knocked over." I suddenly remembered something. "Oh, my Lord, Mitzi, she said the bear looked as if it had been attacked by wild animals."

Mitzi and I sat down at the kitchen table and looked at each other.

"Wild animals?"

"That's what she said."

"That sure doesn't sound good, does it?"

I shook my head. "It sounds like there was a hell of a fight going on in that foyer."

"While Dusk was being kidnapped."

"I don't know," I said truthfully. But I had a good idea that Mitzi was right. And Dusk, tiny as she was, was a superb athlete. She would have given any would-be attacker a good fight.

"It's got to all be connected in some way." Mitzi said. "I don't see how, though, do you?"

I got up, grabbed a Post-it pad and pencil from the junk drawer, and sat back down. Every teacher learns about visual aids in Education 101. I informed Mitzi of this as I set to work.

"This is Griffin Mooncloth," I said, writing his name on the first slip and sticking him to the table.

Mitzi nodded. "Draw an X on him. He's dead."

I drew an X. Then I wrote Dusk on a slip and put it right below Griffin's. Day's went to the side of that trio. Then I wrote Larry, Tammy Sue, Buddy, and Olivia, and I stuck their slips to the table at an angle so Mitzi and I could both see them.

"Okay," I said. "Let's talk."

"Well, Larry couldn't have killed Griffin Mooncloth because the same person tried to kill him. Draw a half X across him, Patricia Anne, for half dead."

I drew the half X. "But he could have, and somebody could have been taking revenge on him." I pointed to Day Armstrong's name. "Maybe her."

"Do you think she was in love with him?" Mitzi pointed to Griffin's name.

"Maybe."

We studied the names. Then Mitzi said, "Why don't we do it

this way?" She moved three slips to the top, Griffin, Larry, and Dusk. "The murdered, the half-murdered, and the missing. Now what connection is there?"

"Griffin was married to Dusk, and he rented an apartment from Larry."

"Hmm. And you learned how to do this in Education 101?"

"Sometimes it works. You want some coffee?"

Mitzi nodded that she did. I stood up and looked down at the names on the table. The answer was there somewhere, I knew. I just couldn't see it.

That was when the phone rang, and Mary Alice told me that Larry had regained consciousness. He was still in intensive care, though.

"Does he know who hit him?" I glanced down at the names, ready to move one.

"He doesn't remember a thing, Virgil says. He doesn't even know what he was doing at the theater. I told Virgil I saw this movie on Lifetime not long ago, and the actress who used to be the bionic woman was wandering around in a supermarket with blood all over her blouse, except she didn't know about the blood because she had on a coat, and she didn't know who in the world she was, not even after her husband came to claim her and took her home. It took her months before she realized that he was the one who tried to kill her. Her husband. At least I think that's what happened. So, it's not unusual not to remember. And I saw a story on *20/20* where the woman was in a wreck and never remembered her husband, and he had to marry her again." Sister paused for a breath. "They're real happy."

"Does Larry know who Tammy Sue is?"

"I hope so. It would be strange having to date your husband, wouldn't it?"

"Yes, it would. Sister? I'm going to hang up and think about this." I slid the phone onto the cradle. "Larry Ludmiller woke up," I told Mitzi. "He doesn't remember anything."

"I'm not surprised," she said. "I saw this movie on Lifetime—"

I poured our coffee while I heard about Lindsay Wagner's amnesia again. Funny, but neither of them could remember the ending. Something to do with the husband being no good, though.

"Tell me about Olivia," Mitzi said, pointing toward her name with the end of the sugar spoon.

"I've only met her a couple of times, but she doesn't seem friendly. She's apparently in love with Buddy Stuckey, who doesn't return her affections." I put a teaspoon of sugar in my coffee and stirred it. "Tammy Sue said yesterday that she thinks Olivia might run him down, though. Stay after him until he gets so used to her that she moves into his life permanently."

Mitzi nodded. "That's what happened to my brother. His wife grabbed on to him like a tick before he was even out of high school. Everywhere he went, there she'd be. He never stood a chance."

"Is he happy?"

"I think he is. He just sits back and lets her adore him."

"There are all kinds of marriages, aren't there?" I said, thinking of Marilyn and Charles Boudreau who had "worked something out."

"Thank goodness." She tapped Tammy Sue's name with her fingernail. "What about them?"

"They seem to be fine. So far." I told Mitzi about Tammy Sue's plans for a Martha Stewart home when Larry got well.

"Probably won't last long," she said sensibly. "I made one of those wreaths last Christmas. Took me forever, and I stole so much holly from yards, it's a miracle I didn't get arrested."

I also told her what Tammy Sue had said about her mother's housekeeping. "Said you could eat off the floor it was so clean, and she ironed Virgil's underwear. I think it upset Mary Alice. If that's what Virgil's expecting, she knows she's in trouble."

"Huh. Mary Alice doesn't have anything to worry about. All she has to do is parade around in those purple boots and Virgil will be happy. Every marriage is different."

"True." We grinned at each other.

"What about the Elvis impersonator here?" Mitzi pointed to Virgil, Jr.'s name. "Seems to me that it's a little strange to dress up like Elvis all the time."

"Being strange doesn't make you a murderer, thank God." I looked at the name, too. "Besides, he doesn't have a motive."

"How about the others?"

"Day and Dusk are the only two that I can see who have a motive. And we know that Day had the knife."

"And Larry could have seen her."

"It's the only thing that makes sense," I agreed. But even as I said it, doubt was jiggling in my brain like lines on a seismograph. She had been protecting someone when she put the switchblade in my purse. Someone she loved.

I reached over, tore off another Post-it sheet and wrote Bernice on it.

Mitzi's eyes widened. "Bernice? Why?"

"Protecting her daughter. If she knew that Griffin Mooncloth was harassing Dusk, she might have done him in."

"No way, Patricia Anne. She brings blueberry muffins every third Sunday for the coffee we have after church."

"We're just throwing out thoughts here, Mitzi."

"Well, unthrow that one." She reached over and carefully unstuck each name from the table. "This is giving me the creeps."

"Me, too," I agreed. "Let's go send Haley an e-mail. The baby's moving."

"Really? Oh, she's into the best part of being pregnant, where you know it's real."

And that's what we did. After Mitzi had left, though, I pulled the Post-its apart and stuck them back on the table. Muffin came to sit in my lap while I studied them.

"Dusk Armstrong is missing," Sister announced as she came in.

"I know. Mitzi told me. It's scary." I was sitting in the den, a book open in my hands, and deep in thought. If you had asked me what book I was reading, I wouldn't have been able to tell you.

"Probably ran away. I've always thought she was involved in the Russian guy's murder." Sister looked over my shoulder. "What are you doing?"

"Reading." I closed the book. Actually I had been thinking about what Mitzi and I had been talking about, how different every marriage is. "Do you think Mama was happy?" I asked.

"Our mama?"

"Of course our mama. Do you think she was happy married to Papa?"

"What are you reading?"

I held the book up and showed her it had nothing to do with my question. "Mitzi and I were talking about marriage, and I just started remembering things. Like her throwing a plate at him one time."

Sister laughed. "She dumped a whole boiler full of black-eyed peas over him once. Don't you remember that?"

I didn't. "Where was I?"

"Out playing, I guess."

"What did Papa do?"

"Scraped a lot of them off and ate them." Sister chuckled. "He'd made one remark too many about her smoking."

"Smoking? Cigarettes?"

"Out in the garage all the time. I think she finally quit because it was too cold out there in the wintertime."

"Are you making this up?"

"Of course I'm not making it up. And close your mouth, Mouse. They were ordinary people just like you and me. And, yes, I think they were happy most of the time. Papa admired her feistiness."

"Mama smoked?"

"Oh, for heaven's sake, Mouse. Why are you worried about that now?"

"I don't know," I said truthfully. "It's just that suddenly there are so many changes. You and Virgil getting married, Haley and Philip having a baby, Marilyn and Charles."

"Speaking of which, Virgil and I had a long talk last night."

"And?"

"It ended up with him picking Bubba Cat up and kissing him several times on the nose."

"You're kidding."

"He swears he loves cats, that Neena, his wife, was allergic to them. He says that's why she had to keep the house so clean, too."

"Makes sense. Were you wearing your purple boots?"

We grinned at each other.

"I'm going over to the hospital to check on Larry and see if Tammy Sue wants to get out for a while. You want to go?"

I shook my head. "I don't think so."

"Sure you do. You're just sitting around here moping. Go put on something decent. I want to go by Parisian and look at shoes, too."

"Mama smoked?" I asked again as I stood up.

"Lucky Strikes." Sister threw a pillow at me.

How could I not have known that?

"Selective memory," Sister said as we cruised down Twentieth Street a half hour later, and I posed the question. "Don't worry about it." She turned on her left signal. "I don't remember high school."

"Really? Was it traumatic or something?"

"Of course not. I just don't remember it."

"Doesn't it bother you?"

"Only when I go to the reunions." Sister drove slowly down Sixth Avenue. "Damn, I wish somebody would come out of a parking place. I hate the deck."

But the deck was what we had to settle for. Both of us were out of breath by the time we got to the intensive care waiting room.

Tammy Sue was asleep on a sofa, Aunt Maude was crocheting, and Buddy, in his Elvis suit, was looking through a *Sports Illustrated*. Aunt Maude looked up and put her finger to her lips.

"How are things going?" Mary Alice whispered.

Aunt Maude put her crocheting down and motioned for us to sit down. "He's in and out of it. They're giving him something for pain that's making him sleep. It's regular sleep, though."

Buddy twisted the magazine into a knot. "That's what I'm going to do to the bastard's neck who did this to him."

"Oh, hush, Buddy. Lord have mercy." Aunt Maude nodded her head toward Tammy Sue. "This is the first time I've seen her sleeping this hard."

We sat down. It was a good day in intensive care. There were only three other people in the waiting room.

"I know you're exhausted," Sister said.

"I am. Buddy's going to take me home in a few minutes. We're just waiting for Olivia to show up."

"And then we're leaving," Buddy added.

"And Larry doesn't have any idea what happened?" I asked.

"None. The last thing he remembers is eating breakfast. Said he had chocolate chip pancakes." Aunt Maude smiled. "He never had chocolate chip pancakes in his life, but the detective said that sounded good, and he wanted the recipe."

"Tim Hawkins?"

"I don't remember. There were two of them." She looked toward the door. "Here's Olivia."

Olivia looked much better than she had the day before. She looked as if she had had some sleep, and she had put on some makeup. Aunt Maude pointed toward the sleeping Tammy Sue, and Olivia sat down quietly. "He okay?" she whispered.

"Sleeping." Aunt Maude stood, put her crocheting in a bag, and said that she had to go home before she dropped.

"Let's go then." Buddy jumped up. "I'll get the car and meet you at the front door." He was in such a hurry that he bumped Tammy Sue's feet.

"What," she said, opening her eyes.

"Sorry, Sis. I'll talk to you later." And he hurried out of the waiting room. I glanced at Olivia, who was looking after him yearningly. I had a feeling that this tick knew she wasn't going to stick.

Tammy Sue yawned. "Hey, y'all."

"We just came by to check on you," Sister said. "To see how Larry's doing."

"He's conscious. But I know Daddy told you that." She rubbed her eyes. "He doesn't remember a thing, though. The police have been questioning him."

"Well, would you like to get out for a while?" Sister asked. "Patrcia Anne and I are going to Parisian to look for shoes. It would do you good to walk around some, get some fresh air."

"Go ahead," Olivia urged her. "I'll go in and visit Larry."

Tammy Sue stiffened. "You are not. Not without me. I'm not going to have you upsetting him with your wild tales about it being your fault he got hurt."

"Well, maybe it was," Olivia said. "I knew Dusk Armstrong was involved with the Mooncloth guy. They were having a knockdown, drag-out argument at his apartment. I heard them when I went to open up the one next door, and then I saw Dusk run out. If I'd told the police about that when he was killed, she wouldn't have been free to hit Larry."

"Why didn't you tell them?" Tammy Sue asked.

"Wasn't any of my business," was Olivia's smug answer.

Please, God, don't let this tick burrow into Virgil, Jr.

Mary Alice stepped between the two of them, which was a good idea. "Come on, Tammy Sue. Let's go down to the cafeteria and get something to drink. It's easy to get dehydrated sitting around a place like this."

Tammy Sue leaned around Sister and spoke to Olivia. "You go in there without me, and I will kill you. And nobody will blame me. I'll start with your skinny toes. I'll cut off every one of them one at a time. And then your legs and your arms and your ears. And then—"

Olivia blanched. Tammy Sue was still dissecting her, and she had gotten as far as her squinty eyes, when Mary Alice led her from the room. One woman sitting in the corner clapped. "Better be careful, honey. I think she means it."

I figured she did, too.

The most you can say for hospital cafeterias is that they try. And University Hospital has tried. The food is decent, their health rating proudly posted above the cashier is a ninety-nine, but let's face it: The ambience doesn't make the grade. Fiberglass trays, metal tables, fluorescent lights, green scrubs, and white coats. The sweetest elevator music in the world wouldn't help out here.

"Vanilla-and-chocolate swirl?" Sister pointed to the frozen yogurt.

Tammy Sue shook her head. "Just something to drink. Tea?"

"Me, too," I said.

She and I found a table by a window. Outside on Nineteenth Street the traffic was moving well. Spring sun angled through the window and drew a line across the floor of the cafeteria.

"Is it warm outside?" Tammy Sue asked.

"Nice. You want to go out and walk around a little?"

"I'd better not." She reached over, got a paper napkin from the dispenser, and wiped the top of the already immaculate table. "You think Olivia knows what she's talking about? That Dusk Armstrong killed Griffin Mooncloth and hit Larry with the bat?"

"I don't know," I said. Then I told her about Dusk's disappearance.

"She could have left town. Run away."

"Maybe."

"Here," Sister said, putting a tray on the table. She had gotten herself a swirl. "I got an extra spoon if you decide you want some of it," she told Tammy Sue.

"The tea's fine. Thanks." Tammy Sue reached for the sugar. "Mrs. Hollowell was just telling me that Dusk Armstrong has run off."

"Yesterday, apparently." Sister dipped into the swirl, tasted it, and declared that we didn't know what we were missing.

"But, y'all," I said, "I didn't say she's run off. There's a good chance she's been kidnapped." I repeated my conversation with Bernice Armstrong.

"A wild animal?" Sister had stopped spooning in yogurt.

"They have a grizzly bear named Maurice in their foyer?" Tammy Sue's tea remained halfway to her mouth.

"Knocked over like there had been a struggle." I paused. "And that's a big, heavy bear."

"Well, why didn't you tell me this sooner, Mouse? I swear."

"I don't know. You were telling me about Mama and the Lucky Strikes and I sort of got sidetracked."

The yogurt and the tea resumed their journeys. Mary Alice and Tammy Sue looked at me as if I were guilty of something. I picked up my tea and looked out at the traffic again. A white police car pulled up to the curb and a black policewoman got out. Bo Mitchell? My good friend who had had me arrested.

Well, you did have a murder weapon in your purse, Patricia Anne, I told myself.

That's beside the point. She's my friend, and she knew I didn't have anything to do with killing anybody.

But rules are rules, and you know that Bo's not going to break any of them. After all, she's planning on being the police chief one day.

But they arrested me! Handcuffed me like a criminal. My neighbors saw me.

Oh, they did not. Nobody was paying any attention to you. Most of the folks in that neighborhood can't see ten feet in front of them, anyway.

I realized that Sister and Tammy Sue were staring at me.

"She has these fugue states," Sister explained. "She goes to white sales at places like Bed Bath & Beyond."

"What do you buy, Mrs. Hollowell?" Tammy Sue asked politely.

"I was not at a white sale. I was thinking." I pointed out the window. "I think I just saw Bo Mitchell come in."

Sister licked her spoon. "She'd be on my list if I were you."

"She was just doing what she had to do." I drank my tea and looked at the sunlight and the traffic, at the people hurrying down the street and ambulances pulling up to the emergency room. Suddenly I longed for Robert Anderson High, the school where I had spent most of my teaching years, the school that was built in the early sixties without windows. Seasons changed, it rained, it snowed, and we sat inside that womb, protected. Inside that womb, I hadn't fallen over a single dead body. I sighed. Today would be fried chicken day in the cafeteria. I'd consumed a lot of good cholesterol at Robert Anderson.

Mary Alice and Tammy Sue had segued to the wedding outfits, which for some reason reminded me that I needed to get Haley's christening dress out and check to see that it was in perfect condition for Joanna. But would Philip want Joanna christened? Surely he wouldn't mind. He'd been happy enough to be blessed by the pope.

"Did you have Debbie christened?" I asked Sister.

She looked surprised. "Of course I did. Don't you remember? She threw up on the preacher."

"That was Debbie? Which christening was it when the hailstorm hit and we thought the windows were going to break?"

"I don't know. Alan's?"

"Your Philip didn't mind having Debbie christened?"

"Of course not." She turned to Tammy Sue. "My second husband, Philip Nachman, Debbie's father, was Jewish. A lovely, lovely man. Patricia Anne's daughter, Haley, is married to his nephew, also a Philip Nachman."

"You didn't tell him you had her christened, did you?"

"For heaven's sake, Mouse. We're talking about important stuff here."

She hadn't told him.

Bo Mitchell walked into the cafeteria, stuck some money in a vending machine, and retrieved a can of Coke. When she turned she saw us and came over looking slightly sheepish.

"Sorry, Patricia Anne," she said.

"It's your job."

"Some job," Sister muttered.

"Sometimes," Bo said, not taking offense. She pointed toward Tammy Sue with the can of Coke. "You're Mrs. Ludmiller?"

Tammy Sue nodded.

"I'm going to be sitting with your husband. He might remember something, and we want to be there if he does."

Tammy Sue narrowed her eyes. "You're there to protect him, aren't you? You think that when whoever hit him hears he's regained consciousness, they'll come after him again."

"That, too," Bo said. "Won't hurt."

"Oh, I saw that on a Lifetime movie once," Sister said. "And the policeman went to sleep, and the killer walked right in and put a pillow over the victim's head and killed him." She paused. "Maybe he didn't die. Maybe he just had brain damage."

"Lot of that going around." Bo grinned, said she would see us later, and left.

"She seems nice," Tammy Sue said.

"Well, now that she's watching Larry, do you want to go with us to Parisian?" Sister asked.

"Are you going to the downtown one?"

"We can. Why?"

"I'd better not leave, but I need you to do me a favor. If it's not too much trouble, could you go by the Alabama and see if you can find his glasses? He didn't get to the hospital with them. The police said they would look for them, but they haven't. Larry's blind as a bat without them, bless his heart."

"You think somebody might have turned them in?" Sister asked. "Reckon somebody's at the theater?"

"Probably." Tammy Sue fished in her purse and brought out some keys. "If they're not, one of these fits the side door. There's usually somebody there, though, practicing for a play or something." She handed Sister the keys. "It's possible they're still on the floor back there where he was hit. I hope nobody's stepped on them." She looked at both of us. "Do y'all mind?"

"Of course not. We're going to be down there anyway. I'll call you if we find them and send them by Virgil tonight."

Tammy Sue's eyes filled with tears. "You just don't know how much I appreciate this. I'd do it myself, but I swear I'm so tired I don't think I could drive my car down there."

"No problem," Sister said.

Famous last words.

Chapter Nineteen

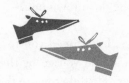

The side door of the Alabama Theater was unlocked. The sun was shining so brightly on the sidewalk outside, that the hall inside seemed black. I looked at the few people walking by us and decided that I wanted to remain where they were, on the outside.

"Looks spooky in there," I declared.

"Don't be silly," Sister said. "And listen."

I took a step inside where I could hear a woman singing "Ave Maria." That certainly wasn't frightening. Nor was the bevy of bridesmaids waiting nervously in the Hall of Mirrors when we came up the steps. The bride herself stood at the foot of the red carpeted stairs that led to the second tier, looking as if she might faint or burst into tears at any minute.

"How about this," Sister said. "A wedding."

I had forgotten that the Alabama Theater was a popular place for weddings, even more popular now that Vulcan Park is closed. All of the weddings that had been planned for the Vulcan site had had to be moved and the Botanical Gardens and the Alabama had immediately been booked.

None of the wedding party paid any attention to us. A lady in a pale yellow suit, obviously the director, was scurrying around, lining up the bridesmaids, straightening dresses. This was a Southern wedding, hoopskirts and all. Fortunately the Alabama boasts double doors and wide aisles.

"Smile, Anna," a photographer said, kneeling before the bride, who was an ethereal looking blonde with wide blue eyes.

"I have to pee," she said through clenched teeth. "Right now."

The photographer motioned frantically. "Mrs. Bolin!"

The lady in yellow came up. "Something wrong?"

"She needs to go to the bathroom."

"Oh, damn. Well, hurry up, Anna."

Anna looked totally miserable. "I don't think I can make it down those steps."

"Of course you can. Just pick up your dress and run." Which Anna did. The woman turned to us. "I swear I can't believe they designed a building with the restrooms in the basement." She looked around. "Where's the father of the bride? Have you seen the father of the bride?"

We said that we hadn't.

"Damn it. He's going to be drunk as a skunk by the time they start down the aisle." She clapped her hands lightly. "Girls, have you seen the father of the bride?"

None of them had. Inside, the woman held the last note of "Ave Maria" an impressively long time. There was rustling, coughing, and then the first majestic notes of "Ode to Joy" from the Mighty Wurlitzer.

"Oh, God!" The woman clutched her chest. She grabbed the

first bridesmaid's arm. "Cheryl, you walk as slow as you can, now. We've got to give Anna time to get back from the bathroom and see if we can find her daddy."

"Mrs. Bolin, there's a man sitting out yonder in the ticket booth," one of the bridesmaids said. "Reckon that's him?"

"It better be him or his ass is in a sling." She pointed toward the photographer. "Go get him." The photographer ran.

"Lord, I love a wedding," Sister murmured to me. "And I love these dresses, don't you?"

"We couldn't walk down the aisle of the church at Tannehill in them. It's too narrow."

"I guess you're right. But I like that each one's a different color. They look like a bouquet of flowers, don't they?"

"Absolutely." And there wasn't a magenta one in the bunch. "I think that's a great idea."

Cheryl, dressed in pink, stepped through the double doors and started down the aisle very slowly. The father of the bride, looking a little sheepish, came back with the photographer. The bride came huffing up the steps just as the last bridesmaid stepped through the door.

There was time to straighten her dress, arrange her veil, and then the sound of "The Wedding March."

Anna froze. "I can't do this. I've changed my mind."

"The hell you have." The director gave her a mighty shove that catapulted her down the aisle. Fortunately Anna was holding on to her father's arm. The audience rose, and the lady in the yellow suit closed the double doors quickly.

"By damn," she said to Mary Alice and me, who were still standing by the steps. "There's got to be an easier way to make a living."

"Everything looked nice," I said.

"Huh. There's still the reception to get through." She went over, sat on a stool behind the candy counter, and closed her eyes.

"Praying?" I whispered to Sister.

"I don't know, but I'm impressed." Sister went over and tapped the praying woman on the shoulder, and the woman cringed. When Sister asked her if she had a business card she said hell no, that wild horses couldn't drag her to another wedding.

"But this is a little one at Tannehill church."

The woman shrugged and closed her eyes again.

"Testy," Sister whispered as she came back to the stairs.

"Well, let's go see if we can find Larry's glasses." I said. "How do we get there from here?"

"I'm not sure. I'm turned around. Last time we went from the stage." Sister went over and tapped the praying woman on the shoulder again. Again, the woman cringed. "How do you get to the dressing rooms from here?"

The woman pointed down the steps toward the basement. "Somewhere down there. The place is a warren. I still think we're missing a bridesmaid."

"What do you think the chances are of our finding Larry's glasses intact?" Sister grumbled as we started down the steps.

The lady was right. The place was a warren. At the very bottom of the steps was the huge living room with the fireplace and round velvet bench, where Sister and I had received so much of our education. About three-fourths of the way down, though, the steps curved, and there was a landing with a door opening onto it. I had never paid any attention to this before. But today the door was open, and the hallway leading from it was lighted.

"Here we go," Sister said. "I had no idea this was here, did you?" I admitted that I hadn't.

She stopped and looked around. "Let's see. Last time, we came in from the stage so it should be way up at the end. Does any of this look familiar?"

I shook my head. It just looked like a hall with a bunch of

doors. "Maybe these are the stars' dressing rooms. When this place was built, they still had vaudeville." I knocked lightly on one and opened it. A broom closet.

"They'd be farther down, closer to the stage."

I closed the door and followed Sister without the least trepidation. Above us Anna was marrying somebody, hopefully. I'll bet it was a pretty scene on that stage, all of the girls in their pastel antebellum dresses and hats. I wondered what the men were wearing. Her father had had on a plain tux. I've been to some of the old South weddings where the groomsmen wore faux-Confederate uniforms, sometimes blue, because gray uniforms are so drab. But they always carried swords. The newlyweds marched under the swords while the photographers took pictures. Real swords. Made me nervous as hell. One careless groomsman and the marriage is a short one.

"Here." Sister stopped suddenly, and I walked into her. "Damn, Mouse. Watch where you're going." She pulled her shoe back on where I had stepped on it. "I think it's one of these rooms." She pointed. "There are the steps we came down the other day."

"Maybe there's still a police ribbon around it," I said.

"Oh, I doubt it. Besides, we're just going to look around on the floor."

I sneezed. "Lord, they need to run over these floors with Endust. Look at the dust bunnies." I casually pushed my foot against one of the larger pieces of dust that had lodged against the wall. It didn't float away like it should. I leaned over and looked at it.

"What?" Sister asked when she saw me looking.

I pushed at the grayish dust again. The whole piece moved.

"What is it? A dead mouse?" she asked. "God, that gives me the creeps."

I squatted down and examined what I had thought was a dust

bunny. Long gray hairs, I realized, attached to a small piece of
dried skin.

"You got any tweezers?" I asked.

"For what? What are you going to do?"

"Pick this up."

"Why? Have you lost your mind?"

"No, damn it. But this looks like a piece of Maurice."

"The grizzly bear?"

"Give me some tweezers."

She fumbled in her purse, fussing that I had lost my mind
and that I was going to get bubonic plague because rats carried
bubonic plague, and I'd better not give it to her. Nevertheless,
she handed me some tweezers and moved back while I picked
up the scrap and examined it. It wouldn't take a forensic scien-
tist to tell that this was a piece of dried skin with long, gray, silver-
tipped hair attached.

"Look," I said, holding out the tweezers to Sister. "I swear I
think it's Maurice."

She backed up. "Maybe somebody got scalped. Or maybe it's
off of a costume."

But I knew what I was looking at. I stood up and looked
around. Much of what I had thought was dust was hair. There
were also a few pieces similar to the one I held with the tweezers.

"We need to call the police," I said. "If Maurice was knocked
over when Dusk was kidnapped, then she might be here somewhere."

"You said Bernice said he looked like he'd been attacked by a
wild animal."

A shiver ran over me. "I know. Maybe what happened was
that Dusk grabbed at the bear while she was being dragged out
of the house. Maybe she tried to push him over on the person
who had her."

"Oh, my Lord, Mouse. I'll call, but they're going to think

we're nuts." She reached into her purse for her cell phone. "You stay away from me with that bubonic patch, though."

"Put the phone away, Mrs. Crane."

Sister and I both jumped. Mr. Taylor was walking down the hall toward us.

"But there's a good chance that Dusk Armstrong may be here somewhere, and we need to call the police," I said.

"Look, you twit. Nobody's calling the police." He grabbed both Sister's purse and mine with his left hand. In his right was a pistol I had failed to notice as he walked toward us. Sister asked later how on God's earth I had missed that detail, and the only thing I could think of was because he was a teacher and teachers don't carry guns. Hah, she said, she'd heard that before.

Mr. Taylor dumped the purses on the floor and handed me a key. "Unlock that door." Which I did. I still wasn't very scared. Things hadn't begun to come together yet.

"Hurry, damn it. I've got to go back and play the recessional."

You see what I mean? Nobody's going to kill you and then run back upstairs and play the recessional at a wedding. Some things just don't fit.

I got the door open. Another broom closet, this one carpeted with green indoor-outdoor carpet.

"Now pick up that green bucket in the corner. Hurry."

I hurried. For a second I considered turning and hurling it at him, but only for a second.

"Pull the carpet back. There's a handle under there. Pull it up."

I did as he said. Nothing happened.

"Move back, you fool. You're standing on the trapdoor."

This was no time to argue that I wasn't a fool. I moved back, lifted the trapdoor, and saw what appeared to be a lighted room beneath it.

"Climb down," was the next order. And again, "Hurry."

I pulled the trapdoor back, said a little prayer, and lowered myself onto a dangling metal ladder that hung between the closet and the floor beneath. It was the kind of ladder that people who have bedrooms on upper stories keep under their beds in case of fire, the kind that hooks over a window, in this case a trapdoor. It swayed as I descended.

"Now you," I heard him tell Mary Alice.

There was no way on God's earth that Sister was going to be able to fit into that trapdoor. And if by some miracle she squeezed through, there was the fragility of the ladder, of the hundred fifty pounds more of Sister than there was of me. Just then my feet touched a carpeted floor. That was a plus. If the ladder broke or came loose, could I cushion her fall someway without getting smushed? I stood to one side, ready to do what I could. But Sister came through the trapdoor and down the ladder with no problem. Mr. Taylor scampered down behind her, holding on to the ladder with one hand, the pistol in the other, still pointed at us.

Afterward, thinking about this, I realized that if we hadn't been so astonished at what we were seeing, we could probably have jumped him as he came down the ladder and knocked the pistol away. He wasn't a large man or a young man, and there were two of us.

We were standing in a Matisse painting. A deep burgundy carpet covered the floor. Atop this was an oriental rug in shades of orange and burgundy. There were several more rugs hanging on the wall and a circular table in the middle of the room with books stacked beside a large arrangement of red lilies. In the corner was an ornate brass bed covered by a floral throw, and on this bed lay a dark-haired, dark-eyed girl. Pure Matisse except for the fact that the girl was tied to the bed and had electrical tape over her mouth. Dusk Armstrong, her eyes large with fear.

"My God," Sister said.

"Here." Mr. Taylor handed her a roll of electrical tape. "Strap your sister to that pipe."

In spite of the ornateness of the room, we were in the bowels of the theater. Mr. Taylor had not been able to hide all of the pipes. He had, however, painted them pink. "Over here in the corner," he said.

Sister took the tape, tore a piece off, and taped my ankles to the pipe.

"Feet and wrists both. And tight." And to me, "Cross your arms."

Sister finished taping me to the pipe. Then it was her turn. Mr. Taylor told her to back up and taped her to a pipe that ran parallel to mine. He pulled off a piece of tape to put over her mouth and then changed his mind. "I'll let you talk," he said, laughing. "See if you two biddies can hatch up anything. You can't be heard, you know."

Then he went over to Dusk, pulled the tape from her mouth, kissed her, and said, "You, too, my darling. I forgot about putting this on you. But such terrible language for a lady." He turned and looked at us. "Well, I'll be back in a few minutes. The recessional, you know. Don't say anything bad about me." He climbed the rope ladder, pulled it up behind him, and closed the trapdoor. We were imprisoned.

Dusk began to cry. "Oh, y'all, I'm so sorry. How did you end up down here?"

"Looking for Larry Ludmiller's glasses," I said. "I saw Maurice's hair all over the hall. You threw it there deliberately, didn't you?"

"I left a trail of it. I was grabbing chunks of Maurice out while Mr. Taylor was trying to drag me out of the house."

Sister pulled ineffectually against her taped wrists. "I was about to call the police when that madman showed up." She tugged again to no avail. "What's wrong with him anyway?"

"He's crazy. He says he's going to protect me, that he's loved me since I used to come and watch Dawn in the Miss Alabama pageants. Oh, God. He's been stalking me for years, and I didn't even know it."

"He knew about Griffin then?" I asked.

"Of course he did." Dusk tried to wipe her face on her arm. Not easy. Her arms were tied above her head. "He killed him to protect me, so he says. And I'm so stupid. I thought it was Day who had killed him to protect me." Dusk gave a half laugh, half sob. "And she thought I had done it because I was so scared I was going to prison for marrying him."

I looked at Mary Alice, but she seemed to be lost in thought. Would she believe me capable of murder? Would she murder someone to protect me? She would if the situation were life threatening, I realized. But Griffin Mooncloth had been a situation that Dusk had entered foolishly. He was no life threat. And the sisters' jumping to the wrong conclusions about each other had caused so much trouble, including my being arrested, Larry Ludmiller almost being killed, and God knows what was going to happen. And yet, I rationalized, they had been trying to protect each other.

My hands were beginning to go to sleep. I leaned my head back against the pipe and took a deep breath. Even the ceiling, I realized, was covered with the burgundy carpet. Mr. Taylor had worked down here for years to create this room, this place to bring his beloved. Oh, my God.

"The Phantom of the Opera," I said to Sister.

"I know. Probably upstairs right now sawing the chandelier loose in the Hall of Mirrors."

"He's not going to let us out of here alive," I said. "We've messed up his plans."

Sister seemed strangely calm. "He'll have to take us out to kill us. Or he'll take Dusk somewhere else and leave us here. My bet is that he'll take us out. This is his lair."

I began to get the shakes. "So if he takes us somewhere like

Huntsville, shoots us, and throws us in a ditch, we're still dead."

"Oh, Lord." Dusk moaned.

"But he's got a problem. He'll have to undo both of us and get us up the ladder. And the one who gets upstairs into the closet first runs like hell. And that'll be you, Mouse."

"Why me?"

"Because I can't fit through the trapdoor."

"You fit coming down."

"I was thinking thin."

"You were thinking thin?"

"It's part of Eastern philosophy. You know the class I was taking at UAB? You think of yourself as a long silver shaft of light, and you can slip right through things."

"Well, can't you slip back up?"

"It's harder. Gravity works against you going up. There's only so much mind over matter. But Mr. Taylor will have to go up the ladder ahead of you so he can hold the gun on you. Then I'll get stuck in the trapdoor, and you run like hell."

I wailed almost as loud as Dusk. My sister had lost her mind. "He'll shoot us both."

"I doubt it. He's going to be too worried about me blocking his way to his room and Dusk. You should have a few minutes."

"Maybe I could hit him over the head with something in the broom closet."

Sister shook her head. "Just run like you've never run before. Run toward the street because the wedding party will probably be gone by then."

"Run," Dusk echoed. "Run like hell."

I would have wrung my hands if I could. "There's got to be another way. I can't leave you stuck in a trapdoor with a maniac."

"Then you tell me what it is."

I couldn't, of course.

Five minutes passed. Ten. Dusk closed her eyes and seemed to be sleeping. Maybe Mr. Taylor had given her something. Mary Alice's eyes were open but had a distant look in them. Maybe she was imagining herself a silver shaft of light. As for me, I was wondering if I would ever see Joanna. And Fred would miss me so.

"What's going to happen to Fred?" I whispered.

"He'll marry Tiffany."

"That's not a damn bit funny."

"Then shut up and let me think."

"Are you thinking you're a blue flame or something?"

"Just shut up."

I lapsed into silence. Maybe if we beat on the pipes? But what did we have to beat on them with but our heads. I thought of the wedding party above us, going out now into the bright warm sunshine of a March day. Going to the reception, probably at the Highland Raquet Club, trying to dance in those hoop skirts. The beauty of the recessional being played by a man who had three women tied up in an exotic room some-where beneath the street. "Thank you, Mr. Taylor," they would say. "It was lovely." And the father of the bride would tip him lavishly.

Had he been trying to decide what to do with us while he sat at the Mighty Wurlitzer? Of course he had. And now he was back to carry out whatever plan he had decided on. We heard the trapdoor being opened, the chain of the ladder clinking as it unfurled and fell to the floor.

Sister and I glanced at each other as Mr. Taylor came down the ladder. He was the least villainous man I had ever seen, small, neatly dressed in a tux, his scarce red hair so plastered with hair oil that you could see the tracks of every comb tooth. But his eyes belied the meek, ordinary look.

"Now what?" he said. We didn't answer, so he answered him-self. "Now I have to get rid of you two pests."

I tried to visualize running down the hall. Which way to the street? What if the doors were locked?

He went over and ran his hand lovingly down Dusk's arm. "So beautiful." She didn't stir.

"She hates you, you know," Sister said. "She told us when you touched her it makes her sick."

Mr. Taylor turned toward Sister, his face contorted.

"You're not the Phantom of the Opera," she continued. "You're nothing but the substitute organist at the Alabama."

"Shut up, you twit."

"What did you call me?" Sister asked.

"A twit. Twit, twit, twit." On each "twit" he took a step forward until he was standing in front of her.

"Yaaa!" Sister screamed her martial arts yell as her foot came up and delivered the hardest kick I've ever seen right between Mr. Taylor's legs. He dropped like a sack of potatoes, and she was on top of him pulling the gun from his pocket. "I hope I broke them, you bastard. I hope you never use them again."

From the looks of him, there was a good chance that she was going to get her wish. In a fetal position, he retched into the oriental rug.

Dusk woke up. "What?" she asked.

But Mary Alice was untaping me and telling me to run like hell for help. "Tell them to bring something to widen the trapdoor. No way I can get out of there."

"Why didn't you tell me you were loose, and how did you do it?" I asked.

"You would have looked guilty. And I just rocked back and forth and stretched the tape."

As I headed up the stairs, she was using the tape that had been on me to secure Mr. Taylor. I don't think I've ever been as proud of anyone in my life.

* * *

"She thought herself thin?"

Fred and I had just turned off the eleven o'clock news where we had watched ambulance attendants carrying Mr. Taylor from the Alabama Theater. He was covered in a blanket as they brought him out, but you could tell that even on the gurney he was still in a fetal position.

I nodded against his shoulder. We were in bed snuggling. He might marry Tiffany when I was gone, but, by damn, I was going to give her something to live up to.

"She says she learned it in a class on Eastern philosophy. You think of yourself as a silver blade of light or a blue flame or something like that, and you can slip right through things."

"I don't believe a word of that," Fred said. "I'll bet Mr. Taylor just shoved her through the trapdoor.

"She was still wonderful. Worked her way right out of that tape and didn't say a word. I didn't have any idea she'd done it."

We lay quietly for a few minutes. Outside the March wind had picked up, and the shadows on the window shades were dancing. I was on the verge of sleep when Fred said, "You know, honey, she didn't have to kick him as hard as she did."

I smiled. And then I fell over the cliff into sleep.

Chapter Twenty

*M*ay fourteenth was a perfect day, weather-wise. A late cold front had slipped through Alabama and the temperature was in the seventies with a light breeze. The old country church at Tannehill State Park is simply one large rectangular room with benches, an aisle down the middle, and windows down both sides. At the front is a slightly raised platform where the minister stands. No dressing rooms, no bathrooms. But the park is undergoing a restoration. It was the site of the first steel mill in the state, built in the early 1800s. The Yankees took care of that. But someone came up with the idea of moving some authentic 1800 cabins to the park, so we could appreciate how our ancestors lived. (They didn't live very well.) And frequently there are Civil War reenactments in the Tannehill woods.

On Sister's wedding day, there was no reenactment, fortunately, since the soldiers tend to do a lot of rebel yelling. But somehow she had managed to get the use of one of the cabins for the bridesmaids to finish getting ready.

We each had on a dress that we had picked out ourselves. The only stipulations were that they be floor length and that our shoes match the color of the dress. We agreed that was fair enough. So Sister had us reach in a hat and pull out the color. Tammy Sue got yellow, but Haley swapped blue with her. Virgil's other daughter, Deena, had declined the invitation to be in the wedding, but I think she was sorry when she saw how much fun we were having.

Haley looked beautiful. She had been home six weeks and was at the good stage of pregnancy. Marilyn, however, was a different matter. She was dressed in lavender and every time I looked at her I thought of the song with the lyrics about "lavender's green."

"I don't think I can make it," she kept saying. But she did, thanks to the tea and crackers that Bonnie Blue kept handing her.

My dress was a pale pink, and Debbie's was a darker pink. Mary Alice, of course, had on the Rubenesque dress, which was a work of art.

Bonnie Blue lined us up, and we walked single-file up a path to the church, trying not to scuff our shoes in the pine straw or snag our dresses on the wild hydrangeas that bloomed on both sides of us. Ray, Sister's son, hadn't been able to make it home from Bora Bora for the wedding, so she had asked Fred to give her away. He had said, "Gladly."

The men were waiting for us at the church. Good-looking, all of them, I decided. Even Buddy in his Elvis outfit. A little strange, but that was okay. Bonnie Blue slipped into the church, and in a minute we heard the first notes of Beethoven's Sixth, the Pastoral Symphony. There was no piano in the church, no organ, thank God. But there was electricity.

"Here we go," somebody said.

The wedding party almost filled up the church. The groomsmen were Mary Alice's sons-in-law, Henry and Charles; her
nephew (and Haley's huband), Philip; and my sons, Freddie and
Alan. Buddy Stuckey was his father's best man. Larry Ludmiller
was doing much better, but Tammy Sue had decided he'd better
not stand that long.

"Too many men anyway," Bonnie Blue grumbled. "Y'all don't
match up."

We marched down the aisle toward the altar that was banked
with spring flowers. I smiled at Miss Bessie and Bo Mitchell. At
Mitzi and Arthur Phizer, Pukey Lukey and Virginia. Fairchild
Weatherby, an old boyfriend of Mary Alice's, was already wiping
his eyes. I looked around. So were several other men.

And then Sister came down the aisle and married Virgil
Stuckey. The only surprise was when the minister said that Virgil, Jr., had asked to sing a song in honor of his father and his
bride. This was right after Fred had given her away and had sat
down in the front row by Bonnie Blue.

Virgil and Sister both looked startled, but Buddy Stuckey
stepped forward and sang "Love Me Tender" so much like Elvis
that it was eerie. To tell the truth, it was the highlight of the
wedding.

The photographer got a lot of pictures of Sister and Virgil on
the steps, and then we headed back to Birmingham for the
reception on the lawn at Sister's house. Half the city was there
partying. I'm sure every drugstore in town was out of aspirin the
next day.

Sister and Virgil didn't change out of their wedding clothes.
Sister hiked up her cream-colored satin dress and climbed into
the RV. That's when I saw the purple boots and started crying.

"Don't cry, honey," Fred said, putting his arms around me.
"They're not going to make it as far as Gardendale."

He was right. They made it only as far as the street before Virgil stopped the RV, and Sister jumped out.

"Mouse!" she yelled.

"What?"

"You and Fred go with us."

"We can't," I said, running down the driveway.

"It's fine with Virgil."

That was when Virgil got out and announced, "The hell it is. Get back in, Mary Alice."

Fred caught up with me and scooped me up. Virgil and Sister got back into the RV, and they turned out of the driveway.

"I love you, man," Fred shouted.

Virgil's arm came out in a wave as they drove off.

Fred slung me over his shoulder like a sack of potatoes and patted me on the behind. He was showing off, of course, but it was really rather nice. Caveman-ish. He chuckled as we started back toward the party.

He staggered about three steps before he put me down, but I thought that was right impressive. We walked the rest of the way, slowly, holding hands.

"Mrs. Hollowell?" Tiffany was on the steps holding out a cell phone. "It's Mrs. Crane. I mean Mrs. Stuckey."

I took it. "Sister?"

"Is Fred all right? I saw the Mr. Macho bit."

"Huffing and puffing so hard he could blow down the little pig's brick house." Fred frowned and walked over to join Haley and Philip. "Where are y'all?"

"Going by Vulcan Park. Do you think everything went all right?"

"Beautiful. Let me go inside and sit down so we can talk."

Sister giggled. "Virgil says hey."